3|17

THE WORLD TO COME

THE WORLD TO COME

Stories

JIM SHEPARD

ALFRED A. KNOPF   NEW YORK   2017

THIS IS A BORZOI BOOK
PUBLISHED BY ALFRED A. KNOPF

Copyright © 2017 by Jim Shepard

All rights reserved. Published in the United States by Alfred A.
Knopf, a division of Penguin Random House LLC, New York, and
distributed in Canada by Random House of Canada, a division of
Penguin Random House Canada Limited, Toronto.

www.aaknopf.com

Knopf, Borzoi Books, and the colophon are registered trademarks
of Penguin Random House LLC.

Several stories were previously published
in the following publications:
Electric Literature: "Safety Tips for Living Alone"; *One Story:* "The World
to Come"; *McSweeney's:* "The Ocean of Air"; *Tin House:* "Positive Train
Control," "Wall-to-Wall Counseling"; *Zoetrope:* "Cretan Love Song,"
"HMS Terror," "Telemachus"

Library of Congress Cataloging-in-Publication Data
Names: Shepard, Jim, author.
Title: The world to come : stories / by Jim Shepard.
Description: First Edition. | New York : Alfred A. Knopf, 2017.
Identifiers: LCCN 2016038353 (print) | LCCN 2016044230 (ebook) |
ISBN 9781524731809 (hardback) | ISBN 9781524731816 (ebook)
Subjects: | BISAC: FICTION / Short Stories (single author). |
FICTION / Literary. | FICTION / Family Life.
Classification: LCC PS3569.H39384 A6 2017 (print) |
LCC PS3569.H39384 (ebook) | DDC 813/.54—dc23
LC record available at https://lccn.loc.gov/2016038353

Jacket photograph by Orietta Corradi / EyeEm / Getty Images
Jacket design by Kelly Blair

Manufactured in the United States of America
First Edition

For Karen, yet again—

Contents

THE WORLD TO COME

Safety Tips for Living Alone

Twenty-five years before Texas Tower no. 4 became one of the Air Force's most unlikely achievements and most lethal peacetime disasters, marooning nineteen wives including Ellie Phelan, Betty Bakke, Edna Kovarick, and Jeannette Laino in their own little stewpots of grief and recrimination, the six-year-old Ellie thought of herself as forever stuck in Kansas: someone who would probably never see Chicago, never mind the Atlantic Ocean. Her grandfather wore his old brown duster whatever the weather, and when riding in her father's convertible he always insisted on sitting in the dead center of the backseat with a hand on each side of the top to maintain the car's balance on the road. This was back when the Army was running the Civilian Conservation Corps, the Navy exploring the Pole with Admiral Byrd, and the Air Corps still flying the mail in open-cockpit biplanes. Gordon had reminded Ellie of her grandfather, and this had stirred her up and set her teeth on edge. She'd first noticed him when he'd stood on the Ferris wheel before the ride had begun, to make certain another family's toddlers had been adequately strapped in, and when they were introduced she'd said, "Who made *you* the Ferris wheel monitor?" And then after he'd answered with a grin, "Isn't it amazing how much guys like me *pretend* we know what we're doing?" she'd been shocked by how exhilarating it was to catch a glimpse of someone who saw the world exactly as she did.

She'd always been moved and appalled by the confidence that men like her grandfather and Gordon projected when it came to getting a handle on their situations. But they each also had a way of responding to her as if she'd come around to the advantages of their caretaking, and she surprised herself by not saying no when after a few months of dating he asked her to marry him. That night she stood in her parents' room in the dark, annoyed at her turmoil, and then switched on their bedside lamp and told them the news. And when they reacted with some of the same dismay she was feeling, she found herself more instead of less resolved to go ahead with the thing.

Her father had pointed out that as a service wife she might see exotic places and her share of excitement, but she'd also never be able to put down roots or buy a house, and year after year she'd get settled in one place and then have to disrupt her life and move to another. Her children would be dragged from school to school. Her husband would never earn what he could as a civilian. And most of all, the Air Force would always come first, and if that seemed too hard for her, then she'd better back out now.

When her mother came into her bedroom a few nights later and asked if she really understood what she was getting herself into, Ellie said that she did. And when her mother scoffed at the idea that her Ellie would ever know why she did anything, Ellie said, "At least I *understand* that about myself," and her mother answered, "Well, what does *that* mean?" and Ellie said she didn't want to talk about it anymore.

"Now that we see you're not going to change your mind, we give up," her father announced a few days later, and she chose not to respond to that, either. His final word on the subject was that he hoped this Gordon realized just how selfish she could be. She lived with her parents for two more months before the wedding and they exchanged maybe ten words in total. Her mother's mother came for a visit and didn't congratulate Ellie on her news but did mention that the military was no place for a woman because the men drank too much and their wives had to raise their children in the unhealthiest climates. She offered as an example the Philippines, that sinkhole of malaria and vice.

They were married by a justice of the peace in Gordon's childhood home in Pasadena, and her parents came all the way out for the ceremony and left before the reception, their wedding present a card that read, *"Take care and all best wishes, Mom."* The following week Gordon was posted to a base in upstate New York and Ellie spent a baffled month alone with his parents before taking the Air Force Wives' Special across the country: Los Angeles to Boston for one hundred and forty dollars, with stops everywhere from Fresno to Providence and seats as hard as benches and twenty infants and children in her compartment alone. The women traveling solo helped out the most overwhelmed mothers, and Ellie spent the trip crawling under seats to retrieve crayons and shushing babies whose bottles were never the right temperature.

In upstate New York, the place Gordon found for her while they waited for quarters on the base was a rooming house that instead of fire escapes had ropes coiled beneath the bedroom windows. She had only a room to herself, with kitchen privileges. "At least it's quiet," he told her when he first saw it, and then asked a few days later if her nightly headaches were related to what he'd said about her room.

She was relieved that he mostly served his time on the base.

Larry was born, and Gordon worked his way up to captain, and when in 1957 he was offered the command of some kind of new offshore platform, he wanted to request another assignment—what Air Force officer wanted to squat in a box over the ocean?—but told Ellie that it was her decision, too. "You have a family now," she answered. "I just want anything that keeps you closer." "I wouldn't get home any more often," he pointed out. "And safer," she added. So after sleeping on it, he told her he'd take the command, though afterward he was so disappointed that he wasn't himself for weeks.

By 1950 the Department of Defense had determined that the radar arrays carried on Navy picket ships and Air Force aircraft on station were not powerful enough to detect incoming Russian bombers sufficiently far offshore to enable fighter interception. The radar stations comprising the Distant Early Warning system across the far north of the continent provided some security in that direction, but given that nearly all of America's highest-priority targets were situated inside its northeastern metropolitan corridor, protection from an attack across the Atlantic seemed both essential and entirely absent. In response, the Air Defense Command urgently ordered the construction of five platforms along the coast from Bangor to Atlantic City. The platforms were called Texas Towers because of their resemblance to oil rigs, were numbered from north to south, and cost eleven million dollars apiece.

They faced engineering problems as unprecedented as the space program's. Tower no. 4 in particular had presented a much greater challenge than the others since its footings would stand in 185 feet of water, more than three times as deep as the others. In 1955 the maximum depth at which anyone had built an undersea structure was sixty feet, and that had been in the Gulf of Mexico. Because of that, the Air Force had decided that this tower would require bold new thinking in its conception and hired a firm known for bridge design. The firm had had no experience at all in the area of ocean engineering for marine structures.

Tower no. 4 stood on three hollow legs nearly three hundred feet long. The legs were only twelve feet in diameter and braced by three submarine tiers of thirty-inch steel struts, and topped with a triangular triple-leveled platform that stood seventy feet above the waves. From its concrete footings on the seafloor to the top of its radomes it was the equivalent of a thirty-story building out in the ocean.

Though oil-drilling platforms had for the most part weathered the storms and seas of the Gulf, the Gulf at its worst was nothing like the North Atlantic.

And something was already wrong with Tower no. 4. Unlike the others, it moved so much in heavy weather or even a good strong wind that everyone who worked on it called it Old Shaky or the Tiltin' Hilton.

The first time Gordon set foot on it he'd stood at the edge of the platform hanging on to the rope railings designed to catch those blown off their feet by wind gusts or prop wash, looked down into the waves so far below, and then out at the horizon, empty in all directions, and asked the officer he was relieving, "What the hell am I doing here?"

The tower housed seventy men. Besides crew and officer quarters and work stations it had a ward room, bakery, galley, mess, recreation area, and sick bay. Seven locomotive-sized diesel engines provided electricity, and on the lower level ionizing machines converted salt water to drinking water. Fuel was stored in the hollow legs.

The crew was half Air Force and half civilian welders and electricians and technicians. For every thirty days on you got thirty days off. The military guys liked it because they got more time than they were used to with their families, but the civilians hated the isolation and complained they were always away for the big holidays, everybody seeming to be stuck out on the platform for New Year's and home for Groundhog Day.

But the tower shuddered and flexed so much in bad weather that whoever had painted *"Old Shaky"* over the door in the mess hall hadn't even been able to get the letters straight, and the floors moved so visibly in the winter that everyone was too seasick to eat. In his first phone call, Gordon told Ellie that the medic who'd flown out with him hadn't even served out his first day; that when he saw how much the platform was pitching he refused to get off the helicopter and took it right back to shore on the next flight out. Once he left, Gordon found a crow hunkered down on the edge of the helipad, its tail feathers pummeled back in the wind. They got blown out here sometimes, the captain he was relieving had explained. Gordon boxed the crow up and carried it to his stateroom and made sure it was ferried back on the last copter out that night. "Well, at least the crow is safe," Ellie told him. "Unless he comes back," her husband answered.

Betty Bakke's husband, Roy, was a medic who hadn't insisted on flying back to the mainland the first time he'd set foot on Tower no. 4, because he believed a man fulfilled his responsibilities. He'd already made master sergeant and been nicknamed for his standard advice, as in *"I thought I was coming down with something but Don't Sweat It said I was okay."* He'd transferred from the Navy, where he'd served on a minesweeper in Korea. The only thing that fazed him, he told Betty in his phone calls, was his separation from her. She and their boy were still stuck in their old bungalow in Mount Laguna on the other side of the country. Roy had put his friend and commanding officer, Gordon Phelan, on the phone during one call, and the captain had regaled her with stories about Roy. Roy had stayed on duty eighty straight hours with an airman second class who'd had a heart attack, and was even better known for having stitched up his own eyebrow after a fall while everyone else watched. He'd organized fishing contests off the deck and also radioed passing trawlers so the guys could trade their cigarettes and beer for fresh fish and lobster. On top of all of that, he'd taken charge of the 16mm movies swapped from tower to tower and had scored big that Thanksgiving by having dealt *The Vikings* with Kirk Douglas for *The Sheriff of Fractured Jaw* with Jayne Mansfield.

Betty had told the captain that her husband sounded like a one-man morale officer, and the captain said that was his point. And when Betty told him she'd heard that long separations were the reefs that sank military marriages, the captain had laughed and said he was going to pass the phone back to her husband. "Sounds like she needs a house call," she heard him say to Roy.

The Navy Bureau of Yards and Docks had advised the engineers that Tower no. 4's platform would need to withstand winds up to 125 miles per hour and breaking waves up to thirty-five feet, based on twenty years' worth of data provided by the Woods Hole Oceanographic Institute. The main deck's planned seventy-foot elevation should then provide plenty of clearance. A few members of the design team dissented, wishing to put on record their belief that wave heights and wind speeds should be calculated on the basis of what might be expected once a century rather than once every twenty years. They were outvoted.

To extend its radar coverage, Tower no. 4 had been given a location as close as possible to the edge of the continental shelf, which meant that just to its east the bottom dropped away thousands of feet and that waves coming from that direction or the north encountered that rising bottom and mounted themselves upward even higher. And in winter storms Tower no. 2, in much shallower water, had already recorded waves breaking *over* its deck.

But wait, Gordon told Ellie once he'd done a little more research: the news got even worse. Because the footings were so deep, no. 4's hollow legs had been designed to be towed to their location, where they'd be upended and anchored to the caissons on the bottom before the main deck was attached and raised. But because the legs were so long, the designers had had to use pin connections—giant bolts—rather than welds in the underwater braces. Though bolts were an innovative modification, they failed to take into account the constant yet random motions of the sea. For that reason, oil rigs and the other towers had used welded connections. The moment the bolts had gone in, they began generating impact stress around their connections. And Gordon had further discovered a storm had so pummeled two of the underwater braces during the towing that they'd sheared off and sunk during the upending, and that everyone had then floated around until the Air Force finally gave the order to improvise repairs at sea to avoid having to haul the entire structure back to shore.

Then, in heavy swells, the five-thousand-ton platform kept smashing up against the legs, so reinforced steel had been flown out and welded over the damage.

"Okay, I think it's time to put in for a change of assignment," Ellie told him in response. "Yeah, well, in for a penny, in for a pound," he answered, by which she took him to mean, *"You got me into this, so I don't want to hear any complaints."*

As soon as the tower had gone operational, Wilbur Kovarick asked to be made its senior electrician so he could be closer to his family on Long Island, and Edna was so grateful that she kept him in bed the entire weekend.

By the time Edna had turned twenty-six, all but two of her friends had married and she'd been a bridesmaid five times. She told Wilbur on their first date that at the last wedding, if the clergyman had dropped dead at the altar, she could have taken over the service. He'd been sweet, and thought she was a riot, but after they said good night, she found herself back in her little rented room with no radio or television and her three pots of ivy, wishing she'd thought to get his home address or telephone number. By the time he called her she had no patience for pretense and told him to come right over, and when he appeared at her door she kissed him until he finally pulled away and she pressed her cheek to his and said, "I'm not fast, I just know what I want," and after a moment he squeezed her even harder than she was squeezing him. Their first apartment after the wedding was so small that neither could get dressed in the bedroom unless the other stayed in bed, and Wilbur swore to do better as a provider and joined the Air Force so they'd send him to electricians school.

He told her that without him, the whole tower went dark and the gigantic antennae stopped spinning, and she answered that this was just how she felt, too. He explained that when the diesels altered their output at odd intervals, the voltage changes caused the radar transmitters to sound their alarms, and every single time the threat had to be assessed, the alarm silenced, the transmitter readjusted, the alarm reset, and a threat assessment report filled out. That meant some of his shifts lasted up to nineteen hours. In those cases he was so wired that he called her when he went off duty and talked and talked. He told her that the windchill was so bad some days that in the sun and behind some shelter he'd be sweating in a T-shirt, while out in the wind, water would freeze in a bucket. He told her that the space heater she'd insisted he take had made his part of the bunk room a popular gathering spot, and that he'd gotten a reputation as a good egg because instead of filing a report about an airman second class who'd dropped a transmitter drawer, he'd spent the night repairing it himself so the guy wouldn't get in trouble.

She asked if that meant he'd made any friends, and he said no, not yet, and there was an awkward pause in which he could hear her disappointment, so he added that he *had* been getting a kick out of a diver who was always sucking helium out of a tank and then cracking everybody up by saying, "Take me to your leader" like he was the man from outer space.

After Gordon had been on the tower for a month, Ellie started hearing about his friend Captain Mangual. Gordon made it sound like he'd known him all his life. "Who is this guy?" she finally asked. "And why are there two captains out there?" He told her that Captain Mangual didn't work on the platform but on the AKL-17 supply ship. "But he has time to visit you on the tower?" she asked. No, they got to know each other by radio, Gordon told her. So he was quite the guy, huh? she wanted to know, and then got even more irritated when he answered, "Honey, there's *nothing* this guy can't do."

Captain Mangual's ship was specially outfitted to unload cargo between the legs of the tower, but it had to be positioned just so, in whatever seas, and it sometimes took three hours just to get its mooring set. And it was no dinghy: 177 feet from stem to stern. He had to have the patience of a saint, boy. And then he had to hold the ship as steady as possible under the crane that unloaded the cargo or personnel onto the platform. The poor crane operator would just get a load in the bucket and the boat would drop fifty feet and then come back up just as fast. And when stuff was unloaded *onto* the boat, that meant dropping it onto a bouncing and pitching cargo area, and once it landed the deckhands had to get it lashed down before it squashed them flat.

Ellie said it sounded like the crane operator and deckhands had it harder than Captain Mangual, and Gordon said, "No, no, no," as though he hadn't been getting through to her at all. No, Captain Mangual was the guy who made it all possible by doing a million different things to keep the boat in the same damn spot no matter what. He started to give another example and then just gave up.

"Oh," Ellie finally said into the silence. After they hung up, she caught sight of her expression in the mirror in the foyer and snapped at herself: "Stupid."

The butterfingers who'd dropped the transmitter drawer was Jeannette Laino's husband, Louie, and the first snapshot he sent to her from the tower showed what looked like a circle of boys in lifejackets high in the air on a fairground ride, on the back of which he'd printed *"On the Crane."* He explained later that that was how the guys got from the ship to the platform, and that spare parts and supplies were always unloaded first, since if anything got smashed or lost, it was better that it was the Coca-Cola pallets. She asked how high the crane lifted them and he said over a hundred feet, and she exclaimed that it looked dangerous, and he told her that the rule was no lifting in winds over forty knots, since that sent the loads spinning like tops. And besides, two guys were always on safety lines trying to control the bucket's swinging.

She asked if they couldn't just go up the stairs. "Baby, if I had a baseball, from the ship's deck I could barely hit the platform. And I was all-state!" he said. "Does anything ever *fall?*" she asked. "I think the crane operators drop stuff on purpose to shake us up before it's our turn," he told her. When it *was* their turn, though, he added, it was funny how everybody stopped joking once they were up in the air.

"So are you keeping busy?" she asked. He reminded her that he *was* a grade 5, so he was as much a specialist as the tech sergeants. She allowed as how that was very impressive, and he answered that whenever she was ready to stop teasing him, that would be great, so she asked how he was getting along otherwise, and he said the same as always: he kept to himself and didn't bother anyone. Those were his mottoes, along with "Stay friendly" and "Don't question stupid orders."

The new policy was that the helicopters would bring in everything except fuel and very heavy equipment. The choppers never shut off their engines, so while you stood there in the noise and wind, the guys coming off duty had to peel off their baggy yellow survival suits and hand them over to the guys coming on, and during the ride everyone did some serious sweating, so those suits were pretty funky. She asked if the helicopters flew in all sorts of weather and he answered that he guessed they had to, since they carried the mail and the beer. He said that you only got helicopter work in the armpits of the world, because in regular places the operating costs were too high with everything that was always going wrong and needing to be replaced. But he loved to see the choppers come in, their double rotors making their own storm and still setting the giant machines down as lightly as a leaf. And then you waited until the rotors lost enough speed to start drooping like they were worn out from the trip.

That night Jeannette lay in bed thinking about what a boy her Louie was, and then she moved on to other boys she'd dated before him. One she remembered had painted flames on his car and asked her to call him Shiv. She fell asleep thinking of that boy sitting in Louie's television chair, and when she woke up her blinds were open and an old man wearing suspenders and no shirt was standing on her front lawn and looking in at her.

The guy that Louie wished Jeannette could meet, though, was Frankie Recupido, one of the divers, and a real Ernie Kovacs type. Louie had been told to watch out for him, and it wasn't hard to see why: he was always pulling stunts like stuffing cut-up rubber bands into someone's pipe tobacco. On their first flight out to the tower he'd emptied a can of vegetable soup into his sick bag before takeoff and then pretended to throw up, so a few minutes later he could call out that he was still hungry before scarfing it down. He kept the noncoms and enlisted men supplied with moonshine he called plonk and made from sugar and banana peels and whatever else he scrounged from the cook. He'd gotten into two fights for punting the basketball off the platform after arguing about fouls during games. They'd had to launch a boat to recover the ball. In bad weather he went out to the railings around the platform and howled into the wind like a wolf.

Jeannette said he sounded like someone to keep away from, but Louie said he was a good guy who really missed his kids. His previous station had been Guam, and his family had gone along, but even so he'd been away so much in the eastern and southern Pacific that he'd been lucky to see them three weeks a year. Frankie told him that two-thirds of the divers he knew were divorced or separated, since whenever the water heater shut down or a kid broke a finger or the roof sprang a leak back at the hacienda, a diver was probably offshore, and after a while the old ball and chain got fed up. He said his wife told him that for her the last straw had been the spiders hanging upside down from the living-room ceiling. When their little girl first saw one, she'd said, "What is that? A cat?"

Louie found it funny that the one thing that Jeannette couldn't get over about Frankie was that he had framed *Playboy* pinups over his bunk. When he told her about that, she just kept saying "Framed?" until he finally said, "You know what? Whether or not you'd run screaming from a guy like that onshore is beside the point. Here the only point is: can he do his job?"

Because, boy, they needed *somebody* to do that job. From day one, the official logs had listed unusual and alarming motions and sounds reported by personnel onboard, and after three or four visits the engineers agreed that the bracing and joints hadn't been as effective in stabilizing the platform as they'd anticipated. They identified which braces and pins were most likely damaged and responsible, and this meant guys like Frankie had to carry out continual underwater inspections and bolt tightenings. The problem, the designers told them, was that the defective portions were not only weakening their immediate area but also shifting stress onto the entire structure.

Despite going down as often as they did, Frankie and the other divers couldn't keep up with the accelerating damage. Even in good weather, the braces' movements under the constant wave loads kept wearing down the pin joints. And what would happen in *bad* weather? The engineers had already figured out that each serious storm would stress a given pin as much as a full year of normal seas.

Frankie would tighten bolts and the next day when he checked them again they'd be so loose he could turn them with his fingers.

At last the designers came up with a new idea, and big T-bolts were flown out and installed at the loosest points to provide more rigidity. That helped some, but a few weeks later they investigated again, and word was that they'd told the Air Force that without radical measures the conditions would continue to worsen, with the ultimate loss of Tower no. 4 the most likely result.

So X-bracing *above* the water was designed and installed in the summer of 1960. The guys felt the difference right away, but when Ellie asked Gordon why he didn't sound more relieved, he told her what Captain Mangual had said when he first saw all that new rigmarole above the surface: since it filled in the space beneath the platform with its crisscrossing diagonals, waves that otherwise would have passed underneath the platform were now colliding head-on into all that brace work. When she asked why that was a problem, Gordon answered that it was like when you were standing in the surf and saw a big wave coming: you wanted to turn sideways so as not to expose your whole chest to the wallop.

Betty Bakke was the first in her family to hear any reports about Hurricane Donna, from a spinster aunt whose telegram announced a ruined vacation in Miami Beach, and in her phone call to Roy that night Betty asked if the hurricane was something that the men on the tower needed to worry about. Gee, Roy answered, he sure hoped not, then asked how she was holding up, all by herself for so long, and she said that so many people now gave her such *"poor you"* glances that she really was starting to look tragic. She'd learned how to run the sewing machine and had made curtains and bedspreads. She told him that she was trying to be as self-sufficient as possible and also doing volunteer work at the Airman's Closet on the base, stocking donated items for the E-4's with dependents. He complimented her on being such a Samaritan, and she told him that she mostly stood embarrassed behind the counter while the less fortunate families picked over what was available. She said she never knew whether to wear her hat to work, so she always carried it in her hand. It was only after they'd gotten off the phone that she realized she hadn't asked what was supposed to happen if the hurricane *was* headed toward the tower.

Edna Kovarick hadn't heard about the hurricane until it was halfway up the North Carolina coast, but when she called Wilbur he was inside a radome watching the height-finder antenna rock in its yoke while making its 360-degree sweep, so he had to call her back. She asked then about the storm and he said they had an evacuation procedure in place and that if the storm got anywhere close he was sure they'd all be safe on dry land before she knew it. Next they talked about babies, and she reminded Wilbur of the story her sister had told them of carrying her infant on the train with an open wicker suitcase for a crib. Maybe they'd get started on that when he got back, he told her.

Maybe, Edna said, feeling wonderful at the notion of it, but when she looked at their little bathroom nook, she wondered what it would be like to bathe a newborn in a shower bath.

Hurricane Donna had already killed 125 people in the Caribbean and Florida by the time Air Force weathermen predicted that it would hit Tower no. 4 dead-on. The evacuation was duly ordered, and a Coast Guard cutter along with Captain Mangual's AKL-17 dispatched from New York Harbor. But the Air Force wanted to wait until the last possible moment so the Russian spy trawlers that were always loitering around the tower couldn't access the classified equipment, and by the time the two ships arrived on-site the outer edge of the hurricane had already hit.

After the first attempts to use the crane, when its bucket was blown into the ocean and the guys in it barely rescued, the evacuation was called off. Captain Phelan called everyone into the mess and gave them the bad news that they were going to have to ride the storm out. Wave crests were now visible through the windows, and with every impact the whole platform screeched and groaned and jolted before settling back into position.

Before the first half of the storm had cleared, the flying bridge underneath the platform had torn loose, and through the lower hatches the men could see it flailing and smashing itself against the two downwind legs. Then the eye passed over, and the storm hit from the other direction. From start to finish it was eight hours, and for the last three there was nothing but shrieking and grinding noises from the structure below.

At one point during the worst of it, Roy dropped by the captain's quarters and asked how long he thought they'd float if they went over. "Float?" Gordon answered, hunkered down in his chair. He told Roy the tower had never been designed for watertight integrity, and that for all intents and purposes it was a building someone had set out over the Atlantic on stilts.

The rest of the time they talked about other subjects. Roy told him that he'd heard that as electronics got more portable, these systems could be airborne instead of platform-based. And what would they do with the platforms then? he wanted to know.

Maybe turn them into prisons, Gordon suggested. Roy informed him that during that last really bad stretch, poor Laino had upchucked into the sink and it had flown back into his face. An hour before the storm ended, the two of them looked in on everyone, and then Gordon wrote in his daily log, *"Men's morale OK."* Afterward, he added in caps, *"NEVER AGAIN."*

When Ellie finally got through on the phone again, once the weather had cleared, her husband sounded like someone who'd been hit by a car. She asked how he was doing and he told her they were all still standing, but just barely. The maintenance platform beneath the main one was gone, and its catwalks just stopped where the waves had snapped the steel. The roof panel on the avionics hangar had rolled up like the top of a sardine can. The colonel who'd flown out for an inspection had said at the end of his tour, "I can't believe you all stayed. I would have ordered everyone off." Gordon said he'd stared at him in response.

By their next phone call, a week later, the news was even worse. There were multiple fractures in the new X-bracing, and Frankie and the other divers had reported that two of the submarine diagonals in the middle tier had torn loose. This required another visit by the entire design and engineering team, who showed up wearing Mae Wests over their business suits, huddled for three hours with the divers in the mess, and then had brought to Gordon's quarters a plan for cable bracing that would extend from 25 to 125 feet below the surface, bypassing the damaged tier. Gordon told Ellie he'd asked if this would really work and they'd all been pretty gung-ho about it. They'd have to fabricate special cables with sufficient tensile strength, but those should be ready by the first of the year.

By the first of the year, though, Frankie and the other divers had discovered more fractures on the lowest tiers, at the 125-foot level, where the cables were meant to be anchored. When the engineers heard that, they threw up their hands and said that stabilizing the tower was such a massive undertaking that it would have to wait until the spring, when conditions would be more favorable.

"So they'll just evacuate you until spring, then?" Jeannette asked Louie once he'd shared that news on his leave. They'd been lying together, and Louie answered that he didn't see what else the Air Force could do, given how badly no. 4 was damaged. And Jeannette startled him by shouting, "Don't *lie* to me about this!" and then rolling away. And after he'd driven back to base, she found under her pillow a note that read *"I love you SO much."* It was paper-clipped to a booklet entitled SAFETY TIPS FOR LIVING ALONE.

A week later Gordon woke Ellie up with a phone call at one a.m. to say the engineers had informed the Air Force the entire bracing system on the A-B side was no longer effective, and they were no longer able to provide an estimate as to the tower's remaining capabilities. Maybe it still retained 30 percent of its initial strength, possibly 40, conceivably 50. But whatever the numbers, they had put in writing that they didn't want to encourage the Air Force to assume it was safe, so another evacuation was scheduled for February 1st.

Ellie cheered so loudly that she woke Larry up. Then she thought: *That's three weeks away.* "Why February 1st?" she asked, and Gordon said a lot of guys were getting off the next day but a skeleton crew of twenty-eight was being left behind for maintenance and to keep the Russians from swarming all over the thing the minute they left.

But how could the Russians get on it with no one working the cranes?, Ellie wanted to know, and Gordon said he'd asked his superior officer the same question. And what did he say?, Ellie asked. He'd said it wasn't as if the Air Force couldn't assume *some* risk here, Gordon told her. And that the only way to keep anybody *completely* safe from the ocean was to leave him on land.

.   .   .

So when Louie rotated back onto the tower a week after New Year's as part of that skeleton crew, Frankie was standing there on the helipad waiting to take his survival suit. After he climbed into it, he shook Louie's hand and said it had been great knowing him but he wasn't coming back. And Louie said, "You mean you guys have already finished all the repairs?" And Frankie answered, "No, I mean I'm not coming back."

Wilbur told Edna on the phone that he wasn't even supposed to still *be* there, that he'd been due to rotate out, but his replacement hadn't reported. For the guys left behind, he said, the atmosphere was like homeroom in junior high on a winter morning: everyone just kept to himself, and those who didn't were surly. The weather was always winter-morning, too, windy and dark and cold. Because they were shorthanded, he now worked as a plotter behind the radar-scope operator, and for longer hours, which was probably good, since nobody could sleep anyway.

Ellie told Gordon that he had to get off there, but he asked how *that* was supposed to work, since he *was* the commanding officer. While she sat on the phone trying to think of what to offer in response, he added it had occurred to him that confidence was like an air bubble that shrank a little every time something went wrong. He said he'd installed a plumb line in his cabin over his desk, to check just how badly the tower was listing, and that now the line never stopped making this wild figure eight. He asked where Ellie had been when he called earlier, and she said she'd been driving Larry around on his paper route. "Why? Should I stay close to the phone?" she asked, and he said yes.

When Roy saw the plumb line he hadn't said anything, but mentioned later that the platform's back-and-forth was like when you bent a wire one way and the other, over and over: sooner or later the wire was going to snap.

It was a mess, all right, Gordon managed to respond. Together they worked out the order of evacuation if it came down to just the lifeboats, though they both knew that trying to lower those boats in anything but good weather would be suicidal. If they were going to get off the tower, they had to do it before a storm was even visible on the horizon. Gordon put himself in the last boat and Roy in the first, but Roy rewrote the list and put himself in the last boat as well. He could always tell when Gordon was making the best of a bad situation, because in those cases he started humming along with whatever he was doing.

Louie told Jeannette that in any kind of wind or seas no one could fall asleep given all the clanging and grinding coming from the legs. She asked if they hadn't been checked, and he told her civilian contractors had come out any number of times and always said when they left that the new fix was the one that was going to last.

When he talked to her now she was always crying. He told her he'd written a letter to the president-elect asking him to override the brass and get them off no. 4, and reminded her that after all they were both Massachusetts guys. He said he'd told Mr. Kennedy that he had to be relieved because his presence here was affecting his wife so much.

That made her cry even harder. "Why did you even *report* when they told you to?" she wanted to know, but he had to say goodbye because his time was up and all twenty-eight guys needed to call home.

The weekend forecast for January 14th and 15th was not so good: sixty-knot winds and possibly higher. The Air Force ordered Captain Mangual's AKL-17 to head for the tower, take on equipment, and stand by for a possible full evacuation. On Saturday the 14th the sky stayed dark but the wind was manageable, and the crane operators offloaded twenty-two tons of radar equipment. Louie traded cigarettes and some of Frankie's hooch for a spot in the front of the line for the phone and called Jeannette back with the happy news that they were removing equipment and there'd be nothing left for him to guard, so he figured everyone would be off the tower by the next day.

Late that afternoon Roy found Gordon at the edge of the platform, staring out to the south at a black wall of clouds that lifted from the horizon to the top of the sky. Wilbur and Louie had pulled maintenance duty and were repainting the two lifeboats on the deck, and stopped to look as well.

"Maybe it's just a local depression," Roy told him. They could already hear the wakes of the tower's legs in the increasing currents.

On the AKL-17's bridge, Captain Mangual read his forecast from the Merchant Marine—it was bad, extreme weather conditions within twelve hours—and radioed his friend Gordon that it was time to get everyone off. And in turn Gordon relayed Captain Mangual's recommendation to his superiors at Otis AFB, who reported back that the Air Force's forecast wasn't nearly so dire, and that the storm would swing wide of them, and that the AKL-17 had already been ordered back to port.

. . .

But Captain Mangual refused to leave. Gordon stayed up all night checking in with him on the radio, and at 0400 went out onto the platform and looked out over the sea. It was blowing hard enough that some of the coffee he'd brought slopped onto his wrist.

The wind was now seventy knots and building fast, the seas already at thirty feet. The lights of the AKL-17 turtled along in the distance off in the blackness and the rain, disappearing behind the wave crests. Sometimes he couldn't even see the green light atop its radar mast.

Farther out, the red lights of the Russian trawlers appeared here and there in the troughs. Because he couldn't think of anything else to do, he spent an hour rigging safety lines over the upper platform, so there'd be something to clip onto if they had to do some emergency troubleshooting or get to the boats.

The next morning the northeaster hit. He climbed up to the helipad deck and opened the hatch just enough to confirm that waves bigger than any he'd ever seen were concussing spray even onto the radomes. Everything was already sheathed in ice. He had to brace himself against the railing because the staircase was swaying.

In the mess near the phone the guys in line let him cut ahead, and Ellie picked up on the first ring and asked if they were getting evacuated. She said the weather was already awful where she was. He told her he kept requesting evacuation and that his requests had been denied. She said *she'd* call instead, and he told her to go ahead. She shouted that his tour was almost over, and he said he knew that already, and that she was going to wake Larry up, and that he'd never wanted to be out here in the first place.

"Are you saying it's *my* fault?" she asked, and he said that as soon as the weather let up he'd be off this tower for good, and that the poor sap assigned to take over was already at Otis.

At 0730 the line at the phone had progressed far enough for Wilbur to call Edna. He had to shout over the awful clanging of metal on metal. "That's outside," he said, as if to reassure her. She heard men screaming. "That's inside," he told her.

At 1030 a huge bang knocked everyone standing off his feet. "I think I shit my pants," Wilbur told Louie once he'd gotten back up off the floor.

Gordon and Roy climbed into their survival suits and humped a hundred feet of nylon rope back up the staircase to the main deck, and Gordon tied a square knot around his waist and clove-hitched the other end to the railing inside the hatch. They popped it open just as a wave exploded over the deck and stripped the crane box of its welding equipment.

They clipped onto the safety lines and crawled forward on their hands and knees. In the wind and spray it took ten minutes to get to the safety netting at the platform's edge, their ropes whipping and spiraling behind them like they were harnessed to furious animals. Roy belayed him and Gordon hung upside-down over the safety netting and the gale blew him out to sea, but the knots held and after a minute or two Roy was able to haul him back in. Both were crying, they were so scared.

Once he got control of himself, Gordon lay out over the netting again, trying to see what had happened below as the wind battered and spun and whirligigged him. Sleet whipped his face and when he looked down the waves erupted to meet him. The bigger ones propelled ice water into his suit and he could hear Roy shrieking along with him.

Finally he signaled they could go back in, and on the staircase they closed the hatch behind them and he gave Roy the bad news.

Some of the X-bracing had broken loose and was smashing against the legs. The joints were failing and the braces buckling. Once that happened, the entire structure was standing on three spindly legs that were three hundred feet long.

Back in the mess, the men helped them out of their wet clothing, wrapped them in blankets, and handed them hot coffee, but they were both shaking so much they knocked the mugs off the tables where they were sitting. Roy lit a cigarette and it kept bobbing in his mouth.

"What have you guys been up to?" Wilbur tried to joke.

"Inspecting the X-braces," Roy finally managed to say.

"Bad day for it," Wilbur told them.

Once he'd warmed up, Roy kept radioing Otis for weather updates. Each time he got off, Gordon asked if it was going to stay this bad, and Roy said that it was going to get worse.

The others climbed into their berths, pulled blankets over their heads, and held their hands over their ears.

The low-frequency beacon antenna ripped loose and disappeared. The last wind-speed reading was 110 knots before the anemometer blew away. The ceiling on the upper floors bowed and the light fixtures popped out and swung free. The outer walls flexed from the air pressure. The dome covering the windward radar collapsed and was torn to pieces. Gordon recorded it all in the log.

Captain Mangual radioed that the AKL-17 was now registering wind velocities of 130 knots, and that the seas were even uglier. He said the only good news was that the wind was so strong it was blowing the tops off the waves.

Afterward, neither Ellie nor Betty nor Edna nor Jeannette, in the face of reporters' questions, could recall a moment when—alone at their kitchen tables or back windows, in the best tradition of military wives—they'd given up hope. But each of them also remembered thinking some version of *"What about me?"*

At one p.m. when Ellie got Gordon's next call, he told her the tower was gyrating, and she registered it as a word he'd never used before. She said she'd called and called the numbers at Otis but couldn't get through to anybody. He said he wasn't surprised, since everyone's families were probably calling. She asked if the tower would float if it went over, and he told her it would go down fast and that no one could be saved. He added that he was worried about Captain Mangual, whose ship was overloaded and swamping. Gordon had ordered him back to port, but he'd refused to obey. He said the last time he'd looked, the ship's entire bow had come out of the water with one wave.

"How did everyone let things *get* to this point?" Ellie shouted, and he answered that he could barely understand her and she had to try to calm down for Larry's sake. When she asked if the men on the ship could help him, he said he doubted they could even help themselves.

When Louie called Jeannette there was no answer, so he dialed again and again and then had to start over at the back of the line, and when he finally got through he shouted at her about where the hell she'd been. "I'm *sorry*," she said, and he told her that he'd needed to tie himself into his bunk, that he'd listened to his buddies crying themselves sick, and that he wanted her to find someone good to take care of her. And she said, "I don't *want* to find someone else," and he said he had to get off now because other guys needed the phone. She said, "You can't just *say* that and hang *up*," but somebody else had grabbed the phone by then and yelled at her to get off the line.

. . .

Betty's phone rang and she snatched it up, and Roy told her their relief ship was in and out of radio contact but had reported it was being lifted off the wave crests and thrown sideways into the troughs. It was just going to have to keep motoring leeward and try to stay within range. He said he and Captain Phelan had started back out on the safety lines but that between the whiteouts from the spray and the force of the water and wind they couldn't make it to the netting to see what was going on below. The deck's steel plates were vibrating. The lower storage areas were awash. But they were all toughing it out.

"My one-man morale officer," Betty snapped, and they were both surprised by her rage. But she wasn't able to make herself apologize.

Otis had agreed to try for an evacuation at the earliest lull, which the forecasters were predicting for 0300, he told her. Copters were already on high alert and ready to go. The aircraft carrier *Wasp* and its entire battle group had been diverted to their location. They just had to hang on.

"For *twelve more hours*?" Betty shouted. He told her that because the weather was a little better over New York, the Coast Guard had already dispatched the cutter *Agassiz* and it was already on its way.

Half an hour later Ellie's phone rang again, and when she answered Gordon said the tower was breaking up. She wailed, and he told her he'd never known he'd had so many religious men in his crew and that even the welders were praying. He said he kept thinking that if this shitbox could last another hour then maybe the storm might blow itself out. He told her that to give everyone something to do he'd ordered them into their survival suits and all hands on deck to keep the helipad clear, so now he had to get back up there because guys were skidding around into the nettings. He told her that she'd been the best thing that ever happened to him. He asked her to wish them all luck.

She was still crying and he was helping Wilbur keep his feet an hour later when, eighteen miles southeast of the tower, the *Wasp*'s captain reported having turned his bow just in time to negotiate a single and monstrously large rogue wave. The crest was 60 feet above the ship's bridge, so he estimated its height at 120 feet. The helicopters strapped to the deck had been demolished, but the ship had careened safely down the wave's back end, which when he'd last seen it had been heading off in the direction of the tower.

Jeannette was trying to call Louie back when the AKL-17's helmsman was knocked unconscious and Captain Mangual had to take over. The seas were like one cliff after another tipping at him from all directions, and between crises all he could do was observe the blip of the tower on his radar screen. At seven thirty by Ellie's clock, as she sat by the phone unable to comfort her hysterical son, the blip vanished. Captain Mangual abandoned the helm and knocked aside his radar operator and watched the wand as its line of light swept through two full revolutions before he grabbed the radio and shouted, "Tower 4! Tower 4!" until his executive officer grabbed his shoulders and brought him back to the situation at hand.

Betty Bakke was trying to get rid of a worried neighbor when her husband was ordered off the deck, to stay with the radio in case of an update about either the weather or an evacuation. Roy had just cinched the top of his survival suit tighter for warmth when everything lurched as though the A-B side of the tower had pitched down a gigantic stairstep, and everything loose or not lashed down was swept into the wall. There was a high-pitched rending of metal like train or subway brakes and he smashed into the top of the door. And then there was another crash and he felt the shock of being underwater and the suction of the sinking platform even there inside the room. The lights flashed out and in the darkness and bitter cold he rose up on waves to the ceiling, and his head surfaced into a pocket of air.

At two a.m. when Ellie's phone rang she ripped it from its cradle on the second ring. She was still in the foyer, with Larry curled at her feet wrapped in the quilt from his bed. The call didn't wake him but his mother's screams did. When he couldn't calm her down he fled to his room and hid under his bed, but then scrambled out again and found their family doctor's number in the address book, and it wasn't until the doctor arrived and Ellie was sedated that all of the screaming stopped.

Jeannette was pulled out of bed by a call from her father, who told her that a New York newspaper had called him at two thirty in the morning to ask if he was aware that the Texas Tower with his son-in-law aboard had sunk. He sounded put out, and when she started shrieking her father was so taken aback that he said he'd call her again later when she was ready to have a conversation.

Edna dreamt of a pounding on her door, and woke to realize it was happening, and with her housecoat on she turned on her porch light to find a man who identified himself as a reporter for *Life* magazine. He wanted her reaction to the tragedy. She made him repeat what he was talking about before she told him to get off her property, instead of collapsing right there in front of him.

. . .

They were all still awake in the wee hours when the senior sonar operator for the destroyer *McCaffery,* part of the *Wasp*'s battle group, reported a rhythmic tapping that was emanating from the wreckage on the sea bottom, as well as what sounded to him like a human voice, and the ship's captain announced that despite the conditions and the water's depth he was attempting to send men down and requesting all possible emergency salvage assistance. Some divers had already reached the site, but had failed to make contact in the limited time they had to search. More help was on its way from multiple shore bases, but by 0330 the tapping and the other noises had stopped.

Four days after the collapse Betty was notified that divers had found Roy's body floating on the ceiling of Captain Phelan's office, still holding the radio mike. The next day they recovered the body of a technician a few miles south. A copter had spotted the yellow of his survival suit. No other remains had been located.

Five months later, on a humid night in June, Edna came in from her screened porch and took a call from a man who explained he was a fisherman out of Montauk. He asked if she was the Edna Kovarick whose husband had been on the Texas Tower, and she was about to hang up when he said he had something for her: her husband's billfold. It had been dredged up inside a giant sea scallop's shell three miles from where the tower went down. He was looking at her photograph as he talked to her.

. . .

The report by the Senate Committee on Armed Services on the inquiry into the collapse of Texas Tower no. 4 ran to 288 pages and ended by acknowledging the tower had represented a spectacular achievement, but that due to various factors, it had never really approached its intended design strength, and stipulated that the committee was not so much attempting to assess blame as to follow up on the dollars that Congress had drawn from taxpayers to pay for programs such as this and others deemed vital to national defense. The committee sought to protect all individuals involved, whether contractors or service personnel, where protection was justified, and felt the facts it had uncovered afforded a proper and necessary background against which any individual who might have charges preferred against him could be tried properly. But the report's conclusion stressed that those twenty-eight men in and out of the service who had sacrificed their lives deserved the same recognition as those who had died in combat, since it had certainly been a battle station to which they'd been assigned. And the committee wanted to make clear to one and all that those men had been patriots in every sense of the word.

Ellie read the report and then took it out into the backyard with Larry and set it on fire. Jeannette read it once and stored it afterward in a trunk with the rest of her husband's papers. And Edna found that whenever she read it she lost her Wilbur all over again, so after the fifth or sixth time she stopped.

Each of them despised herself for her own contributions to the disaster. Ellie thought her father had turned out to be right about her selfishness, and Jeannette spent weeks remembering having asked only about nest eggs; Edna told friends that a more confident wife would have worried less about her husband being well liked and more about where he would be stationed, and Betty kept hearing

Roy's silence on the phone after she had shocked them both with her rage.

What the Senate report spared them was the last thing their husbands had seen that night while they slewed across the pitching and ice-covered platform in the rain and sleet and wind in their survival suits, waiting for their rescue. While Jeannette and Edna and Betty and Ellie had sat by their phones castigating themselves for ever having entrusted their lives to other people's promises, off to the southeast of their husbands' platform as if in a silent movie the sea was rising, and one after the other their husbands had turned in that direction, confused that everything was black until they realized they weren't seeing any crests or spray because they weren't looking high enough. And once they did they saw, like a line across the sky, the thin white edge of the top of the wave. And they recognized it as the implacability that would no longer indulge their mistakes and would sweep from them all they had ever loved.

Wall-to-Wall Counseling

The boys were haggling at the dinner table about which was worse, circumcision or getting hit in the nuts. One is twelve and the other nine but they already know everything. I was finishing the chardonnay and fielding questions from my daughter, Maeve, about how late she could stay out. Across the country, my sister was coming apart and waiting for me to call back, but of course I hadn't picked up the phone yet.

Maeve told her younger brothers that they were driving her up the wall but they wouldn't let up, so she finally asked what about a catheter. They wanted to know what that was and after she told them there was a lot of shrieking and crotch grabbing. Sean said there was no way doctors really did that and Neil said that nobody was sticking anything up Nolan. The noise around the table quieted a bit.

Who was Nolan, Maeve wanted to know. And when Sean saw his brother's face, he said, "Oh my God—did you just call your dick Nolan?"

"What?" Neil said. "I always call it Nolan."

We were all a little openmouthed. The dog stood in the doorway, wondering if it was safe to cross the kitchen to check on his dish.

"*Why* do you call it Nolan?" I asked. These were the kinds of weekends I was having now.

He immediately started crying, and looked down at his lap like he wanted to kill it.

"Neil," I said. I could've helped a little more than that. When he gets miserable I always find myself thinking: *The kid's nine years old.*

"*Nobody* in this family understands me," he said.

"Nobody on *earth* understands you," his brother told him.

When he was getting ready for bed that night, I checked on him in the bathroom and he had my toothbrush and was brushing Nolan with it.

"What are you *doing*?" I yelled.

"What?" he shouted. I'd scared him.

"What are you *doing*?" I asked him again. "That's my *toothbrush*." I pulled it out of his hand.

He started crying again. Of course the other kids wanted to know what was going on and everybody piled into the bathroom.

"Get *out* of here," I told them. "This is none of your business." Their brother had already pulled up his pajama bottoms and pushed past them into the hall.

I found him in bed with the covers over his face. When I pulled them down he pulled them back up again. "You're *such* a bad mom," he told me. He was still crying. "You're *such* a bad mom."

"Why am I such a bad mom?" I wanted to know. "Because I don't let you brush your wienis with my toothbrush?"

"And that's why you're so evil to me, too," he said.

"Evil," I said, at a loss. I was pinning his arms so he couldn't twist away. "Why am *I* so evil to *you*?"

"Because I'm adopted," he said.

"What is going *on*?" Maeve called from her bedroom, and it took me a minute to say something.

"What makes you think you're *adopted*?" I finally asked.

"Look at me and look at you," he said.

I glanced at myself in the mirror over his dresser. "We look alike," I told him. This seemed to make him feel even worse.

I was going to ask his father about it but fell asleep waiting for his call. Monday everybody went off to school, no problem, and when Neil got back we had a talk. I left work early for it. I took him by the sleeve after he dumped his backpack and he wasn't going outside until we set a few things straight. He said he didn't know why he needed to brush Nolan, he just did. I told him if he did need to brush Nolan we'd get him a special toothbrush, but that he wasn't using mine.

"Well, I don't want to use *mine*," he said.

"Right. We don't want to do that, either," I told him. "We'll get a special Nolan brush."

And that was fine with him, though he was still weepy about it. That night after he was supposed to be in bed he found me just sitting there with my head in my hands in front of my e-mail.

"Wait—are those all for you?" he wanted to know.

He was talking about my Horror Stories inbox, which was so nuts by that point it took me a full five minutes to scroll through it. I work for the PR arm of America's largest health insurance company, and the last few months the entire Eastern Seaboard had apparently been denied claims for reasons that would make any self-respecting media outlet sit up and take notice, and I was having trouble writing up the explanations as to why. Some of the clients, if you had any kind of heart, it wasn't so easy to explain why they should be shit out of luck.

"These are just the ones *I* have to deal with," I told him. "Some of the people I work with have even more."

He made one of his *I'm so glad I'm not you* noises. Again: he's nine years old.

"I'm happy you're so sympathetic," I told him.

"Well, a woman's work is never done," my husband said when we finally got ahold of each other. He was trying to be heard over what sounded like karaoke and Polynesian music in the background.

"What are you, in a *tiki* bar?" I asked.

He laughed. "I'm taking Nolan out for a good time," he said. He'd liked the Nolan story, though he otherwise hadn't commented much.

"It's getting so I don't even want to go into the office," I told him. "I think that's why Janine developed her migraines."

"Hey, it's like your father always said about people buying insurance," he reminded me. "If they wanted security they should've put their money into hedge funds."

My father spent his life representing the carriers in product-liability cases, so whatever story you told, he always had an ear out for the deadbeats who wanted to soak the poor insurance companies.

Like all its competitors, our company collects data on the number of claims we deny and why. But it turned out that only California made us report that information. Anybody else who asked was told it was a trade secret. A state senator during a hearing last December asked our regional manager just how many claims from state policy-holders our company had rejected that year. "Aw, jeez," our guy said into the mike with a straight face. "Who can say?"

People sometimes came in after they'd been denied, and there were lots of phone calls, but our supervisor was always telling us to thank God and deregulation that it wasn't as much work as it could have been. What he meant was that the previous year about half of all respondents to a national survey said they'd experienced some kind of serious problem with their health insurance, but only 2 percent managed to file a formal complaint. And the even better news, as far as the company was concerned, was that 92 percent of those surveyed couldn't name the agency that regulated health insurance in their state.

All of which meant that when I asked my boss just what was *not* permissible, when it came to reasons our MDs and case managers could reject claims, he said, "Hey, it's the Wild West out there." We made his answer into an acronym and used it for everything, as in *"Hey, there's no toilet paper in the ladies' bathroom! Well, HITWWOT."* Every so often our company polices itself, but that's just being extra careful because nobody's minding the store. Our state regulators not only no longer know percentages on denied or dropped coverage; they can't even keep track of the policies in effect in their own jurisdictions, or even which companies in the state *offer* policies.

Not everybody getting culled out took it lying down. Every so often we picked up an outside line and got our hair blown back. It took however many minutes just to calm some people down enough to make clear we were transferring their call. We had fewer happy customers than the average mortgage company.

After some of the worst abuse we kidded one another to remember Asshole Jimmy's Two-Step Program: Confuse your customers and dump the sick. You could never go wrong if you stayed on task when it came to confusing your customers and dumping the sick.

"We'll be more than happy to initiate the appeals process," Janine would tell someone. "We'll just need to make an initial assessment as to whether the process would have an impact on either the case under consideration or the relevant subgrouping of parallel cases. And that could take an indeterminate amount of time, depending on the availability status of the case managers as well as, on an entirely different calendar, the consulting physicians."

"I hope *that* cleared things up," sometimes she'd say to herself once she hung up.

Asshole Jimmy was this guy whose picture was on the wall in the main conference room for having posted the best numbers in the company's history. He was based in Oklahoma City. It wasn't really his Two-Step Program, but it might as well have been.

"So has your sister called?" my husband asked. The Polynesian music had faded a little, and it sounded like there was an auctioneer somewhere in the background.

"I haven't heard from her in a week," I told him.

"She's probably en route," he said. "Police the perimeter and set the trip wires."

When he was being funny my husband liked to talk like Janine, whose fiancé was an NCO in the 3rd Infantry Division, or the "Broken TV," as they called it, because their unit patch was a square with blue and white diagonals like a TV on the fritz.

My husband had had what he'd claimed was a hilarious talk with her at an office party about my sistering, which she classified as total FISHDO, as in *"Fuck It, Shit Happens, Drive On."* She had enough information in that regard to know what she was talking about. She'd had to sit through any number of calls I fielded at the office and had also heard a lot of my stories. The day after Jennifer's thirteenth birthday, to pick just one, I'd come home with two twist-tied baggies and shut her bedroom door behind me and announced it was time we got into drugs. This was the week after I'd taught her to play backgammon. She'd had maybe the shittiest birthday party I'd ever seen, so though I didn't have a clue what the drugs would do to her I figured things could only improve.

I was two years older and better at putting up with boys' crap and our parents' crap, so my sister always thought of me as the cool one. When I told Janine that, she gave me such a look I had to go, "I know. I don't get it, either."

My sister was the kind of kid who whatever we were doing always looked like she wanted to be doing something else. Once when she was fifteen I had to tell her to cheer up when we were snorting cocaine. After she got involved with boys, her favorite way of asking me to be quiet was to tell me to shut my cock holster.

My parents had their own problems and every so often my mother would say that it would be nice if I could look after my sister. That was usually after a call from the school or the police.

Now the problem was that her boyfriend was kicking her out. She hadn't mentioned coming east, but then she doesn't do a lot of what other people call "planning," and she doesn't tend to have a lot of other options.

"So listen," my husband said. The music had stopped entirely and now there were only normal bar sounds behind him. "I'm gonna finish here early because it turns out we didn't need to meet with these people. I can change my flight and be back tomorrow."

He's also in PR and his firm was working with the city of Buffalo to put together a bid for the 2026 Winter Olympics. "I shit you not," I told Janine after explaining it to her. So far the plan involved sprucing up some of the old Lake Placid venues, which were only 350 miles away. The working slogan they'd come up with was *"Recapture the Magic!"*

"Inspired by our marriage," he said, when he first told me.

"Does this make even the remotest bit of sense?" I'd asked him then.

"Hey, it's business, isn't it?" he said.

"The city of Buffalo has money to piss away on this?" I asked.

"What can I tell you?" he answered. "The checks haven't bounced."

. . .

The next day I hadn't even gotten my coffee yet when Janine groaned from her cubicle, "Oh, man, did *you* pick the wrong day to come in." My answering machine had forty-eight messages on it, all from local TV stations. Turned out the parents of a little girl from Oswego—a local celebrity who'd gotten past the first two rounds of *America's Got Talent,* no less—had just been informed that we were refusing to cover her liver transplant because they owned a second home.

"What'd you do, turn off your cell last night?" Janine wanted to know. "BOB is not pleased."

BOB is what we call our boss. It's another one of her fiancé's 3rd Infantry acronyms, for the sun, and stands for *"Big Orange Ball."* She'd been on the story since late the previous night, since nobody could reach me after I gave up on e-mail after another Neil melt-down. She'd sent out the standard-issue response but this time no one had bought it. NBC's morning show out of Albany had already gone with "Members of a local family say they're living a nightmare, and they blame their insurance company," and by the time I listened to half of my messages it was clear the story was going national. Calls had come in from CNN, ABC, MSNBC, and *Last Week Tonight with John Oliver.*

Before I even finished with the messages I called the babysitter, who thank God was able to extend her hours even beyond what we'd planned. No chance I was getting home before ten. Then I got the lowdown from BOB, who had both our CEO and the company's chief medical officer on the phone.

It turned out that the part about the second home was wrong; the CMO explained that the kid had Alpha-1 and things had progressed to the point where the transplant director thought a procedure for someone in her condition would constitute an experimental or unproven service, which we don't cover. In other words, he thought a transplant was unlikely to result in a successful outcome, and he stood by his decision.

"*How* unlikely?" our CEO asked over the phone.

"I'd say a 70 to 75 percent chance of things going kablooie," the CMO told him.

But here was the thing, I had to point out: If this were some fifty-year-old guy, we could ride that out. But this was a twelve-year-old girl. And one who'd been on TV besides.

"NBC in Albany just ran a clip of her singing Clint Black's 'Like the Rain,'" the CEO added glumly.

I spent the morning going back and forth with them. The CEO understood it was a PR nightmare but also felt that we were in the right and was annoyed we were getting hammered for it. According to a lawyer for the girl's family, New York Presbyterian had a perfect match and would hold the liver for forty-eight hours, so that was our window. I was sent back to the phones to see what I could accomplish with the TV people.

It wasn't much. When I left that night, BOB was still at his desk.

"Look who's here," Maeve said when I finally walked through the door.

"You're shitting me, right?" I said to both her and, mostly, my sister. I dropped my briefcase on the dog's back paws. He was climbing on me with his front ones to express his hellos.

"Hey," Jennifer said. She'd feathered her hair and put on some weight. The thighs and knees of her jeans were slashed but maybe that was the new look. She smelled like an ashtray and cleaning products, and was leaning against the sink.

I walked over and gave her a hug.

She said she'd sent the babysitter home and told her I'd settle up with her the next time around. "You better deal with Neil," she said.

Neil had barricaded himself in his room because his big brother hadn't been able to resist spreading the word about Nolan.

"That was helpful, Sean. Thanks," I called down the hall. Neil's door was locked but if you knew how to jiggle the knob you could pop it open.

"Hey, nobody said it was a secret," Sean called back.

"I'm not going to school," Neil told me once I finally got in.

"You *are* going to school," Sean called.

"Sean, stay out of it," I told him. "Neil, why are you under the bed?"

"Do you even know who my teachers are?" he asked. "Do you know what it's like for me on the bus?"

"Aw, honey, times're tough all over," my sister said from the doorway. It was hard to tell whether she was commiserating or busting his stones. "I had a rough time in school, too." She squatted to get down to our level.

"Mrs. Willison," I told him. "Mrs. Durrant for music. Mr. Ham for phys ed."

"All right, Mom, I'll see you later," Maeve called from the stairs.

"You'll see me later? What does *that* mean?" I asked.

"I'm staying over at John's," she said.

"Has everyone here gone nuts?" I asked. "Who's John? You are *not* staying over at John's."

"He's just this *guy* I know," Maeve said. "We talked about this."

"No we haven't," I told her. "And you're not."

She gave me a little more grief before she made some end-of-the-world noises and stomped into her bedroom.

It took me another fifteen minutes to get Neil calmed down and into bed. Then I made the rounds and went downstairs. Everyone I said good night to looked back at me like I was the worst mother in the world.

"Some day, huh?" Jennifer said when I flopped down at the kitchen table.

I stood right back up and got some wine from the fridge, found two clean glasses, and held one out to her.

"I'd better not," she said.

"So how are *you*?" I asked. I didn't do a very good job of keeping the impatience out of my voice.

She told me about the most recent guy, who evidently was obsessed with anal sex. "And I'm not," she said.

I could hear my cell buzzing in my bag in the front hall.

"You need to get that?" she asked.

I wiped my face like I was trying to rub out a mark. "Yeah, at some point," I said.

The anal-sex thing wasn't the real issue, it turned out. The real issue was the verbal abuse, and his stealing. She'd given him however many warnings. She provided a few examples and then started crying. We put our heads on each other's shoulders.

"So where's Andrew?" she asked, when she got ahold of herself.

"That's a good question," I told her. "He said he'd be home by now."

We stayed up talking about the boyfriend. She said the one good thing about him was that he kept her straight. She never could've stayed on the wagon without him.

"Well, there is that," I said.

She seemed discouraged by my lack of enthusiasm. She said she had to crash and I got her some blankets and made a bed on the sofa while she changed. After she conked out I checked my cell and dealt with more e-mail.

Things had gone downhill. The little girl's mom told CNN her daughter couldn't get the treatment that would save her life because some administrator thought it was too expensive. BOB sent an enraged e-mail to Janine asking why I hadn't been on top of this. She'd forwarded it to me with the subject line BOHICA, which is 3rd Infantry for *"Bend Over, Here It Comes Again."*

My husband finally got home and ditzed around the kitchen for a while. The dog was all excited. I scrolled through as many more e-mails as I could stand and then went to say hi. He didn't look at me and then did and made a face.

"So what's up with you?" I asked.

"Nothing. I'm used to being the last priority," he said.

"It's one o'clock in the morning," I told him. "Now *you* have a complaint to lodge? What haven't I done for *you*?"

"Like I said, nothing," he answered. He washed my wineglass and stuck it on the rack. "I wouldn't want to add to your troubles."

"How about you help with the parenting, if you're looking for something to do?" I said. "I don't need four kids to deal with. I already got three."

He clomped upstairs and went to bed. I didn't even know if he'd noticed my sister on the sofa.

They were both unconscious the next morning when I left, after getting the kids up and fed and out the door. At work, things were so bad that for a little while Janine and I just sat around the coffee machine like there was nothing to do.

"No *way*," she said, sitting forward to hear more once I told her that on top of everything else my sister had shown up. I gave her the details and she joked about starting an office pool on who'd be arrested first, me or Jennifer, and for what. She said she didn't know who'd been meaner to her sister over the years, her or me.

I answered it was me, easy. I told her that when I was in the *need-my-privacy* phase, Jennifer decided she was Nancy Drew, so I put a childproof lock on my door and before I got home from school she'd gotten a wrench and torn it off. And that she later claimed I'd chased her around the house with the wrench. I told her that once when I was eight and was supposed to be watching her for *five lousy minutes,* as my mother used to put it, I tied her to our porch rail because I was dying to go off with my friends. And that my mother didn't get back to cut her loose for like forty minutes. And that my mother said that when she got there my sister had just been getting the knot undone.

Her phone buzzed and she looked at it and then held it facing me so I could read BOB's text: *"Why isn't anyone at their DESKS?"*

There'd been no movement on the firm's decision to deny the transplant, so the task of the day was to tweak the talking points in advance of the meeting to prep the CEO on all the media events coming up. Since the meeting wasn't until eleven, we were left alone until then. We kept our conversation about Jennifer going across the cubicles while e-mailing each other tweaks. Janine said her sister always treated advice like it was character assassination, and that she'd never once got her to change, though she *had* usually managed to make her feel bad about it. I told her that all those afternoons when my sister and I sat around with pot laced with PCP, I'd go on and on telling her what to do and Jennifer would just sit there watching me like I was a talk show. I told her that when our dad found out we not only hadn't stopped using but also had started dealing, he broke down the door and took me by the shoulders and slammed me from wall to wall.

"Oh, yeah, good old wall-to-wall counseling," Janine said. Which turned out to be another 3rd Infantry term.

My sister called to ask where the coffee was. Then called back to ask if we had sugar. Then to ask if I could drive her to the airport when I got home. I told her I couldn't. Finally she called to ask if I'd lend her money for a cab to the airport. I told her I couldn't do that, either.

"Don't be such an *asshole*," she said. Nobody I knew could sound so desperate. "I wouldn't ask if it wasn't an emergency."

"It's always an emergency," I told her. I told her I had to hang up, which was true, because BOB was standing over my desk looking at the cell in my hand like I'd beaten his dog to death with it.

He called us into his office, apparently just so he could swear and keep us from listening to the TV. More people packed in behind us, curious about what was going on.

Every time he changed channels the news got worse. CNN had instituted a countdown scroll onscreen once there were only twenty-four hours left for that liver deadline at New York Presbyterian. *Good Morning America* was looping footage of the family's flight down to the city so Lindsay could be ready if and when the life-saving operation came through. Somebody at Fox had wrangled an interview with the CMO's wife over a hedge in her backyard, and she was saying on camera that she didn't have all the facts but was sure the firm was trying to do its best by its customers, though it sounded to her like Lindsay should be allowed to have her transplant. When she finished, the room erupted like a sports bar where the home team had just lost.

We struggled back to our cubicles through the crowd. BOB and his betters were having another emergency meeting.

"They gotta cave, don't they?" Janine asked. "I mean, how much is publicity like this costing them?"

"You would think," I told her.

There were four calls on my cell from home. When I called back, Maeve answered. "What're you doing at home?" I said.

"I didn't feel good," she said. "But Aunt Jennifer's really sick. She threw up all over the sofa. I can't get her up. And I can't understand what she's saying."

I asked where her father was and she didn't know. She sounded panicked. I told her to sit tight and called his cell and office and left messages. Then I called 911. When I called Maeve back she was crying. "Where *are* you?" she said. "Her fingernails and lips are like blue."

So naturally when I got all the way home, the paramedics had come and gone and Jennifer was sitting up at the kitchen table with a glass of water. She wouldn't tell me what she'd taken but said she told the paramedics she'd fainted.

Maeve was in her room, traumatized. When I came back downstairs and reported that to my sister, she apologized.

The whole time my cell kept ringing because BOB couldn't believe that I'd actually left the office. While I cleaned the sofa, Jennifer stayed in the kitchen. I heard her get more water from the tap.

"Go," she told me when I went in to put away the Febreze. "I'll be fine."

When Janine heard about all of this she got the two little travel bottles of Johnnie Walker out of her desk and poured them into Dixie cups.

"It's two in the afternoon," I pointed out. "And we're probably going to be here until midnight."

"Will Andrew be awake when you get back?" she asked. "You look like you could use some I&I." She was always saying she needed some Intoxication and Intercourse, her fiancé's version of R&R.

We'd just gotten our final tweak on the hard-line position approved when BOB sent word that we'd be doing a one-eighty, and you could hear cheering and complaining all over the floor. So we worked straight through dinner on why the company was reversing its position on something it claimed it had been right about in the first place, and how that decision had nothing to do with rotten publicity.

Janine asked what I thought Jennifer had taken and I answered that I had no idea. She said, "So she's off the wagon again, huh?" and I said it sure looked like it. That was more work for me, she said, and I told her it wasn't like I'd auditioned for the role of big sister. I told her that being a big sister was like being a mother, but with even less power. That little sisters mouthed off and then did what they wanted to do anyway. And that they followed your example, so every bad thing you did was bad twice over.

"I hear you," Janine said.

"My mother was so useless," I told her. Our first draft had already been judged by BOB as not aggressive enough in our own defense. "Years after we were in high school, somebody would mention a blowout party at our house and how our friends broke the picture window or the gas grill or the railing on the porch, and our mother would go, 'Where was *I* when all that was going on?'"

Janine made a sympathetic noise and we went through two more drafts.

"Is your sister going to be all right at your house alone?" she finally asked.

"My father would get so mad at me," I said. "'She's just a kid!' he would always yell."

"Well, she *was* just a kid, wasn't she?" Janine asked.

"After she finally had boyfriends she threw out all her toys but her Ken doll, Sun Set Malibu Ken," I told her. "She kept him on the windowsill by her bed and when her boyfriends asked what he was doing there she said he liked to watch."

"I remember Sun Set Malibu Ken," Janine said.

"My sister picked Japanese beetles off the rosebushes and planted them in rows and announced she was making a beetle farm," I told her. "Any poor beetles that tried to dig themselves out she buried deeper."

BOB showed up with another crisis: the concession letter was ready to go but nobody could find the family. CNN seemed to believe that Lindsay and her entourage were heading to some kind of protest meeting outside the company's New York headquarters.

"At nine o'clock at night?" Janine said.

No, he told us, it was scheduled for the next morning. He had his hands in his pockets and was looking around the office like everything was in a shambles, which it was. He told us we might as well go home, though we'd better keep our cells on.

In the elevator I asked Janine what *she* was so cheery about, and she said her fiancé just sent an e-mail reminding her that in a month he was processing out and getting transferred to Fort Living Room, which is what he called her apartment.

"Sounds like nonstop I&I," I told her.

"Breakfast, lunch, and dinner," she said. "We'll be turning over tables and kicking over potted plants."

We laughed.

"You're happy for me, right?" she said, looking like she really needed to know.

"I really am," I told her.

.   .   .

By the time I got home she'd called my cell and left a message. The girl had died en route to the protest. No one had realized she was that far gone.

"I don't know why I can't stop crying," Janine said. "Call me when you get this."

I dropped my keys on the counter and poured a glass of wine. The dog came over and said hello. I planted my feet so he wouldn't knock me over.

It was as if the news had gone straight to my equilibrium. While I was standing there BOB called the cell and the home phone and left messages. Everyone needed to reassemble right away.

"I hear we had some excitement today," my husband said when I sat down next to him on the sofa with the wine. Maeve must've filled him in, though how she'd found out I didn't know.

I told him I didn't have much to add and ran my hand over his forearm.

He said he'd gotten all three kids into bed by nine, though they'd had calamities of their own: Sean had been moved by his coach from short to third, Neil got into a fight on the bus and had to walk half a mile home, and Maeve had packed a bag and tried to argue that I'd said it was all right if she spent the night at John's.

"She told you that?" I wanted to know. "How long did she think *that* was going to hold up?"

"Who's John?" he asked, and I shrugged.

He took a sip of my wine and handed it back and we both sat there for a little while.

"I'm sorry about the little girl," he said.

"Yeah," I said. And I must've sounded so sad that he put his arm around me.

"Don't you want to know where your sister is?" Jennifer called from the front porch. She was far enough away that I couldn't tell if she'd been able to make out what we'd been saying or not.

"How're you?" I called back, then exchanged a look with my husband and gathered some energy and got up to go see her.

"I need money," she said when I stepped onto the porch.

"Maybe you need to get back with that guy who helped you before," I told her. "The guru."

"What are you crying about?" she asked.

I shook my head.

"You worried about your little sister?" she suggested.

"A little girl died," I finally explained. "We were trying to help her."

"Trying to help her?" she asked.

"No," I said. "We weren't trying to help her."

"I thought that sounded weird," she said.

"I don't know what you want from me," I finally said. "You want me to give you money for drugs? You want me to bankroll your trip? You want me to come out west and live with you?"

"I don't want anything from you," she said.

"You just said you wanted money," I told her.

"It's a loan," she said. "You'll get it back."

"Are you okay now?" I asked. "I heard you were in pretty bad shape."

"I was pouring myself some juice this morning and your daughter took the bottle out of my hands and finished the pouring," Jennifer said.

"It sounds like you didn't even know where you were," I told her.

"This was *before* then," she said.

"She was probably trying to be helpful," I suggested.

"She's fifteen years old," Jennifer said. "Doesn't she think I know how to pour my own juice?"

"Did you bite her head off about it?" I asked.

"We're talking about *me*, here," she said.

"Whoa, ladies," my husband said from the living room.

We sat there looking at each other as if in the next yard a bunch of kids were spraying the hose through their kitchen screen: not *our* problem. Though someone a little more responsible might have intervened.

"Do you remember what I said that first day you brought the hash home?" she asked.

I shook my head. Even then she'd had self-esteem issues. She used to complain that no matter where she was in her room, her turtle turned in its dish so it wouldn't have to look at her. Everything was poor me. And even with all that, she never stopped messing with you: she used to not towel off after showers so she could come up and drip on me.

"I guess I never told you why my boyfriend kicked me out," she said.

I felt like I really had to go to bed. Like I couldn't even lift my arms. "So why'd he kick you out?" I asked.

"Sal's back in the picture," she said. She watched for my response. "Remember Sal?"

My husband finally got up and went into the kitchen.

"Nice expression," she said, staring at me.

Sal had been our whole summer one year. He was eighteen, I was sixteen, she was fourteen. I'd brought him around because I thought if I could be one-tenth as attractive as he was I could die happy. He also sold just about everything and had no trouble getting his hands on whatever I couldn't find. We used to go over to his rec-room basement. He always acted like we'd asked a cliff diver into the kiddie pool, and we really wanted to wipe that look off his face.

"How did Sal get back on the radar?" I asked.

"Same way anybody does," she said.

The last time we hung out together his stepfather came by with his biker buddy. Jennifer had done mushrooms and I made out with Sal and the biker buddy while she fell asleep on the floor with her hand in the dog's mouth. They had this ancient Lab who never got off his bed. Then she was throwing up and crying and throwing up and crying and Sal and the biker buddy had passed out, and by that point it was almost midnight, and I was ready to go do something else for a while. I left her over the toilet and went to the 7-Eleven to get sodas for everybody and ran into some people there. When I got back, she was under the covers in Sal's bed.

Sal and the biker looked like our dog when he'd pissed on the rug and we hadn't seen it yet. When I asked if everything was all right, they both looked at me. "Why wouldn't everything be all right?" Sal answered.

When I got Jennifer home she told me the whole sad story, and I helped her clean up. I tucked her into bed and asked if she was okay or if we needed to call the police.

"No, they were nice enough," she said.

And the way she said it made me want to kill them myself.

She spent the next day in bed and I stayed in the house with her.

There was nothing on TV. There was nothing out the windows. There was no one I could imagine talking to for the rest of my life. Sometime that afternoon I called Sal and told him that if I ever saw him near my sister again, I'd kill him with a garden hoe.

"All right, whatever, don't get your panties in a bunch," he said before I hung up on him.

Once she was better, she shut herself in my room and dumped all the stuff in my drawers out. I tried to get her to stop and finally our mom threw us out of the house and told us to go piss off somebody else's mother for a while.

We walked for miles and finally she flopped down in the grass along the river and let me sit next to her. She didn't say a word for almost the whole afternoon until out of nowhere she said she was working on making herself less godawful. Then we were quiet and just watched the kids floating past us on inner tubes. And I promised her I would do the same thing.

"Neil's having some kind of nightmare," my husband said, standing over us. Who knew where he'd come from. "And your boss called like four more times."

"Just gimme a little money and I can get out of your hair," my sister told me. And I said we'd talk about it in the morning. And I thought, *Am I really just going to let her go again?* Then I wandered around the house in the dark the whole night because I couldn't sleep.

And in every room there were other versions of my sister and me. They gave me that look and they dragged their feet. Or they reached for my hand and then knocked it away. They saw right through me, but even so they kept perking up, like they'd never stopped thinking I was someone they should stay in contact with, or they'd never stopped believing I might be about to step in and make things better.

HMS *Terror*

3 July 1845

There is a feeling generally entertained in scientific societies and among officers of the Navy that the costs of discovery are never so great that we should shirk from the immensity of the endeavor. I was actuated by this idea at a very early age. One August morning when I was a few days short of eight years old my father found me idling in a mangy patch of park beside his establishment and announced on the spot that we would take an excursion by foot. We lived in Sleaford, a town so minuscule that the public excitement was the communal pelting with stones of any wayward donkey that got into the kitchen gardens, and where my father ran a shop in which you might buy anything you wanted, provided it was a secondhand campstool or a broken-down wheelbarrow. He proposed a walk of some distance to Scrane End, on the coast, where we would, as he put it, gather data at the outer limits of human knowledge.

He saw me as one of those solitary and openmouthed boys who

possessed the gift of lethargy in its highest perfection, though he never glimpsed the comprehensive intransigence of my isolation, and he never lost an opportunity to provide me with what he liked to call moral hints to the young on the value of time. My mother had died in childbirth, and while I never saw him read, he had the scholarly air of someone with neither a wife nor a child at home, and a basic humanity so considerate that at night in my bed I shook with a devotion to him that I felt unable to fully express.

We set off without hesitation that morning, me with my walking stick and my father sporting his ancient ruin of a hat, and we followed for a time the rail line, passing stations so small they were nothing but a platform and a bell. He held forth about his business as though I were a confidant, and seemed never able to make out why no one was entirely satisfied with him. By late afternoon he was teasing me that for every step of which I approved I complained of two more. I had by then developed an awful case of blisters but was proud of having resolved to keep that information to myself, so as not to shame him about the state of our shoes. And when we finally arrived, Scrane End's waterfront opened before us to a glorious eastern expanse of sea and sky, and its market featured heather brooms so fresh the purple flowers still flourished among the bristles. Together we assayed the sheep stalls and the pig stalls, through which a naval recruiting sergeant watchfully elbowed his way. And it was there, seeing my father's response to the sergeant's passage through the town, and the three-masted schooner in its harbor, that I first conceived of a career at sea.

4 July 1845

The finder of this journal should know that its author is Lieutenant Edward Little, serving under Captain Francis Crozier aboard the HMS *Terror* as part of the Franklin Expedition, and though the author is not the keeper of the officers' log, his record and observations will be of sufficient interest, in the event of the expedition's failure to return, that the Admiralty has offered in advance a reward of one hundred pounds for the recovery of such information.

Her Majesty's government having deemed it expedient that a further attempt be made for the accomplishment of a sea route north of the American continents to the opportunities of the Indian and Pacific Oceans, the *Erebus* and the *Terror* were fitted out for that service and placed under the command of Captain Sir John Franklin, KCH. In addition the expedition's charge is to correct and amend the highly defective geography of the Arctic regions, most especially those adjacent to the Americas, and to ascertain the precise location of the North Magnetic Pole, given that improved understanding of magnetic deviation in the high latitudes is essential for accurate charts and navigation. The site of the Pole is clearly beyond the reach of overland expeditions and can be attained only by overwintering ships which then would be in position to pursue the exploration of the Northwest Passage.

Upon having attained the latitude of 74° 30'N, we have been commissioned to push on westward until we reach the longitude of Cape Walker, which is situated at 98° W, and from there to follow as direct a course for Bering's Straits as circumstances might permit. Captain Franklin has been further instructed to transmit accounts of his proceedings to the Admiralty by means of the natives and the Hudson's Bay Company, should opportunities offer, and otherwise by throwing airtight copper cylinders overboard. He has also been charged to erect cairns or signal posts when convenience allows.

We may be so circumstanced at the end of our first winter, or even the second, as to wish to assay some other route. But having an abundance of provisions and fuel, we may do so with safety.

We could not be more ably led. A fortnight short of his fifteenth birthday Captain Franklin saw his first naval ship, the sixty-four-gun *Polyphemus,* take part in Nelson's assault on the Danes at Copenhagen; and at Trafalgar, on the *Bellerophon,* forty of the forty-seven men on the quarterdeck beside him were killed. In those days they called the quarterdeck the slaughter pen because it rode level with the enemy's gunports. He participated in the first circumnavigation of Australia, and during one shipwreck subsisted on whelks and land crabs for six weeks. After he published his account of his Hudson's Bay expedition he was known as "the man who ate his boots," and an Arctic panorama including his portrait opened in Leicester Square. I remember it as having a garnish of polar bears.

Captain Crozier is Northern Irish and Presbyterian, but as Tom notes, this verifies only that he has worked his way from cabin boy to command without assistance from well-placed patrons. He has served aboard every sort of vessel that floats, from tenders to cutters to sloops-of-war to gun brigs to frigates to ships of the line, and he sailed as a midshipman on Parry's first expedition in search of the Passage, which came very near to succeeding. He's had more experience among the ice at both Poles than any man alive. Does it matter he's not the sort that other officers might invite to their club? We hold with Cromwell, who said, Give me one of those plain Captains who knows what he fights for and loves what he does, instead of one you can call a Gentleman and nothing else.

Tom Hall served as steward on our captain's Antarctic expedition, and not only allowed himself to be cajoled into serving in the same capacity on this one but also induced me to sign on as well. This required no great eloquence. It was said that Discovery Service pay was enough to make a man forget that he might be dead before he earned it, and there was also two months' river pay in advance while the expedition was fitting out. And when he made his proposal I had just settled upon the notion that there was nothing for me ashore.

I had conceived of an irrational and precipitous love for an old schoolmate, Miss Sophie Carr, with whom I had recently become reacquainted on a series of walks. Together with her aunt, who kept a discreet distance, we had perambulated two towns in a soft, fine rain. It seemed everywhere we went chimneys were being swept, and the wet cinders in the drizzle gave the streets the appearance of having been set afire and put out. Occasionally we stopped at inns for tea. She had an affecting habit when first sitting of nervously pleating her skirts. She was endlessly inquisitive and well informed and wished to know everything about life aboard ship. Her uncle said she had a furious curiosity and had taught her to play chess, which had scandalized his wife. My previous experience had taught me that as for love, it was trouble enough to fall out of it once you had tumbled into it, and thus I had kept clear of it altogether. But I found the precipitation on her eyelashes and lips acutely stirring, and believed her to be so similar in taste, feelings, and the impulse to moderate desire that by the end of our second walk I had taken her hand and expressed the hope that we might together, some time in the future, find the full enjoyment of every earthly blessing.

I immediately recognized my mistake. She had assumed the pained expression of someone asked an immense favor by a stranger on a public conveyance. In the silence that followed, she attempted not without compassion to resume our previous ease, only to discover that her co-respondent sat disconsolate, inveigled to talk but refusing to do so.

I was thrown back upon my previous isolation. I felt I had made an honest attempt at being like other young men, and the result left me morose and impatient and impossible to admire. Since my father's death two summers before I had seemed to my acquaintances in the very last degree constrained and reserved, if not troubled outright, and at times even the leverage of strong drink failed to move others to good fellowship in my company. After this latest misfortune I saw no prospect ahead for any joyous feeling whatsoever, at least not before Tom returned from a year's sailing among the Indies, and whiled away the time in my rented room exclaiming aloud every so often about my limitations while gazing at the flies upon the ceiling.

6 July 1845

The *Terror* was originally built as a bombardment vessel, and has the bluff form and secure frame and capacious hold of that class. The decks and hulls are designed to withstand the Olympian recoil of five-ton mortars, with oak ribs and beams two foot square, and have been as fully braced to resist the pressures of the ice as the resources of science can ensure. Five belts of timber ten inches thick have been laid along her waterline and her bows armored with inch-thick plates of sheet iron. And even before her recent reinforcement, on her voyage to Repulse Bay she was beset for more than eleven months in drifting ice and exposed to every variety of assault to which a vessel in such a position is liable, even squeezed entirely out of the water and thrown over onto her side, yet sustained damage only to her stern post.

Both ships have been refitted for steam at Woolwich, and I'm informed that the engines will be critical for pushing through the ever-narrowing masses of ice when there are no other means for doing so.

The conjoined crews of the two ships, officers and men, amount to 133 souls. Junior officers like myself journeyed from far and wide to serve in the expedition—it was said these would-be explorers had crowded into Captain Franklin's house to plead their cases in person—but when it came to the crew, despite his fame and the high wages offered, there was a scarcity of volunteers. Those who had never served in the polar regions anticipated with apprehension three years of extreme hardship there, while those who *had* served almost never volunteered for such service again. So that even as late as March it was still necessary to engage ice masters, warrant officers, and able seamen. And our sailmaker, caulker's mate, blacksmith, and quartermasters have none of them voyaged above the middle latitudes.

7 July 1845

We have anchored in a narrow channel at the entrance to Disko Bay on the western coast of Greenland, in as convenient a place for our purpose as can be found. The Greenland Ice Sheet extends from horizon to horizon and rises fully one mile high. It blots out the heavens and sends an unremitting and frigid wind roaring over us even in midsummer. We have already obtained a very satisfactory set of magnetic and other observations. On board we are as comfortable as it is possible to be. We are very much crowded, as not an inch of stowage has been neglected, and food is crammed into every conceivable space. The corners of my berth are packed with tinned potatoes. But as we will consume coal and provisions as we go, that evil will continually be lessened.

On 12 May the ships were towed from Woolwich to Greenhithe, where they took on the last of the provisions and the magnetic instruments. The officers and crew then assembled aboard to offer thanks to God for mercies already vouchsafed to us, and we commenced our hazard in the highest spirits. A crowd of ten thousand saw the Franklin Expedition off at the wharf, the ships' companies mustered on deck in their blues. Near Aldeburgh we anchored to wait out a storm, and in the Orkneys we took on fresh beef, and then we struck out across the Atlantic, so heavily laden that our sealed gunports were four feet above the waves. During the reach to Greenland we were accompanied by the *Barretto Junior* carrying extra coal and supplies. She lies anchored beside us, her crews joining ours in salting down freshly killed seabirds. This morning I presided unhappily over the slaughter of the last ten oxen, pitying them in their cages overhung with icicles, their eyes dulled to the surrounding terrors. Nearly everyone else spent the day engaged with the final transfer of coal, the dust having blackened everyone and everything, even the dried fish hung in the rigging. Four men have been invalided home.

12 July 1845

We have learned from a Danish carpenter in charge of the Esquimaux on this coast that though the winter was severe, the spring arrived no later than usual, and that the ice is now loose as far south as 74 degrees or thereabouts. And with three hearty cheers from the *Barretto Junior* our expedition set sail to the west, across Baffin Bay. Taking leave of that great landmass we could spy, even that far astern, walruses in the channels, and a polar bear on one of the floes.

16 July 1845

Four days of matchless conditions and exhilarating progress. Our ponderously overburdened and flat-bottomed little fleet seems to leap over the waves. And even the least sanguine of us under such headway has begun to entertain aloud hopes of spending a part of the next winter in the South Seas.

20 July 1845

Worked to windward all night against a stiff breeze. The sky is lurid though the horizon is tolerably clear. A dinner in the officers' mess of canned oxtail soup, jugged hare, Finnan haddock, pickled onions, and hot bread and butter, followed by cheese and Normandy pippins and brandy. Many have said no ships could go to sea better appointed. As steward managing the provisioning, Tom reports the stowing of 18,000 cans of biscuit, 150 casks of salt meat, and 1,200 kegs of lemon juice for proof against scurvy. There is raillery about the *Erebus* having retained the lion's share, because of her commander. Captain Franklin from a distance resembles one of those gallant admirals from the stage who always feature ample fortunes, pretty wards, and gout. He is so obese it is said that whenever he moves out of earshot his crew loves to mutter, "Who ate all the pies?"

Wedged in wherever possible amidst the coal and provisions are all manner of medical supplies and wintering habiliments. We have a library of 1,200 books on the *Terror* alone, and enough magnetic instruments to equip a colonial observatory. A popular subscription provided each ship a mechanical hand organ capable of playing fifty tunes, ten of them hymns. And Sir John's wife, Lady Franklin, anxious to add her own touch to the voyage, procured a monkey for the *Erebus,* in the belief that dressing him up would prove a source of amusement for the crew.

26 July 1845

A safe anchorage within a bowshot of land at the entrance to Lancaster Sound, and an invitation to dine with the officers of the whalers *Enterprise* and *Prince of Wales,* but we cannot pass up a favorable wind. They are the last other souls we are likely to see for at least a year. The song of an unknown bird has been heard at night so loudly as to deprive us of rest. The men claim it whistles the first bars of "Oh Dear! What Can the Matter Be?" This morning a lynx was observed swimming across the strait.

3 August 1845

Westerly progress along the southern coast of Devon Island. For an hour fog detained our departure from anchorage until, finally unwilling to lose all of the morning, Sir John signaled that we should proceed some distance in the thick weather under the guidance of the *Erebus*'s ice master, who hung from its bow with a lantern. The cliffs ashore seem composed of micaceous slate traversed by large veins of granite. The precipices are three hundred feet high.

Once the weather cleared, all hands lined the deck to starboard for a full hour to pole away growlers, small icebergs the size of cottages that rotate in the chop and, besides complaining noisily against the hull, can tear away great sections of a ship's rigging or even the anchor stays. Here came my first chance to talk with Tom in some days. It requires great self-control to moderate my inquiries about these regions, as I always seek to benefit from his experience, and requests too rudimentary produce in him the kind of expression a not-uncaring father has for a sorely afflicted son. As it is, much of the time his look suggests he is awaiting that inevitable occasion on which I will overstep my capacities. Though I have neither polar nor scientific experience, I have served three ships as administrator and officer of the watch. I asked if he calculated we were but a few days from Barrow Strait and Cape Walker, and the opening beyond to the west, and he responded after some silent work with his pole that even supposing the state of the ice permitted us to attempt that route, we remained ignorant of the exact position of the opening, the entire tract between Cape Walker and Bank's Land—some five hundred miles—being unknown. And moreover, wherever that opening we presumed to exist might be situated, the channels among the islands are likely indirect and more probably fiendishly intricate, so that vessels pushing into any one of them in late summer might be exposed to the ice closing behind and barring all regress. When I rejoined that Parry had by all accounts negotiated the passage around Cape Walker with dispatch, he reminded me that in polar seas one navigator might be graced to pass through a tortured archipelago in a single season, while any number of successors might find impassable barriers thrown across the same path.

"With perhaps new avenues opened," I remarked. And after he continued his poling, he granted the possibility.

8 August 1845

Landfall at Cornwallis Island just NE of Cape Walker. More magnetic observations recorded amidst red-throated birds that utter the most mournful cries upon the invasion of their territory. A strong headwind blowing this morning detained us at the post, as it were, until we at last embarked by creeping alongshore under the shelter of leeward ice and rock. In blowing weather our only resource is to keep a good offing, as the surf breaks high on the shelving flats. Many black whales and two white ones recorded to the east. Eider ducks now in immense flocks are migrating to the SW.

As a petty officer, Tom is below my station. He notes that I speak to him less when other officers are about. But I remind him that the irregularity of having an Irish Presbyterian for a captain does emphasize that our current enterprise is not a promenade in Regent's Park.

He first made my acquaintance at a mourning outfitter's to

which I'd finally dragged myself before my father's funeral service. Having suffered through some minutes of my intercourse with the proprietor, he spoke up on my behalf, reminding us both that though I had arrived for the purposes of being suited for an inextinguishable sorrow, it did not necessarily follow that I was to be bankrupted. He then led me to a competing establishment across the lane, taking my arm and informing me that we'd had enough of Messrs. Moan and Groan and that Navy men needed to stick together. He had a history of himself to relate that had its likeness to mine. Though of a lesser rank, he, too, had not known his mother and had recently lost his father to a fever. And I remember my sense of his spirit as confirmed some weeks into our association when, at my glum remark that we both lacked a classical education, he noted that all of those who devoted themselves in passing to the subject of his self-reform could go hang. He had gotten from *Barkham Burroughs' Encyclopaedia,* he said, all he needed as a life's philosophy: Rise early. Be abstemious. Attend to your own business. Use knowledge to plan and enterprise to execute. And stand by your friends. He taught me that when it came to fellowship, ninety-nine might say no, but the hundredth yes.

13 August 1845

A partial circumnavigation of Cornwallis Island and now an anchorage in a NW gale and a high sea. Twenty-five miles accomplished around the bays but only six attained in direct distance. Passed through jagged drift ice by very devious channels and not without risk, if fortunately without damage. By day the icebergs refract a vividness of color beyond the power of art or words to represent.

16 August 1845

A monstrous southerly swell has raised spray over the distant ice-bergs to a height of one hundred feet. The concussions are at once shocking and sublime.

The deterioration of the climate is daily ever more evident. During the night much ice drifted past, and in the morning we were beset on all sides. It must happen that the pressure of the ice on this coast even in the summer is relieved for only a brief time. By midday a strong NW wind cleared away a channel closer in to shore, though all remained white to seaward. We were able to run before the wind for three hours until we arrived at a bay through which there was no passage. Sunset found us anchored beneath precipices of columnar basalt. The ice below the cliffs is loaded with many tons of gravel, on which the snowdrifts are continually undermined by the action of the waves. Some last migratory stragglers: a brood of long-tailed ducks with the mother bird in the van. From above, before darkness fell, our captain of the foretop recorded open water at a distance of thirty miles.

17 August 1845

From the mastheads lookouts are reporting massive ice fields to the SW. The abruptness with which summer ends! The ice before us by noon was still negotiable if we repeatedly backed our engines and went full ahead to break through. Those of us on the stern could literally see the ice knitting itself out into the channels we created. A day's pursuit of ever-narrowing leads, when unexpected contact with submerged pack ice causes all hands to lose their footing and the masts to bend with the impetus. Mist freezes on the ropes and sails, making them too stiff to manage. By late afternoon the sea as far as our view extended had formed one closed pack, and no lanes of open water could be discerned from even our crow's nest. We are off the north side of Beechey Island, a short row from a shingle beach, providentially sheltered. Captain Crozier has already announced Captain Franklin's decision that it is here we will winter. At lat. 74° 44' N, long. 91° 55' W, it is the most northerly position in which any ship is known to have laid itself up.

27 August 1845

Our upperworks have been entirely dismantled and carried ashore; otherwise, weighted with ice, they would dismast or capsize the ships. Snow on the upper decks has been packed down tight for insulation and then covered with a layer of sand for footing. Lower spars have been turned fore and aft to form a ridgepole for a canvas shelter. Storehouses have been built ashore to relieve conditions aboard. One of our Royal Marines fell into the sea and was hauled back to ship, wrapped in blankets, and thawed near the stove, and it was still hours before he again could speak.

27 September 1845

Two and a half hours of daylight. A candle is required to write at eleven in the morning. One of my captain's ideas has been to hold theatricals to occupy the men. There are also classes in reading, writing, navigation, and astronomy. I assisted the captain this morning ashore with his magnetic dip circle. The instrument performed perfectly, though the adjusting screws were too small for our frozen fingers.

27 October 1845

However firm the mind, nature continues to do her utmost. The stark intensity of the cold is scarcely to be credited. Fish thrown onto the ice freeze mid-writhe. A wet shirt exposed to the open air cracks in half if bent. A storm wind last night funneled the devils of hell into our little metal chimney. On deck, lights shone out into the teeth of the blizzard revealed hosts of snow figures in wild career and flight. The *Erebus* is now reporting that its monkey is wearing wool trousers and a frock.

20 November 1845

Yesterday we greeted the sun for a final time. It set upon rising, in a piercing line of crimson that became a brief green shimmer, then darkness. All around us the heavens are a black wall down to the horizon. Our lower decks are lit like the catacombs, with oil lamps and candle lanterns.

29 December 1845

The coldest days of the month have been the 26th and today, our instruments reading 72 degrees below zero Fahrenheit. Since this constitutes one of the lowest temperatures on record, great pains were taken with its accuracy. An ounce of lemon juice leavened with a second of sugar is the regulation daily issue for each man. We have also provisioned as antiscorbutics pickled cucumbers and cabbages. An hour on deck out of the wind is all that can be managed. When the ship is asleep, in the profound silence there is a deadness with which the human spectator seems out of keeping.

New Year's Day, 1846

Our lead stoker has expired of tuberculosis. Having been on nothing but rice and wine for a month, he succumbed early this morning. He'd celebrated his twentieth birthday under the surgeons' care just two weeks ago. He was buried ashore by lamplight, Sir John himself presiding over the service.

7 February 1846

Another month of darkness. As my spirits flag I find myself increasingly inclined to neglect this journal. Two more are dead, a seaman and a marine, both from the *Erebus.* The surgeons are said to be perplexed. Yesterday I labored beside Tom and William Gibson, the subordinate officers' steward, and Lieutenant Hodgson to clear snow from the upper deck, and the latter reminded us that if we were the sort to fret about what might happen we would better have stayed home in bed. As my father liked to claim, work is good medicine for morbid thoughts. The sun has returned, if only for an hour a day.

28 March 1846

Tom has clearly taken a liking to this young William, his assistant. At mess the boy spoke humorously of his own father, a grocer, and his town, the sort in which something of amusement happens once a month. He proclaimed himself an ignoramus, having as a child abstained from opening his schoolbooks and preferring instead to fall asleep on them. Everything he expresses seems to bring his fellows pleasure.

2 April 1846

I can feel a change in the men's temper when I'm relieved on watch by an officer more personable. Tom pulled me aside as we passed in the fore hatch and asked why I was moping, now that we had got to where we had so long strove to be. I see why good cheer, appealing as a private virtue, is even more a public duty. The boatswain has taken to chanting in his hammock, "Here we sit for the eighth month running, the eighth month running, the eighth month running."

5 May 1846

An elevation in my disposition. The snow is clearly softening on south-facing surfaces. Snowbirds have been observed in small flocks. A first goose.

19 May 1846

Thaw is under way. The pack ahead has begun to separate into looser floes and brash ice. Bowhead whales surface in the spaces between. Guillemots and little auks are visible ashore. Bands of snow geese pass to the NW at a great height. Sunset tints the sky scarlet and aquamarine. The lookouts report the undersides of clouds to the south are dark, indicating open water beneath. And yet for three days the pack has still been too thick to negotiate. Three days so unimportant elsewhere that are of vital consequence in these regions.

20 May 1846

This morning to our astonishment much of the ice had vanished, and a great opening lay before us. "I predicted as much!" young William exclaimed to myself and Tom as we gazed at the sight, as though he assailed us from the fortress of common sense. All aboard are electrified by that signal elevation of spirits produced by rapid motion of any kind after so many months of immobility. Despite our ordeal, the expedition is in highly effective order. Only moderate inroads have been made into our provisions, Tom reporting that only some seven hundred cans of biscuits are spent out of the eighteen thousand with which we began.

14 June 1846

Slow progress through Peel Sound, which remains open to the S. Each inlet of any size to the W might be a key to the Passage. We endure as many disappointments as there are stones on a beach. A narrows at the end of Prince of Wales Island we christened Franklin Strait. According to our instruments it is a direct route to the Magnetic Pole.

18 July 1846

In the strait the ice fields have returned but with our engines we thread through the pack into winds out of the S/SE with low temperatures and sleet and the occasional fog. The state of the weather has for the last week prevented all but magnetic observations. Captain Crozier was overheard to remark in the officers' mess that the presence of so much ice at this point in the year is an occasion for melancholy. A single boulder on a little cape looked to be over sixty feet in height.

9 August 1846

Some damage to the rudder. Two seamen were lowered over the side to remove the gudgeon pins from the sternpost so it could be hauled aboard and repaired. While overseeing this work with me Lieutenant Hodgson made a joke about our sister ship's name and when he saw my incomprehension said, with some impatience, "*Erebus*, from the Greek: the place of darkness between earth and Hades. Springing from chaos." And then he capitulated to my ignorance.

The ships have hove to and the captains and ice masters are in conference. There is an entire array before us of low and wide icebergs the latter call hummocky floes. The deep snow atop them and the tidemarks on their waterlines apparently indicate a monstrous lot of ice ahead. And yet lookouts have spied the rounded promontory of King William Land, which is less than 150 miles from the North American mainland. We stand at the very portal to the Passage. Captain Crozier has made no secret of his conviction that we must find safe harbor now, and that should we overestimate the season by even a day we will find ourselves locked in pack ice in open water and at the mercy of those cyclopean forces for the better part of eight months or more. Captain Franklin has already indicated his optimism about the open leads ahead and the possibility that in perhaps a week or two we could be into the Passage itself.

10 August 1846

We are under way at all speed. The success of our wager requires a good deal of luck and nearly flawless ice navigation. All is well as long as the winds and temperatures hold. Our progress gratifies everyone aboard even as the young ice interlaces in the channels with appalling ingenuity.

15 August 1846

Fatigue parties are toiling around the clock to keep the leads before us open. Two men each work the ice saws hung from great tripods. Our anchors are also set into the pack ahead and the vessels then winched forward. Eleven hours of labor for four miles' progress. To make use of even our respite from these exertions, our afternoons are concluded by sallying: running en masse from one rail to the other to effect a rocking of the hull in order to break the ice's grip. To our E and N, unbroken fields of pack ice extend as far as the eye can see. The yardarms, ratlines, and footropes are all now lethally slippery with the freeze. "What sort of a name is *Erebus*?" Tom asked, exasperated, while we all took a moment's ease on deck. To his consternation Lieutenant Hodgson laughed, and I laughed with him.

2 September 1846

A change in wind direction has occasioned an instant drop in temperature and a precipitous consolidation of the ice. The only movement now possible is a slow southern drift with the ocean's current. The situation, as Captain Crozier has put it, is not ideal. And thus our luck has collapsed, just as the Arabian Wizard's money turned to leaves.

2 October 1846

A solid month belowdecks. In the pack ice in the open sea, there is no recourse of going ashore and offloading to relieve the suffocation. Even the captain's cabin is half the size of a Newgate cell. My own offers not enough room to stand and dress. Rationed lamp oil means cabin light only two hours a day. Because of our storage needs the crew's quarters afford a headroom of less than five feet. Each man's hammock width has been allotted at fourteen inches. Moisture on the beams and berths warmed by the stoves drips onto the bedding.

15 October 1846

Each morning the night's topside ice has to be chopped and sledge-hammered away to keep the ship riding high in the constriction. The pressure ridges from the great packs in collision all around us continually fracture and explode. Under the larboard quarters we can see the ship's great beams bending, being compressed with such force that turpentine is oozing from their extremities. The *Erebus*, just off our stern, reports the same.

3 November 1846

The metal plates have sheared off fore and aft. The crew report leaks on every level. The ship is under such audible distress from the ice that when speaking with me the officer of the watch is obliged to put his mouth to my ear.

2 December 1846

In three months ice-bound we have recorded two days absent of sleet or heavy snow. I am afflicted by pain and swelling in the joints. No one can explain why the daily issue of lemon juice is proving ineffective. The ship has held together all of this time, though the rudder is now very awkwardly situated.

New Year's Day, 1847

A special breakfast of ship's biscuit with jam, hot cocoa, and Scotch barley mush with sugar. Then inspection. The forepeak is filled with the sick waiting to see our surgeons. Work parties are topside in a gale clearing ice and sleet. I visited the captain's cabin to secure permission for the crew's holiday ration of hot bread and butter, and found him reading Blane's *Observations on the Diseases of Seamen.* "You don't assay much in the way of opinions, do you, Little?" he remarked. I asked if he might elaborate. "Have you any friends of your own station aboard?" he said instead. At my reticence, with some charity he inquired, "I haven't posed one of the eternal mysteries here, have I?" And after half a minute's study of my face, he added, "Oh, go on with you."

14 February 1847

The weather is so awful that the latter part of the day had to be devoted to overseeing the make-and-mend near the cookstove. I was empowered to grant five seamen and two marines reprieve from deck duty to set them to unraveling old rope into hemp that caulkers can use to seal the ship's seams. "Cheer up, sir," one of the marines suggested, a recommendation the assembly found droll. It had occurred to me that I could have chosen Tom for this duty and had not. What could I offer him about the reasons for my decision? My companions eyed me and I smiled to register my satisfaction at their good fortune, while for the duration of their chore they seemed struck by my inability to find any reason for my poor spirits.

23 April 1847

A year after my failure with Miss Sophie Carr I attempted to again open a correspondence with her. I had sent an apology immediately following our walk. In the later note I made mention of a storm my previous ship had weathered off the Irish coast, and my achievement of a lieutenant's certification. She wrote back only that I had caused her great distress and would I please desist. Her declaration immersed me in shame and an incomprehension that even Tom, when I beseeched him to read the note, was not able to dispel.

16 May 1847

The summer my father died, a letter detailing the severity of his fever managed to reach me at my lodging house above a slopseller's near the Cutler Street warehouses. I read it looking out my little window at a forest of masts beyond the chimneys. He did not know if this letter would find me in time, my father wrote, but if it did I should make all haste to Sleaford. Cargo chains loosed of their weights down below gave off great rattles, and empty casks rolled along the cobblestones like hollow drums. I sat in a kind of daze until I finally left that afternoon, but in addition visited a public house where like a victim of mesmerism I partook of an unhurried luncheon before setting off for my train. I arrived just after nine and was informed my father had expired shortly after eight. At the end he had been attended by a fellow shop owner he had befriended.

20 May 1847

Sharing a watch with me, young William spoke without surcease until nearly four bells. He related the loss of his fiancée to a rival, and asked if I thought it better to have had such happiness and lost it or to have never had it at all. He said the fault was his and that he was continually the source of his own ruin. He added that it was as if his discomfort found him somewhere in his sleep and there expressed itself to him. He asked if I had any advice to give and I told him I did not, and he thanked me for my patience.

24 May 1847

The ice is unchanged and midsummer is scarcely four weeks away. Tom estimates that on full allowance the expedition has but eleven months of provisions remaining. The coal situation is even more worrisome. Since we can no longer wait to find an escape from the pack, Captain Franklin has sent a sledge party under Lieutenant Gore beyond where lookouts in the mastheads can see to search for any signs of breakup or open leads. Gore has been ordered to cache a message ashore on King William Island in the cairn erected by Ross seventeen years ago on the headlands he christened Victory Point.

1 June 1847

Gore has returned. His party required five days to traverse the twenty-three miles to the landfall, so monstrous was the condition of the ice field. He reports neither open leads nor indications of such possibility. The pack at its thinnest still retains a thickness of seven feet. When the messenger conveyed the news from the *Erebus,* Captain Crozier reminded me by example that it is the practice of our countrymen to receive all great disasters in dead silence.

3 June 1847

Captain Franklin has addressed the crew at full muster. He wore for his short trip across the ice a frock coat of twilled wool over his dress blues and wire mesh goggles atop his head for snow blindness. He spoke for only a few minutes. The wind at one point blew him very nearly off his feet. There is to be no release this summer, no attempt at the Passage. All of that will have to wait another full year. As for rations, for the upcoming winter every six men will be issued the allowance for four. Some meals must be taken cold. And the lower decks heated only during the most frigid hours.

"Now everyone's going about with your expression," Tom remarked to me some time later, on the ladderway.

11 June 1847

Captain Franklin is dead. Belowdecks there is as awful a silence as can be heard among men aboard ship.

12 June 1847

Captain Crozier is now Senior Officer, with Lieutenant Fitzjames commanding the *Erebus.* Both ships' surgeons proclaim themselves without explanation of the calamity's cause.

28 June 1847

Awoke this morning to consternation throughout the crew occasioned by seamen from the *Erebus* who in their panic had crossed
the ice and attempted to board the *Terror,* their Lieutenant Gore having been found dead in his bunk.

28 July 1847

Four full weeks since the wild alarm and confusion that was for the
most part allayed by our captain's steadying addresses to each crew.
He has that excellent officer's capacity to put catastrophes behind
him, accustomed as he is, when facing what appear to be insurmount-
able troubles, to do whatever might be done. An energetic series of
exploratory sledging parties have failed to produce alternatives to
our entrapment. All hands have taken part. On the sledges, meals are
cooked over stoves fueled by pint bottles of pyroligneous ether. The
men complain it takes an Arctic winter to bring their pan to a boil.

28 September 1847

I am continually confronted by dreams in which I play the role of
handmaiden in the scene of my interview with Sophie Carr. In these
I am given to strolling about with a downcast face and asking her
occupation, and her hair is always in a knot constantly coming down
behind. In one she says to me with some heat, "Let's know what to
make of you. Say something plain." And of course my answers are
always lost to me when I awake.

I seem to be negotiating the awfulness of yet another winter by
means of a comprehensive internal inertia while going about my

duties. It has not hindered my efficiency but has I'm sure rendered me even more remote to my fellows. And yet today Lieutenant Hodgson shared with me a piece of his pie.

3 November 1847

Two more officers, Thomas Blanky and Frederick Hornby, are dead. Now we are without our ice master. The pack is so thick it can't be penetrated for their burial, necessitating their storage in the hold.

Thirty men are sick, almost half the ship's complement. Lieutenant Hodgson's gums have receded and his mouth is black. We are all of us losing teeth to the ship's biscuit. Old wounds reopen under the strain of work. The surgeons still have no comprehension of the lemon juice's inefficacy.

New Year's Day, 1848

Night watch on New Year's Eve. A singular scene of desolation. All around us a great heap and preposterous jumble of ice blocks, some halfway as tall as our crow's nest.

1 April 1848

Months of the same round of endless toil in the cold and dark. A fever of some sort has been overcome, and a portion of my vigor has returned. My recovery apparently has been protracted. The surgeon reports that when Tom was able he took extra pains to see to my comfort.

3 April 1848

The captain gave an address I was strong enough to attend. There is coal left for only a week's worth of steaming, even if the ice were to release the ships, of which it shows no intention. We can either wait and hope that later this summer the pack does break up and then attempt to sail home, or else abandon the vessels. The former requires not only the separation of the pack in the next few weeks but also favorable winds to allow us to negotiate under sail the narrows of Peel Sound and Franklin and Barrow Straits, and requires as well open avenues through all three waterways. The latter necessitates sledging over the ice while we yet possess the strength to do so. If there is by next week still no sign of change in the ice, the latter will have to be our course. To the question of where we will go our captain answered there are but two alternatives: east to Baffin's Bay in hopes of reaching some part of the whaling fleet before its summer departure, or south to the Hudson's Bay outpost on Great Slave Lake. Given that the first option means traveling over pack ice for most of a route that stretches over 1,200 miles, and that Lieutenant Gore's party spent five days to traverse 23 miles of a comparable nightmarish chaos of colliding ridges and slabs, our second option seems preferable. The outpost is some 850 miles to the south, but by summer much of that will be overland or on a river that may be ice-free and, most importantly, would provide us with the possibility of taking fish and game from along its banks.

21 April 1848

The ships' whaleboats, shallow-drafted and long, are well suited for river travel, and can be carried one each on four strongly built hauling sledges. All have been fitted out with tool chests and as many necessities as they can hold, and their oars cut short for river work. Our caulkers' and carpenters' mates have driven brass screws through the soles of our sea boots to provide purchase on both snow and ice. The remaining flour has been baked down into hard biscuit and the salt meat packed into sacks. The provisions have been divided into eight hundred pounds per hauling party, thirty men pulling, Tom reckons, upwards of 2,500 pounds.

22 April 1848

The order has been given to desert the ships. Captain Crozier in his final address before our departure expressed the hope that in the country running NE from Great Slave Lake we might find the farthest outlying settlements of a people called the Red Knives, thereby shortening our journey. Lieutenant Irving, most junior among the officers of the *Terror,* died hours before the announcement, our departure then delayed by his burial. He was sewn into his canvas with his arms about his beloved marine telescope. A record of our decision and plans and our losses has been left behind in the cairn at Victory Point.

29 April 1848

The frightful disarray of the floes dictates entire half days given over to work with axes and picks. Some of the ridges are fifty feet high, and paths need to be hacked up the slopes before the sledges can be dragged forward. It is apparent to all that getting the boats to landfall and ultimately the river's mouth will require far longer than was anticipated. Just the six miles to Gore Point has consumed a week.

For the pulling Tom is harnessed beside me. He estimates the sledges hold forty days' supply of food. Even ten miles a day will carry us only four hundred miles, or less than halfway. The Arctic fog makes the man beside you a phantom, while the man beyond him disappears entire. The ship's biscuit is an ongoing torment for softened gums and loosened teeth.

3 May 1848

A SE storm pins us in our tents and spares us the hauling. We labored to pull through it until a gale of ice crystals that stung like bees turned us back in defeat. No one has seen such effort or misery. We have to remove our mittens to use our hands to thaw our faces and feet, rubbing them with snow frozen so hard it bloodies our skin. And then the melting snow turns our hands white and numb, and they in turn have to be rubbed in our armpits, while we shriek and wail as feeling returns. A fear of diminishing options follows us like an invisible companion impossible to elude.

5 May 1848

The thaw has finally begun. The weather ranges from overcast with thick snow to abominably cold even though all is turning wet underfoot. Every so often seals break the surface to track us with their round eyes. Open leads have started to bar our progress, visible only when we come right to their brink. When one presses a body part affected by the scurvy, there remains a hollow as if in a piece of dough. Blood weeps from our hair follicles. My joint pain is intensifying.

9 May 1848

The shore ice has turned to meltwater and slush, soaking everyone to the bone. We break again and again through the rotten floes, cutting our legs in the process. The sledges continually capsize and it takes the combined efforts of all hands to right them. We're often waist-deep in trenches baling the frigid slurry or beating it down to compact it sufficiently to bear the sledges' weight. For respites we climb shivering onto the heaped provisions and shake ourselves like dogs. Endless cold wind. Endless fog. No trace of edible game, or of any other living thing; neither track nor footprint, apart from those we've made.

12 May 1848

Lieutenant Le Vesconte expired after being hauled to his feet having collapsed in his traces. The point where we buried him now bears his name. His loss raised the officers' mortality rate to 40 percent. The surgeons are treating frostbite with amputations and chloroform and rum. The sounds of the afflicted at night are nearly too much to bear. My right foot is the worst; my left is all right. Meals cooked on our little stoves are ringed about with haggard beards and sunken eyes. We are like Egyptian slaves harnessed to our pyramid blocks but with frozen feet and bodies that can barely stand.

27 May 1848

Two days' rest beside a flat bay whose stony foreshore is overhung with a low and gloomy line of cliffs. Our party must divide. The strongest will continue to make for the river while those who can no longer proceed will wait here under Lieutenant Fairholme for our return. There has been weeping all around at this leave-taking. Keepsakes have been passed along for us to carry to relatives. We have left shotguns behind so the men might lose no opportunity should the seabirds return.

28 May 1848

When the sun dips the wool freezes into the most awful and punishing twists and configurations. After only one day's pulling, two Royal Marines were unable to rise this morning and have arranged themselves on the wayside. Our fingers are so frozen and rope-burned that to undo a half hitch requires an hour. During breaks we perch on the sledges like children, stupefied with agony. We no longer distinguish one death from another. Captain Crozier conveys himself from group to group, promising smoother passages and better progress ahead. Our blanket-bags are never dry and thaw with us inside them. Tom has presented me with fresh boots from the boat to replace my soaking ones. He said he felt that since he had landed his friend, a man of no polar experience, into this, he must do what he could to see me safely out of it. Whenever I rouse from my lethargy I find him watching me, always alert to mitigate what he can. "A bit better now, isn't it?" he'll sometimes suggest. He takes special care of his young William, as well.

18 June 1848

Two more died in the night and when we set off in the morning two others, when it came time to pull, were unable to tighten their traces. We haul until everything goes black before our eyes. We sink to our chests in ponds of meltwater a quarter-mile across. My feet at days' end are yellow and wooden and swollen, and the toenails sugarcoat with frost while I inspect them. The soles have started to peel off. A party has foraged for saxifrage with some success, and mudworms have been thrown into the kettle as well. Rhodes and Peglar can no longer eat and have taken themselves outside our circle of blanket-bags. Young William's cheek has been laid open by frostbite and his hands are like great gray mittens, the fingers fused. He has taken to comforting himself by recalling the disasters that taxed his patience in his early years. Before sleep tonight, Tom said into my ear in a small, gratified voice, "And what a good thing it is, too, that we still have a little tea."

25 June 1848

Not once has the route ahead stimulated us by its novelty. Nothing moves and nothing changes. All is forever frigid, cheerless, and still. When the wind dies the only noise is our desperate gasping as the going becomes too rough.

Our progress has been further impeded by the necessity of sending out hunting parties, which have met with no success. The provisions are gone. Foraging groups have continued to gather saxifrage and lichen. The latter seems to mitigate some effects of the scurvy.

9 July 1848

William is unable to go on. As if by agreement the sledges have stopped for the day where he collapsed. For the last few hours he'd hoped to continue to pull with us but soon found that he could only stumble on in front in an effort to trample a bit of track and thereby ease our passage. Even in that role he continually pitched forward into the slush and remained there until we dropped our traces and dragged him to his feet. Each time he then tottered on, weeping that it was awful wanting to walk and not having the fortitude to do so.

For a short period before he lost consciousness he lay on his back, listening to our dinner preparations with enormous composure. Said meal was a few ounces of boiled lichen. He remarked, when Tom and I left the fire to sit with him, that here he was, sick and alone and soon dead in a strange place with no one but strangers to pity him.

With the day's inactivity, I recover the stamina to return to this journal. We camp by the gleam of a single lantern against the almost palpable polar darkness. No one has retained any vitality, so we accomplish what little we can very slowly, as if miming our own actions.

10 July 1848

Tom's legs are swollen and inflamed. William cannot move at all. The side of his face is frozen hard as a mask with the flayed portion drawn away to expose the teeth. One of the sledges has tipped and the snow is strewn with kettles, pans, clothing, barrel-hoops, mallets, bottles.

24 July 1848

William's body has been stripped of his heavy coat and boots. There is little compassion in the human frame when in a state of privation. His clothes brush lies in the snow just beyond his hand.

28 July 1848

Captain Crozier has continued in his notebook to map the geography of this coastline, and he asks for recommendations to christen our present location. Some of us suggest Awful Cove. Tom in his blanket-bag proposes Starvation Cove.

12 August 1848

Should the veil be torn from those acts of which we are still capable—those acts that fix what we are? I have for the last two days been peering at my hands. The earth has refused to open up and swallow us. We have gained strength and been partially returned to ourselves. And no one can look his companion in the eye. Fourteen days ago, with all prospects gone, our captain asked our surgeon how long we could expect to survive without sustenance, and upon receiving his answer he proposed that given our circumstances the question was whether we should extinguish hope here or carry on. And if the latter, he said, the only route lay through this lost soul who had served so long and so faithfully. He was referring to William, whose shirttail lay flapping in the wind.

His meaning became apparent to us by degrees. We were aghast; we were appalled; we were terrorized by the rapacious extremity of our response. We knew when he suggested it that we would not do this. And then we knew that we would not do otherwise.

The corpse was thawed by the fire and carried a short distance down the beach and laid on a sledge. The surgeon, since he had both the skills and callousness indispensable to the profession, was assigned to the butchering. I accompanied the party as if to hold William's hand. From his bag the surgeon arranged on a crate a hacksaw, a straight-bladed saw, two filleting knives, and a soup ladle. When his assistant gripped William's shoulders and he began to saw through the neck I turned my eyes away.

The flesh from the arms and legs was cut into strips and dropped into a communal kettle that had been set to boil. His ligaments resisted the knife to the point that the surgeon had to change hands. The sternum was cracked and the shield of ribs and muscles sawn through and opened to reveal viscera among the recesses and cavities, and tortured organs like wrecks in a frozen sea. Severed surfaces in all their ghastly detail.

Nothing was wasted. The longer bones were split and the marrow scraped with a woodcarver's gouge. The head was covered in a canvas bag and crushed with a mallet and its contents emptied into the pot as well.

The effect of the meal was miraculous. We were rejuvenated. We were able to haul once again. I stood in the traces suffused with my body's joy at the restoration of its machinery, and as the cook was lashing the lid onto our great stewpot and the stewpot to the sledge, I glimpsed the little keel of a breastplate.

22 August 1848

Our campsites resemble a gathering of ragpickers adjacent to a hospital and a butcher's shop. Boats and sledges that can no longer be pulled as our numbers decrease are chopped up for firewood. Bones that have been sheared clean and broken open are piled within sight. A special waterproof bag has been dedicated to the carrying of joints on the march. Lieutenant Hodgson has found himself alone at our gatherings about the fire because he makes such ugly sounds while eating. Tom will no longer suffer anyone to touch him.

24 August 1848

We are now forced to a halt. We had been following King William Land SE toward Back's River until the shoreline angled sharply to the NE as far as the horizon. This is not a part of the American mainland but an island, and the strait blocking our way S is some miles wide. "Why have we stopped?" Tom asked, with cadaverous disinterest. "Because we've found it," Captain Crozier told him. "Found what?" I managed to ask. "The Northwest Passage," our captain answered finally and quietly.

And so a man labors to the very top of the tallest tree only to discover there's no prospect. While we sank in the snow, our captain fetched a sextant and chronometer from the sledge and fixed and recorded our position in the log he still carries in his greatcoat. We will have to wait for the entire strait to freeze over before we can proceed.

25 August 1848

It was only when I returned to Tom the day I helped cart William away that I saw my coat sleeve had been spattered with blood. He was so affected by the sight of it as to become perfectly motionless, and once roused from his trance he burst into tears. We spent the night with our blanket-bags within reach but not touching, reanimated by what we had ingested even as we were beset by our involuntary humanity. And I was recalled to a much earlier exchange that had occasioned an impassioned outburst on his part, when I had brought him the news of our lead stoker having become the expedition's first fatality. He had searched my features without satisfaction and then reminded me that the man's name had been John Torrington, with whom I had shared any number of exchanges, and that he had counted Tom and myself as his friends.

28 August 1848

The strait has frozen, and we have negotiated it. Captain Crozier estimates that we have pulled these sledges 125 miles.

29 August 1848

After three full years, other human beings. We spied the dark figures at a great distance and the sight occasioned a wild celebration. But they revealed themselves to be not a rescue party from Great Slave Lake, but a small group of Esquimaux—men, women, and children—out on the ice. Their faces evinced even more shock than ours. Despite our precautions our captain thinks they have peered into the boats and seen what we carry as provision. They left us two seals and withdrew, refusing any further entreaty.

1 September 1848

September. It beggars the imagination. A heavy snow last night. Captain Crozier estimates the mouth of the river to lie only 60 miles ahead. The thermometer fifteen feet from the fire reads 22 below zero, and the wind sweeps across us with a frigid and relentless purpose. The sun rose this morning veiled by frost smoke. A day has been spent recovering and waiting for someone to die.

8 September 1848

The days continue to shorten. The dreadful darkness blots out all features of even the roughest ice and compels us to stumble blindly along. Unable to see where we tread, we slip on stones and pitch into holes. Captain Crozier has fallen. Lieutenant Hodgson is dead. Tom and I have left all behind to keep going forward. He carries only his blanket-bag; I'm unable to manage even that. Time and again one of us exhorts the other, "Up you go, and on with you, and soon we'll come to food." The first night we sheltered from a sleet storm in a cleft of rock, chest to chest and then chest to back, clinging to each other so desperately that not even the icy wind could slip between us. We have nothing warm inside us now, for there is nothing left to burn. When dozing I find myself in the presence of all those lunches that awaited me on the shelf outside my schoolroom. This morning a lone caribou appeared in the distance but neither of us had the strength to leave our bag. In my dream my father was holding a dish of something out to me and saying with great understanding that I should eat, because I must be so hungry after so long a walk. The hollowness of our voices produces in us more horror than our appearances.

An unteachable portion of me still seeks to record everything in this little log, the same portion that can still imagine the river achieved and a life for us among other nomadic hunters in the cold and dark.

I have always been unfit for the company of men. All that one could not suppress I suppressed, and all that one could not restrain I restrained. My father's largesse in the face of my failure was never a mystery; it was simply that he loved his son. If William had come back that day I carted him off, Tom would have wept and given everything up to him in joy. For that reason our discoverers should recoil not from him but from me. For that reason I have continued to let him sleep, rather than exhorting him once more to his feet. For that reason I have fixed my attentions on his embrace, as if in glimpsing his humanity I might confirm my own.

Cretan Love Song

Imagine you're part of the Minoan civilization, just hanging out with your effete painted face down by the water's edge on the north shore of Crete, circa 1600 BC. Biting flies knit the breeze around your head. Wavelets slap discreetly ashore. When the volcanic island of Thera detonates seventy miles to the north, the concussion, even where you're standing, knocks passing waterfowl out of the air. Oxen are jolted to their knees.

Back where Thera used to be, more than thirty-five cubic miles of the equivalent of dense rock have been blown out of the water and up into the troposphere. That's all of Manhattan and the bedrock beneath it concussing upward thirty thousand feet. It's as if something has convulsed the horizon and churned the bowl of the sky above. What you're looking at no one in recorded history has ever seen, before or since.

Long before the blast column has reached the upper atmosphere, the shock wave coalesces in a grim line that radiates from the outer edge of your field of vision all the way to your little inlet. The oxen,

still on their knees, low in terror and struggle to regain their footing. Your boy—your primary responsibility—seems to have slipped
from your grasp. Everyone just gapes while the surge flashes across
the last of the distance, and when it hits you're knocked flat like the
oxen, the palms above and around you stripped of their leaves in a
roaring turmoil of wind and sand.

The woman beside you is on her hands and knees. The infant
she'd been holding is facedown and crying nearby, at the end of a
swaddling cloth that apparently unspooled in the impact. One ox is
up and lumbering inland.

Off the beach a dark blue band races like a furrow back out to
sea. Your boy calls to you, through air alive with grit and glittering
in the sun. He has only one eye open, which may make the view a
little less painful.

Once the undersea furrow finally aligns with the farthest edge
of the sea it holds steady for a moment. Your boy is still calling. The
infant is still crying. Then the horizon line darkens still more, and
widens, all of this accompanied by a continuous rolling thunder that
seems to emanate from somewhere beyond the curve of the earth.
Another ox has gotten to its feet and bulled in panic past its han-
dler. It's only when you look to the east and west that you realize
the band is widening because it's rising, into a wave whose size is
without precedent. At sixty miles away it already appears an inch
tall, its upper edge frayed and filigreed in white. Its reverberations
are already oscillating through your hands and feet. You have time
to run, but unless you're able to cover half the island in the next four
minutes you might as well stay where you are.

Your boy finds you, since you've done so little to find him. He
asks what's happening. He asks what you're going to do. He asks as
if the very extent of your love and responsibility might carry with it
sufficient power to avert even something like this. He reminds you

that you have to run, and you understand him to mean that though you won't reach safety you could maybe reach your home, his mother and your wife. In the interval you have left you might even make clear with just a moment's embrace and the time to hold her face still and engage her eyes that despite your lassitude and arrogance and petulance and selfishness and pettiness, she's granted you a gift for which you've never adequately expressed your joy. She's buoyed and nurtured you and weathered your despotism, and continued to envision what you could've become rather than what you are. She's put wings to your feet for the entirety of your lives together, and with them you run. Your boy mostly keeps pace, clutching at your arm when you begin to pull away. He's the one who got you moving but is now receding, and you reach back your hand at his cry. The wave behind you is an all-enveloping sonic domain. The road before you is one you've traversed a thousand times. The woman waiting in the courtyard is your best chance to accomplish one more panegyric before the world upheaves and confirms that, whatever other self-renovations you may have had planned, your time is gone.

The World to Come

Sunday 1 January

Fair and very cold. Ice in our bedroom this morning for the first time all winter, and in the kitchen, the water froze on the potatoes as soon as they were washed. Landscapes of frost on the windowpanes.

With little pride and less hope and only occasional and uncertain intervals of happiness, we begin the new year. Let me at least learn to be uncomplaining and unselfish. Let me feel gratitude for what I have: some strength, some sense of purpose, some capacity for progress. Some esteem, some respect, and some affection. Yet I cannot say I am improved in any manner, unless it is preferable to be wider in sensation and experience.

My husband has since our acquisition of this farm kept a diary to help him see the year whole and plan and space his work. In his memorandum book he numbers each field and charges to each the manure, labor, seed &c and then credits each with the value of each crop. This way he knows what each crop and field pays from year to year. As of last spring once we lost our Nellie he asked me to keep in addition a notebook list of matters that might otherwise go overlooked, from tools lent out to bills outstanding. But there is no record in these dull and simple pages of the most passionate circumstances of our seasons past, no record of our emotions or fears, our greatest joys or most piercing sorrows.

When I think of our old farm I think of rocks. My father hauled rocks for our driveway and rocks for our dooryard and rocks for the base on which our chimney was set. There were rock piles in every fence corner, miles of stone walls separating our fields, and stone bridges so we might cross dry-shod over our numerous little water courses. Piles of rocks were always appearing and growing, and every time we plowed we would have a new supply. My first tasks as a toddler were picking rocks out of new-plowed ground and filling the woodbox. My father before his day began would say to me, "While I'm gone you can pick up the rocks on this piece, and after you get that done you can play." And when he returned at sundown I'd still be in the field at which he'd pointed, on my hands and knees, in tears, the job always less than half done.

My sister's features were so fine that our mother liked to sketch them by lamplight, and her spirit was equally engaging, but when it came to the affections of others, circumstances doomed me to striving and anxiety. I grew like a pot-bound root all curled in upon itself.

I resolve to recover some of my former patience. And to remember that it was got at by practice. What most of us truly require is to make habitual what we already know.

————

"Welcome, sweet day of rest," says the hymn, and Sunday is most welcome for its few hours of quiet ease. A series of phaetons on the road despite the cold. Were it not for worship all of the ladies hereabouts would be in danger of becoming perfect recluses. As for me, I no longer attend. After the calamity of Nellie's loss what calm I enjoy does not derive from the notion of a better world to come. In the far field, foxes at play on their hind legs, wrestling like boys. The wind heavy at intervals. The snow is falling from the trees about the house until their limbs straighten up like men released from debt.

Old Mr. Manning who's been very low for several weeks died this morning.

The ink stopper has rolled on me and ruined a whole half-entry. Why is ink like a fire? Because it is a good servant and a hard master.

Sunday 8 January

A strong cold wind blowing all day from the west. Fried two chickens and made biscuits for breakfast. I want to purchase a dictionary. I have two dollars to spare and can't imagine how better to expend it to my own satisfaction. My self-education seems the only way to keep my unhappiness from overwhelming me. I will recommence as well with my long-neglected algebra. Some time not spent working is always wise. The bow forever bent loses its power.

An hour this morning chopping and spreading old turnips on the snow for the sheep. Dyer has culled the wisest of the rams to be set aside for sale in the spring, to allow someone else the pleasure of matching wits with them.

Nothing stirring outside except Tallie's dog, who makes the rounds of the neighboring farms for woodchucks the way a doctor visits patients. Lurid clouds are rolling up against the wind. Dyer holds that the first twelve days of January portend the weather for the next twelve months. Thus our fine day on the 4th promises good weather for the spring planting in April, the fourth month, and a storm tomorrow will guarantee trouble for the September harvest. He has used the time I've been writing this to read an article in *The Rural New Yorker* on "The Inutility of Sporadic Reform." He seems pained by my skepticism as to his weather acumen and smiles at me every so often. My heart to him is like a pond to a crane: he wades into it as far as he dares, and then attempts to snatch up what little fish come shoreward from the center.

He has a severe cut through the thumbnail.

Sunday 15 January

Deep snow. Bitter cold. A shovel and broom necessary on the porch before light. Tallie called here after breakfast. She and Dyer chatted a few minutes in the sitting room before he left to see to the cows. Her husband is today killing his hogs with a hired hand. She said after Dyer left that she didn't mean to intrude, and that it was the dullest of all things to have an ignorant neighbor come by and spoil an entire Sunday afternoon. I assured her that she was more than welcome and that I knew the feeling of which she spoke, and that during the widow Weldon's visits I always imagine I've been plunged up to my eyes in a vat of the prosaic. She took my hand as she laughed. She said she'd once gotten the widow started on the county levy and that the woman's few ideas were like marbles on a level floor: they had no power to move themselves but rolled equally well in whichever direction you pushed them.

There seems to be something going on between us that I cannot unravel. Her manner is calm and mild and gracious, and yet her spirits seem to quicken at the prospect of further conversation with me. In the winter sun through the window, her skin had an underflush of rose and violet that disconcerted me until I looked away. I told her how pleasant it was to finally be getting to know her, and she responded that the first few times she'd spied me she had kept to herself and thought, "Oh, I wish to get acquainted with her." And then, she said, she'd wondered what she would do if we were introduced.

She asked if Dyer was as sober when it came to the cows as he sounded and I told her that he deemed cows needed not only a uniform and plentiful diet but also perfect quiet, and warm and dry stabling in the winter. He was continually exhorting our neighbors to either enlarge their barns or diminish their stock. I admitted that at times if a cow was provokingly slow to drink I might push its head down into the bucket, and he would tell me that anyone who couldn't school herself to patience had no business with cows. Tallie said her father had scolded her the same way, having assigned her work in the dairy barn at a very early age, which had soon become an ongoing vexation for him because she had never been in favor of the idea. We compared childhood beds, mine whose straw was always breaking up and matting together and hers which was as hard, she claimed, as the Pharaoh's heart. She asked if Dyer had also been raised Free Will Baptist and I told her he liked to say he was indeed a member of the church but that he didn't work very hard at the trade. She said she felt the same.

She described how restlessness had been her lot for as far back as she could conceive, and I told her how when I was young I would think, "What a wasted day! I have accomplished nothing, and have neither learned anything nor grown in any way." She said her mother had always assured her that having children would resolve this dilemma, and I told her my mother had made the same claim. A short silence followed. Eventually we heard Dyer tromping about with his boots in the mudroom, and she exclaimed about the time and said she must be getting on. I thanked her for coming, and told her that I'd missed her. She answered that it was pleasant to be missed.

Sunday 22 January

Frigid night. Wintry morning. Dyer's third day with the fever. At sunup he had a spasm but was restored by an enema of molasses, warm water, and lard. Also a drop of turpentine next to his nose. His feet are now soaking in a warm basin. After breakfast I was emptying the kitchen slops and heard, off by the canal, several discharges of guns or pistols.

Dyer brought me as his bride to his house five years after he had begun to farm. In the journal I kept for a few months back then, I noted the night to have been cloudy and cool. We had about thirty-six acres that was not muck swamp or bottomland. Of those perhaps one-third was hillside covered with scattered timber from which all of the best woods had been culled. It was not an ideal situation but we all wish to have land of only the best quality and laid out just right in every respect for tillage.

My mother had married my father when she was very young, without much consideration and after a short acquaintance, and had had to learn in the bitter way of experience that there was no sympathy between them. She always felt she had not the energy to avert an evil, but the fortitude to bear most that would be laid upon her. She seemed possessed of a secret conviction she had left much undone that she still ought to do.

Dyer as the second son of my father's closest neighbor helped out with numberless tasks around our farm for many years. He admired what he viewed as my practical good sense, my efficient habits, and my handy ways. As a suitor he was generous if not just, and affectionate if not constant. I was appreciative of his virtues and unconvinced of his suitability, but reminded by my family that more improvement might be in the offing. Because, as they say, it's a long lane that never turns. And so our hands were joined if our hearts not yet knitted together.

As a boy he made his own steam engines by fashioning boilers out of discarded teakettles and sled shoes, and I have no doubt he would have been happier if allowed to follow the natural bent of his mind; but forces of circumstance compelled him to take up a business for which he had not the least love. He admitted this to me frankly during his courtship, but also maintained that with good health and discipline and a level head, there is always an excellent chance for a fellow willing to work. And if one's head went wrong, one could always straighten it up in good time, particularly if one was fortunate in one's choice of partner.

He believes that one should always live within one's income, misfortune excepted. He believes every farmer should talk over business matters with his wife, so when he preaches thrift she will know its necessity as well. Or she will be able to demonstrate to him that he worries too excessively. He feels he can never fully rid himself of his load. And I believe that because his mind is in such a bad state it affects his whole system. He said to me this morning that contentment was like a friend he never gets to see.

Sunday 29 January

The night once again bitter cold. Despite an amaranthine fatigue, I'm unable to sleep. No sounds outside but the cracking and popping of the porch joints. Up in the dark to lay the kitchen fire, and through the window in the moonlight I could see one lean hare and not a creature stirring to chase it.

Snowpudding and corncakes for breakfast. Dyer up and about. He is much improved and has been given a dose of calomel and rhubarb. He intends running panels of new fence later this afternoon. Yesterday the timber was so hard-frozen the wedges wouldn't drive.

The previous night's unhappiness hangs between us like a veil.

My reluctance seems to have become his shame. His nightly pleasures, which were never numerous, I have curtailed even more. He
has been patient for what he considered a reasonable interval when
it came to my grieving, but lately has begun to pursue with more
persistence the subject of another child. And in our bed, when he
asks only for what is his right, I take his hand and lay it aside and
tell him it is too soon, too soon, too soon. And so the one on whom
all happiness should depend is the one who causes the discontent.

I can see that when I am unhappy his mind is in all ways out of
turn, and so throughout the morning I made a greater effort at cheer.
I shook out and stropped his coat while with a good deal of fuss
he prepared himself for the long walk to the timberline. Inside his
boots he wears his heavy woolen socks greased with a thick mixture
of beeswax and tallow. Before leaving he suggested once again that
perhaps the time had come for us to have our sleigh. He's laid aside
in the barn's workroom some oak planks and a borrowed compass
saw, which can make a cut following a curved line. He seemed to
want only a smile and yet I was unable to provide it.

My mother told me more than once that when she prayed,
her first object was to thank God that we'd been spared from harm
throughout the day; her second was to ask forgiveness for all of her
sins of omission and commission; and her third was to thank Him
for not having dealt with her in a manner commensurate to all of the
offenses for which she was responsible.

Sunday 5 February

Not so very cold, though the moon this morning indicated foul
weather. On the porch after sunup I could hear the low chirping of
the sparrows in the snow-buried hedgerows. Breakfast of hot biscuit,
sweet potatoes, oatmeal, and coffee. Dyer cutting timber for firewood.

. . .

A visit from Tallie yet again, and she came bearing gifts for my birthday! She arrayed on the table before us a horse chestnut and a pear—in February!—in addition to a needle case and a pocket atlas. She brought as well for us to share a little pot of applesauce with an egg on top. While it was warming she reported that Mrs. Nottoway had suffered an accident; a horse fell on her, on the ice. Her leg by all accounts is crushed and Tallie is planning to pay a visit there later this afternoon. Tallie herself had an accident, she noted, coming here today, her foot having plunged into the brook through the thin ice in our field. I made her remove her boot and stocking and warmed her toes and ankle in my hands. For some few minutes we sat just so. The heat of the stove and the smell of the applesauce filled our little room, and she closed her eyes and murmured as though speaking to herself how pleasant it was.

I asked after her health and she said she had generally been well, though she suffered chronically from painful tooth infections and the rash they call St. Anthony's fire. I asked after her husband's health and she said that at times they seemed yoked in opposition to each other. I asked what had caused the latest disagreement and she said that he recorded the names of trespassers, whom he easily sighted across the open fields, in his journals, and that when she asked what sort of retribution he planned they had an exchange that was so cheerless and dismaying that they agreed to shun the subject, since it was one on which they clearly had no common feeling. She had then resolved to come visit me, in hopes her day would not be given over entirely to such meanness.

I was still holding her foot and unsure how to express the fervor with which I wished her a greater share of happiness. I reminded myself: (1) Others first. (2) Correct and necessary speech only. And

(3) Don't waste a moment. I told her that Dyer thought Finney had many estimable qualities. She responded that her husband had a separate ledger as well in which he kept an accounting of whom she visited and how long she stayed. I asked why, and she said she was sure she had no idea. When in my surprise I had nothing to add to her response, she fell silent for some minutes and then finally removed her foot from my hands' cradle and brought the topic to a close by remarking that she'd given up trying to fathom all the queer varieties of his little world. I was oddly moved watching her try to wriggle her foot back into her stocking. We enjoyed the applesauce and I exclaimed again on the delight of my gifts and we chatted for another three-quarters of an hour before she took her leave. As she stood on the porch, bundled against the cold, and stepped forward into the wind, I told her I thought she was quite the most pleasing and thoughtful person I knew. Because I remember how appreciation made me feel when I was just a girl, and I had resolved back then to praise those who took up important roles in my future life whenever they seemed worthy of it. Dyer returned with two wagon-loads of timber minutes after she departed, and once it was fully unloaded and stacked and he was able to take his ease before the fire, he gave me his birthday gifts as well: a box of raisins, another needle case, and six tins of sardines.

Sunday 12 February

The blizzard that began last Wednesday continues with a stupendous northeasterly wind. The snow has drifted eight feet deep. The barn is holding up well and there is feed for the stock but the henhouse has fallen in on one side. Half the chickens are lost. We dug ice and snow from their dead open mouths in an attempt to revive them. I'm told the Friday newspaper reported a train of forty-two cars from the center of Vermont having arrived at the Albany depot with snow nearly two feet thick atop its roofs. Of course there is no question of visiting or receiving anyone; we are in all ways weather-bound. I found myself vexed all afternoon by the realization that I might have taken a walk to Tallie's farm during a clear spell on Friday, but milk spilled on dry ground can't be gathered up. By the fire Dyer and I made ready to sketch out on some writing paper our plans for the sleigh but soon laid them by, since as a project it was so ill conceived and weakly begun. We retreated to separate corners, myself to darn and mend and my husband to his ledger books.

He finally looked so distraught that I asked how long the feed in the barn would sustain the stock, should the weather not improve. He estimated five days before he'd have to go to the mill whatever the conditions. He said the newspaper had quoted a prediction that the storm would let up by Tuesday, based on an expert's consultation of a goose bone. I let that prognostication sit between us while I repaired the heel of a sock, and he took his hair in both his hands and said with surprising vehemence that we offered and offered our hard work and God refused it by delivering such brutal weather.

I joined him on the settee and reminded him that the best management always succeeds best but in a real crisis of Nature we are all at Another's mercy. He seemed unconsoled. We listened to the wind. We watched the fire. He recounted again the story of his poor mother's ordeal when just a child.

She had been seven and had awoken before dawn and gone to her window, and she told him that a flash of light that had seemed to run along the ground had preceded the earthquake. Her dogs when they saw it had given a sudden bark. A far-off murmur had floated to her on the still night air, followed by a slight, ruffling wind. And then came the rumbling, and a sudden shock under which the house and barn had tottered and reeled. Latches leapt up and doors flew open.

Timbers shook from mortises, hearthstones grated apart, pan lids sprang up and clattered back down in the kitchen, and pewter and glass pitched from their shelves. Their chimney tumbled down. The oxen and cows bellowed. She told him that she'd heard her mother calling for her but she'd been unable to tear herself from her window, where even in the dark she could see the birds fluttering in the air as if fearing to again alight, and she could hear the river writhe and roil. She'd had to jump as her brothers had down the collapsed staircase, and then the sun had risen and greeted with its complacent face her disconsolate and fearful family. And as soon as it set again that night, their fright had returned, a fright, his mother later told him, she had never fully dispelled. For what was safe if the solid earth could do this?

Before he finished his account, I stopped his lips with my fingers and led him to our bed, undressing him as one would a boy. We shared any number of caresses and he seized my hair in his fists and held my head to his own and passionately declared his love. Early this evening I rose while he slept and made us some beef tea and cornbread for dinner. For dessert I cooked a very unsatisfactory rice pudding.

Sunday 19 February

Sleet, and ice, and a gloom so pervasive all our lamps had to remain lit at midday. Both of us much borne down of mind all morning, as for the past five days. Dyer able at last to get to the mill.

Sunday 26 February

Bright sun. Biscuit and dried mackerel for breakfast. Tallie visiting her father in Oneonta. A lonesome and tedious week.

The Cobbs lost their son to pneumonia a few days ago. I think last week. Their only child. Dyer was loath to tell me, but the memories of Nellie came on only slowly after he had done so.

I never showed our daughter a face free of fatigue; the night I bore her I had just finished dipping twenty-four dozen candles. She never seemed to lose her head colds, and we had many hard nights. I never felt blessed with enough time for her when she was well and it was that much harder watching over her during her illnesses. I spent my days beyond distress, fearing the consequences of her sickliness, until when she was two years and five months on she suffered an attack of the bilious fever, pleurisy, bowel problems, and croup. She was treated with bayberry and marsh rosemary to scour the stomach and bowels, and a tea of valerian and lady's slipper for the fever, though when she rallied for a day or two and gazed at me she seemed to know that even if her condition were coaxed into a small clemency it wouldn't spare her. The night came when she asked, "Mommy, take me up," and I lifted her from her bed while Dyer slept. She asked for my comb, and when I gave it to her she combed my hair and then smoothed it with her palm and then asked me to lie down with her, put her arms around my neck, and did not rise again.

Since the norms of polite society require that private woe be concealed from public view, I was allowed to sequester myself away for some months following. There I remained speechless. I was surrounded by objects that, if silent everywhere else, here had a voice that rang out with her presence. And I never forgot her face that final night, because there is nothing so affecting as mute and motionless grief in a child so young.

Sunday 4 March

Windy and very bright. Dined with the Hill family last evening. On our way there we saw hunters with ducks over their shoulders and boys skating on the river. A most excellent dinner of seven dishes of meat, four of vegetables, pickles and a pie, tarts, and cheese, wine and cider. This morning a breakfast of only oatmeal, jam, and coffee. Mr. Tarbell came and hung the bacon. Dyer is augmenting the padding in the cow stables with his hoardings of leaves and old straw, which he believes will increase the output of manure.

It seemed Tallie would never appear, but time and the needle wear through the longest morning. When she arrived my heart was like a leaf borne over a rock by rapidly moving water. She said that a few days earlier their hired hand had pulled down a box of eggs and broke nearly two dozen, whereupon Finney informed him that he was unlucky to eggs and was no longer allowed to approach them. Her husband believed that he suffered a great deal from the carelessness of hired hands, she said. She reported further that old Mr. Holt was said to have swum his horse over the canal despite the cold, and that the widow Weldon's son had been contracted to carry the mail on skis, but that otherwise there was no news. She was much better in her health, and overjoyed to see me.

She said she'd spent the previous two days rendering the lard from the hogs and making soap. She said her husband was even more out of sorts than usual, and had again mentioned the idea of migrating west. I told her that I considered this a bad idea since my uncle had moved to Ohio only to come to a desperate end. She asked if that wasn't where my sister had also settled, and I said no, she was out near Lackawanna, and that her husband was a manufacturer of horse cultivators. She asked me to tell her more about my sister and I told her that Rebecca had always loved legends of Indians and Quakers and county witches, and that while our church had frowned on dancing it allowed kissing games and she had been a champion at Copenhagen and Needle's Eye, and that she'd met her future husband at an agricultural society fair in which she was named Queen of the Livery. Tallie remarked with some wryness this all sounded very grand, and I wanted to embrace her for that kindness alone.

I asked about her brothers and she answered only about the one who had survived. She said that once he was old enough to stand he'd gone round with a sling he claimed was identical to the weapon with which David had slain Goliath. He never killed anyone but did give his family some anxious moments. When he was fourteen she'd caught him skinning baby rabbits alive, and he'd told her the rabbits were used to it. A year later, she said, he'd knotted a rope to his wrist and their steer's horn and had been dragged cross-country. When their mother asked what made him do such a thing, he said he hadn't gone half a mile before realizing his mistake.

We talked of parents. I told her of remembering my father telling my mother that she shouldn't feel bad about me because sometimes the plain grew up to be enormously wise. She told me that only once in her life did her father say an encouraging word, though he said plenty of the other kind. She said that she refused to offer an excuse for her constant disobedience to him, but believed now that her father had done her a far greater wrong. I said that I was sure she'd been as good as gold and she answered that she had been the willful kind of child whom no frown would deny nor words restrain, and that accordingly her father had often taken her in one hand with a strap in the other and brought the two together until she had had enough.

By then we were in late afternoon light and Dyer had again returned to shed his outer clothing in the mudroom with maximum fidget and fuss. She stood and composed herself, then touched a finger to my shoulder. I felt, looking at her expression, as if she were in full sail on a flood tide while I bobbed along down backwaters. And yet I never saw in her the indifference of the fortunate toward those less so. At the mudroom door my husband greeted us before passing inside, and Tallie put her cheek to mine before leaving. I watched her ascend the snowy path toward her land, her dog running to greet her. While Dyer rubbed his lower extremities for warmth, I added to our hearth fire, contrary to my usual custom. It cheered the room a bit but everything still looked desolate. That is me, I thought, taking my chair. One emotion succeeds another.

Sunday 11 March

A sloppy day. The wind chilly but with hints of a warmth. Up early. Ham and potatoes and coffee for breakfast. Scalded my wrist with boiling fat. Applied flour and hamamelis, since we have no plaster.

A bad week for burns. Dyer and Finney were summoned on Thursday to tend to Mrs. Manning's little girl, who had just been severely burned, and they accomplished all they could before the doctor arrived. It's thought she didn't die of the burn but of pneumonia from taking a chill from the water thrown upon her. She complained of being cold from that moment until she died.

A cardinal pair has adopted the house. I've been laying out seed to sustain them, and when I forget sometimes they fly to the kitchen window to remind me. The female is the prettiest muted green.

The week spent sowing clover. What's needed are still mornings, ideally after frost heaves, when the sun has thawed the soil's surface just enough to fasten the seed in the mud. We sow with a Cahoon, which hangs on a pair of suspenders, and throws out a continuous stream with a handle-crank. On Friday we had to finish in a headwind, which was hard on the eyes. I look as if I've been on a spree.

My mother's mother was born in 1780 in a log house right here in Schoharie County. I wonder now at the courage and the resourcefulness of those women who fared forth, not knowing where they were being led, to begin to chip into the wilderness the foundations of a civilization. Maybe they found love and kisses in their loved ones' regard, and a certain high hopefulness that we no longer possess.

Astonishment and joy. Astonishment and joy. Astonishment and joy. I write with only the small hand lamp burning, as late as it is.

After breakfast Dyer asked apropos of nothing if my friend Tallie intended to visit us again today and when I said I expected she would he gave no sign of having heard me, but went about the business of gathering his outer garments and left the house.

Tallie arrived some minutes later with a handkerchief to her nose. When she heard I was well she claimed to be disappointed and said she'd hoped to compare colds. I showed her my burn.

When she completed quizzing me on the various remedies I'd applied, we expressed our admiration for each other. She said she had from her earliest childhood an instinct to shrink from others' selfishness or icy regard, and that she cherished the safety she felt when in my presence. She said she'd lately composed a poem entitled "O Sick and Miserable Heart, Be Still."

I told her how as a little girl I'd always imagined cultivating my intellect and doing something for the world, and she gazed at me as though I'd said the absolute perfect thing, a possibility I found thrilling. And when I said nothing more she wrung both of my hands with hers, and said that those moments in which we were carried in triumph somewhere for having done something great and good, or we were received at home in a shower of tears of joy: was it really possible that such moments had not yet come for either of us? When I regained my voice, I said I thought that now one had. Or that it could. She asked what I imagined. And I said, astonishing myself with my own dauntlessness, that I loved how our encircling feelings left out nothing for us to seek or miss.

When her expression remained as before, I added that perhaps I presumed too much. The pyre in the hearth collapsed with a little show of sparks, and we both gazed at the flaming logs. Finally she murmured, so softly that I could scarcely hear, that it was not those who showed the least who felt the least.

Her pacing dog's toenails were audible on the ice on the porch. She leaned forward and offered me her lips to kiss and then turned her cheek, which I then kissed instead. I asked why she hadn't done as she was going to do, and she had no reply. So I took her hands and then her shoulders and, with our eyes fully open, brought my mouth to hers.

She smelled of rosewater and an herb I couldn't identify. Her taste was suffusing and sweet and entirely full. Her mouth was at first diffident, and then feathery and tender, and finally welcoming and immersive.

She worried I would catch her cold. She took in her breath at the passion of my response. We skidded our chairs closer and had no thought of peril nor satiety, hearing the wind's increase outside as an index of our exhilaration and starting up at every sound of her dog on the porch. There was a sweet biscuity smell to her hairline. Eventually she pulled free and after I kissed her again bade me open my eyes and said she was leaving.

Dyer noted when he returned all that I still had not yet accomplished when it came to my responsibilities, and asked with some irritation as I stood over the pump and sink if I required assistance. I came very near to answering that I did, I felt so undone by my Tallie's departure. The moment she had left I was like a skiff pushed out to sea with neither hand nor helm to guide it.

Sunday 18 March

Falling weather soon, whether rain or snow. For three straight days my bowels have remained unmoved. A spell of dizziness and shortness of breath this morning, and no appetite, so Dyer prepared his own breakfast. He says that old Mr. Holt while returning from a sale in town was badly beaten by two strangers and had to be hauled home in his own cart. Their intention had been to kill him though it seemed they were mistaken as to who he was.

Dyer also claims to have had many unpleasant dreams, owing again to his mind. Otherwise he has been notably silent through the day. I am happy to be left to my solitude. Thankful to my Maker for such blessings &c.

When still a little girl I used to hope God with a voice as loud as thunder would proclaim that all of my sins were forgiven. Now I know I can wait until doomsday and never hear any such thing. And yet the repentant sinner must actively seek God's forgiveness instead of waiting for Him to act.

Hard labor all week, sunup to sundown, helping Dyer in the outer fields with the smoothing harrow and the roller. Old Bill our horse has the heaves. Both of us fit to drop by Saturday eve. Both mournful this morning, and have since spent the day as if listening for footfalls on the porch. Yet when my thoughts turn to her I wonder with special heat *why* we must be divided. Merciful Father, turn the channel of events.

Still feeling poorly by nightfall, and so unable even to cook. A dinner of tea, bread and butter, and cold ham.

Sunday 25 March

A wild mix of wind and rain and clouds and sunshine. Muddy March has dragged on like a log through a wet field.

Downhearted and woebegone. A poor night. Fried corncakes and ham for breakfast. Poor Dyer suffering from a painful cough.

Opened the mudroom door this afternoon to Dyer having returned from the fields, and he said with some asperity that it was pleasant to be greeted by the smile one values above all others only to see that smile vanish because it's been met by one's own presence, instead of someone else's.

He then sat with me a while, still in his boots. I asked if he wanted more of the ham and he said no. I told him that when he next went to town we needed calico and muslin and buttons and shoe thread. He asked if it was troubling, sitting with him like this, and when I assured him it was not he remarked that he had learned consideration of others. And that he had learned the need of human sympathy by the unfulfilled want of it. I told him that I felt as though I had provided him with much sympathy throughout our years together, and he allowed as to how that was true. We then waited again, sitting facing each other, and I thought with some pity how his life seems equal parts furious work and resignation. When Tallie arrived he greeted her and seemed in no hurry to take his leave. He remained sunk in his chair for nearly a half hour while we exchanged pleasantries and news before he finally rose to his feet and left without announcing his business.

Once his figure was out of sight through the windows, I asked in a low voice after her spirits. She was content to repeat only that she was feeling doleful and unreasonable and unaware of what she

wished for. I asked what it was she then required of me, and responding to my tone she said she wished me to be gentler. I asked again,
chastened, what she desired, and she answered that she wanted to
lay bare for me all of the hoardings of her imagination. I said nothing. Although I often speak before thinking, I can keep still on occasion. She said our kisses had swept through her much like measles
had the poor Indians, laying waste to everything. She said she had
told herself to abolish all desire for comfort or any sort of happiness
before immediately abandoning this resolution.

She asked that I speak. I almost cried out that how should I
have known what was happening to me? There were no instruction
booklets of which I was aware. I told her I could feel something rising in me as she approached, like hair on the back of a dog. I told
her the thought of her through the week was my shelter, the way the
chickadees took to the depths of the evergreens to keep the snow and
ice and wind at bay. I told her I believed we were now encountering
a species of education that proceeds from being forced to confront
what we never before had acknowledged.

She asked if we might share some tea and was silent until it was
brewed. She said she believed intimacy increased goodwill, and that
if so then every moment we spent together would further tie happiness to utility. Wouldn't our farms benefit from our more joyful
labor? Wouldn't our husbands' burdens be lightened?

We spent the interval thereafter consoling each other and
allowed ourselves some gentle excitement. And once she departed I
looked around the room and thought, "She's gone and it's as if she'd
never been."

Sunday 1 April

Warm and windy with the appearance of rain. First day this spring we could go all afternoon without a fire. Fried chicken and potatoes for breakfast. The morning spent manuring the onions.

Dyer took the wagon after breakfast without explanation. My burn seems to be healing poorly. Tallie here earlier than her usual time, and we embraced in the mudroom as if rescued. She mentioned as if in passing that her dog would provide ample notice of arriving friends or strangers, then led me to our chairs and delivered herself over to our kissing as if it were the most urgent of errands. When I withdrew for breath she kept her face close, describing delicate patterns along my mouth with her tongue. During our longer kisses her breathing grew stronger.

When separated we took each other in, myself over-quiet and Tallie flushed and on the lookout. Together we made for a distressing pair.

I took her hands and she expressed pain at my sadness. She asked if I'd been to town during the week, and reported when I told her I hadn't that they were cleaning out the drain under the streets along the fork and that several people were down with the fever.

She added that her husband had said he no longer believed he had a wife and that he would not lie with a woman if it required a contention. She said that she had informed him that he shouldn't have anything to do with her; that she was opposed to it; that she was not willing. I was shocked and asked what his response had been. She said he had had no response. I asked if she believed he had given up on the notion of children, and she told me she had no insights on that question.

We were silent for some time, then, out of respect for our predicament. I inquired of her husband's age and she said he was nineteen years her senior and had been born in 1811, which would make him forty-five. I asked about his demeanor and she said that as mealtime conversation he had lately begun giving great credit to reports of men living far from town who had worked to poison and thereby kill their wives.

I asked if she really believed he would acquiesce to the notion of no sons. I asked if she believed he resented her visits here with any special fervor, and she said she thought not. We worked ourselves nonetheless into a state of alarm that could be assuaged only by more embraces and two or three extended kisses of great sobriety.

She admitted to having been at work on another poem she had brought to show me, but allowed me to see just the opening lines. "*I love to have gardens, I love to have plants / I love to have air but I don't love ants.*" I told her I could not support the rhyme, which saddened her. She held the poem between us and together we studied it as if it were the incomplete map of our escape route. Finally she said she feared that when she drew near I would retreat, and when she kept still I would return but remain at a fixed distance, like those sparrows that stay in the farmyard yet never enter the house. I responded that in her presence I felt perpetually prepared to take her by the hand, lead her to my garden gate, and proclaim: "Everything in here is yours, so come and go and gather as you like."

She also unwrapped from the same packet where she had secreted the poem a sprig from her favorite cedar, which I told her I would plant in a place it would forever stay green.

Once she left I took myself outside into the sunshine and spread some feed for the surviving chickens. Upon Dyer's return he found me taking my rest in the shade and kissed me, before withdrawing to refill the water buckets. After a dinner of duck and beets and sweet potatoes we enjoyed some little company together.

Sunday 8 April

Very damp, cloudy, and cool. Smoky. Perhaps the forest is somewhere on fire. A breakfast of hotcakes and custard and pickled peaches. Dyer seems now quite worn down at bedtime with grievance and care. We suspect his cough is producing a decline. A syrup of old wine, flaxseed, and a medicinal called Balsam of Life seems to have helped. This morning he made me a trellis for the lima beans and shot a crow and filled it with salt to be hung in the shed over the corn to warn off others of its kind. The whole house seems both angry and repentant. God help us.

No word from Tallie. At midday I stood off the back porch in the sun, my face turned in her direction. Above me a circling hawk used a single cloud as his parasol.

Sunday 15 April

Rain in torrents nearly all night. The lane is flooded and the ditches brim full. This morning only a slight shower.

A breakfast of oatmeal alone. Prepared the pea sticks for the first crop of peas and drowned the barn cat's kittens. Because of the holes in the fencing our new wheat is still exposed to the hogs, which we have driven out several times already. We can identify the gaps yet for lack of time cannot adequately repair them. Thus we find our enterprise sinking level by level.

A dispute with Dyer over the windows, open vs. shut. Unable to sit still afterward. Our quarrels always throw me out of harness. How many are there who have a happy fireside? Broad is the gate that leads to dissatisfaction, and many wander through it. Such is the effect of absence from what we love. But I have always been morose.

My mother used to call me her raincrow because time with me was like standing in an endless drizzle.

After Dyer retired I took his spyglass and in the darkness crossed the fields to Tallie's farm, approaching her front windows as close as I dared, and after some patient searching, fixed through the kitchen glass on her motionless figure in relief against the darkness within. Her features were still. By turning the lens-piece I drew her face nearer to mine and held it there until she turned away. Could I have been seen from the inside? I felt a giddiness like the violence of the impulse that sends a floating branch far out over a waterfall's precipice before it plummets. Her dog's barking drew her husband out onto the porch, and I retreated, plunging in over my boots in the mud.

At sunset, earlier, a good three minutes of honking mallards winging northward. By what faith do they arrive at their destination? I imagine them alighting on some marshy pond, where one by one their scattered kind arrives in safety, there to be together.

A terribly bad spring so far but the clover has come up through it and is all right.

Sunday 22 April

Finally a glimpse of her after three weeks of no word. She and her husband stopped their wagon outside our house to invite us to dinner on Saturday next. They departed before Tallie and I could exchange much more than a look.

The Nottoways report that our hogs have continued to stray into their fields as well and threaten increasingly harsh measures against them, including putting out their eyes and driving them into the river. The cardinals are enjoying the hornbeam and catkins on the birches. The female seems to prefer feeding on the ground.

Cool, but warm enough for no fire in the sitting room.

Sunday 29 April

Rain all week long, so heavy that it broke down the mill. All our ditches are running to overflow. The lower clover field is swamped.

Two of our hogs are still loose, as they are ailing and Dyer believes a hog is a good doctor and can cure himself by finding the medicine he needs.

For dinner last night Tallie served us ham, beef, duck, potatoes, beets, pickled cucumbers, biscuits, and cornbread. We commended her on this feast and her husband said he recalled the day when every family was fed, clothed, shod, sheltered, and warmed from the products a wife gathered from within her own fence line. I said Tallie must have spent two full days on our behalf, and she responded that her mother always said the hardest part of the week fell at its end.

Her husband offered up while we ate what news had lately occurred. We were all uneasy to find him so voluble. He mentioned the Mannings' third daughter was now one week old. He said that by some means old Mr. Holt had apparently pitched himself forward out of his cart, which had then passed over his back with its load of five hundred pounds, and that the doctor says he was not severely hurt because of the mud. He said he had heard, when examining the damage at the mill, of news from Middleburgh: that a man down there had last week been admitted to jail for shooting his wife in the face.

There were silences. Tallie seemed to be keeping strict custody of her eyes. I remarked upon the duck and the men discussed for an interval the old shovel plow, which Dyer compared to dragging a cat by the tail. I marveled at the size and power of their hanging lamp, and Tallie answered it was eighty candlepower and that she had induced her husband to purchase it so everyone might read with equal ease all around the room. Finney said he believed that even if he had been brought up not to read overmuch, he should give his children every chance to do so.

The rain next came under discussion. Finney said that no matter what misfortunes arrived at his doorstep, he would seek to improve his lot by means of his own industry; he would study his options closely and address vehemently even things he'd already thought adequately attended. Dyer commended him and reminded the table that success came because someone had been working hard. Finney stated as an example that when he first began farming he'd been so vexed by his dog's barking one January that during a storm he held the animal around the corner of his barn in a gale until it had frozen to death.

I replied after a moment that I found that reprehensible, but he seemed not to hear. I felt sure I was white as a sheet. I could see from Tallie's face that she'd heard this story before. He held forth to Dyer about his hinged harrow, complaining that its spikes caught the rocks and roots and were forever breaking. He told Tallie, once we had finished eating, to bring the dessert, and I said we were stuffed and she explained he insisted on his pastries and preserved fruits and creams, then rose to clear the table and fetch them. I excused myself to assist her, and in the kitchen I asked in a whisper about her situation and she shushed me with a shake of her head. When I noted the bruise on her neck she said she'd taken a fall over the fence. I answered with some petulance and anxiety that I hadn't heard, and she responded that many things happened to her about which I didn't hear.

Back at table her husband's mood seemed to have darkened. He served the pastries and fruit and creams himself, leaving only her plate empty. "Is your wife being punished?" Dyer joked. And when Finney chose not to answer, Tallie finally said that it was not in her husband's temper either to give or to receive. He replied that he had lately been sick in the chest, but as she had expressed no concern for him, he had been hardened.

The entire ride home my speculation was hectic with dread. I finally was able to ask if Dyer had felt anything amiss, but he shook his head while keeping his attention on Old Bill. Along the river he pointed out a flooding so extensive it had carried away the long wooden bridge at Washington; fragments of it, with the railing still intact, came floating down past us. Hard behind followed a tree of enormous length with its uptorn roots and branches lashing the current. Upon reaching our property he remarked with disgust of one of our line fences that it hadn't been cleared in all the years I'd been here. I said that it looked perfectly serviceable to me and he said it would be ideal as a hedge.

Sunday 6 May

No word from Tallie. No visit. A mild and lonesome night. My anxieties cause me between tasks to pace the house like a prisoner. The windows wide open.

My mother told me once in a fury when I was just a girl that my father asked nothing of her except that she work the garden, harvest the vegetables, pick and preserve the fruit, supervise the poultry, milk the cows, do the dairy work, manage the cooking and cleaning and mending and doctoring, and help out in the fields when needed. She said she appeared in his ledger only when she purchased a dress. And how have things changed? Daughters are married off so young that everywhere you look a slender and unwilling girl is being forced into a sea of tribulations before she's even full-grown in height.

Dyer keeps his distance seeing me in such a state. The night fair and warm with the appearance of a coming rain. A shower.

Sunday 13 May

My heart a maelstrom, my head a bedlam. Tallie gone. This morning the widow Weldon on the way to town reported their house and barn were abandoned. Rushed over there myself, Dyer galloping along behind and calling to me. Their barn, which I passed first, had been emptied of stock and feed. Their front door was open. Some furniture &c yet remained but most was gone. A dishtowel lay on the kitchen floor. A spatter of blood spread up the wall above the sink. A handprint of the same marked the lintel above the door.

Furious colloquy with Dyer most of the night about the county sheriff's office. He promises tomorrow to make the rounds of the neighbors and, if unsatisfied, to take our fears there.

Monday 14 May

No work. The Nottoways recalled spotting their caravan on the county road in the late evening on Friday the 4th, heading northwest. Dyer said Mrs. Nottoway believed she spied Tallie's figure alongside her husband's but was unsure. A hired hand, she thought, was driving the second wagon. The sheriff refuses to investigate. Dyer says if I refuse to calm myself he'll lash me to a chair and administer laudanum.

Sunday 20 May

I'm a library without books. I'm a sea of agitation and trepidation and grief. Dyer speaks every so often of how much we have for which to be grateful. The two of us sit violently conscious of the ticking of the clock while he continues to weep at what he imagines to be his own poor forgotten self.

Sunday 3 June

A letter this Friday—!—delivered into my hands by the widow Weldon's son. In it Tallie apologized for all it lacked. She said she understood that the best of letters were but fractions of fractions. She begged my pardon for having been prevented from offering a proper farewell and regretted that we'd traded one sort of anguish for another.

She said that houses deep in the backwoods always seem to feature something awful and unnatural in their loneliness, and were there only a ruined abbey at theirs, the view would be perfect. The ramshackle roof was fine in dry weather but required them to spread milk pans around the floor when it rained. Still, outside the kitchen there were already anemones and heart's ease and even lovelier flowers which her ignorance prevented her from naming. She joked that in this new situation only the resilience of her nature allowed her to overcome such a dismal start.

She said that during what little time she had to herself Finney read to her from the New Testament, but that when it came to the Bible he was familiar with many passages that had neither entered his understanding nor touched his heart.

She said she had enjoyed herself less these last few weeks than any other female who had ever lived. She said she could not account for her husband's state of mind except that her company must be intensely disagreeable to him, and if that were the case she was sorry for it.

She said that force alone would never have carried her to this spot and she had been induced to act in support of the interest, happiness, and reputation of one she professed to love.

She said that as far as she might estimate we were now only eighty-five miles apart, though she realized that poor people rarely visit.

She said she had always marveled that her name was so close to mine; didn't I think it strange? But as with most things, she said, it probably gave her a greater pleasure to tell me than it did me to hear.

She said it was so difficult to write of gratitude, yet she had to begin, and did so by saying my companionship had been a spacious community. She said she felt for me a tenderness closer than that of sisters, since her passion had all the honor of election. She said the memory she most cherished was of that smile I wore when I saw that I was loved. She said she wished to see me more than she had any chance of making me understand. She said she was unsure what was to come, but that our occasions of joy and trust and care and courage would shine on us and protect us. She said that though the future seemed to admit no relief she would hold me by her fire until we found a season of hope and the beginnings of mercy. She said she had always believed in me. She offered again her heart's thanks for all that I had given her. She closed by pledging that any letter with which I responded would become her most closely guarded treasure, and would be preserved and returned to me in the event of her passing.

Cleaned the shed of rusty and dusty rubbish. Washed windows and swept for the summer. Beneath it all, the irresistible current of the ongoing composition of my reply. I will tell her that God caused this connection, and that what He has joined together let no man put asunder. I will tell her that I imagine the happiest of unions, of the sort in which two families previously at daggers-drawn are miraculously brought together on love's account. I will tell her that our cardinals have come to love the acacia, where I today counted twelve full branches in flower. I'll describe for her the sudden wealth of fireflies blown about in the evening breezes.

Fourteen dollars from the sale of our milk and butter.

Tuesday 5 June

A letter from Finney to Dyer informing him that his wife died on the 24th of May in the full enjoyment of her Christian faith. She was taken on a Wednesday and gone on Thursday. Her husband said he wished all to know that her last prayers were for God to help her love His will even in her bitterness.

Thursday 7 June

Bleary and short of breath from the laudanum. I wake weeping, retire weeping, stand before my duties weeping. Dyer takes the many implements from my hands and finishes whatever tasks I've begun. I still move about the house as though performing in their appointed order my various offices.

He has conveyed my accusations to the sheriff, who was finally induced to visit. Despite some hours without the laudanum I was so befogged and wild with anger and grief that the sheriff was left unsettled and wary of my state. Moreover he claims to have satisfied himself in person after a two-day ride and interviews with both the bereaved husband and the sheriff of Oneida County that there has been an absence of foul play.

Monday 11 June

Took the wagon and rode to see Finney myself. Dyer refused first to permit my departure and then to accompany me and only caught up to the cart at the end of our property and climbed aboard. We were the very picture of anguish, rattling along side by side. A quiet but heavy rain persisted the entire second day.

The house even for that country had a wild and lonely situation. No one answered Dyer's knock or call but the door was ajar and when he pushed it open wider we saw Finney sunk in a chair in the middle of the room, facing us. He seemed unsurprised at our appearance and asked us our business.

At Dyer's silence I gathered enough resolve to overcome my fear and said that we had come in order to learn what had happened to Tallie.

He said he thought that might have been our errand. He said he'd heard our approach and taken us for the tin knocker and brought out all the pails and kettles that needed mending.

It was a hideously dark and dirty kitchen and it grieved me to think of Tallie among its spiders and yellow flies. I asked again for his account and he offered us nothing more than the sheriff had repeated. He remained in his chair and we remained in the doorway. He made no move to light a second lamp.

I said I had ridden three days for more particulars and would not leave without their receipt, and he replied that he was not concerned with my desires. None of us said anything further and a mouse scuttled across the floor. Finney looked at Dyer with contempt. He related, finally, that Tallie had taken a chill and had continued ill for two days. He'd treated her with among other remedies a tea of soot and pine-tree roots which had had some good effect, but added that sickness always tests our willingness to bow before the greatest Authority.

He said nothing more after that. I was weeping such that I could barely see. I asked to view her grave and he told me he'd buried her up in the woods. I commanded him to show me the location and he said that if he found us anywhere else on his land once we left his porch we would see what would happen. Dyer told him sharply there was no cause for threats and that he should keep a civil tongue. He then took my arm to lead me out and I pulled free and asked Finney how he could live with himself. He said he'd been sleeping well except for some rheumatism in the knees. He came onto the porch once we were seated on the wagon and said that on the final day Tallie had been able to sit up with a little help, and that her expression at the very end had reminded him of the last afflictions of Mrs. Manning's little girl, who had suffered so with her burns. And I could see on his face that he could see on mine the effect he had desired.

Sunday 24 June

A cut on my hand from a paring knife. Dyer at work in the barn. Night after night we enact our separation. Anxiety is now his family, discord his home, and dark spirits his company. Captious dignity and moonlit tears his two prevailing states. This love he seeks to win back he fails to apprehend would be only the hulk of a wrecked affection, fitted with new sails.

No business is more uphill than farming. The most fortunate of us persist without prospering.

Carried off in the night by the immensity of what we promise ourselves and fail to do.

At one point during Tallie's last visit she expressed regret that I had never crossed the fields to visit her. I considered telling her of my midnight expedition with the spyglass, but refrained. Instead I joked about the need to preserve one's self-respect, and that I sometimes seemed to believe the only safety to be within. She'd had to look away as though sharing my shame. Finally she said she always feared that she called misfortune down onto those she loved because of her intemperance, and that this thought on occasion had terrorized her. After another silence she asked if I didn't think it eloquent that I had contributed nothing in response to her remark. I told her I could not imagine what more we could do for each other, and she answered that the imagination could always be cultivated. And in the interval that followed her fingers intertwined with mine but her silence was like the sight of a leafless tree in an arbor with everything else blooming green.

Found Dyer in the late afternoon sitting beside Nellie's gravestone. Sat with him in the dry grass. As though it were someone else's I reread the poem I composed for her epitaph: *"One sweet flower has bloomed and faded / One dear infant voice has fled / One sweet bud the grave has shaded / One sweet girl O now is dead."*

After dark I walked across our upper fields over the hills for the wide, wide view. I stood there with my child's face and selfish love. I imagined my Tallie living in a home that existed only in our thoughts. I imagined myself ungoverned by the fear that holds the wretch in place. I imagined my response to her crying, "What do I know about you at this moment? Nothing!" I imagined cherishing a life touched by such alchemy. I imagined the story of a girl made human. I imagined Tallie's grave, forsaken and remote. I imagined banishing forever those sentiments that she chastened and refined. I imagined everyone I knew sick to the point of death. I imagined a creature even more slow-hearted than myself. I imagined continuing to write in this ledger, as if this were life, as though life were not elsewhere.

The Ocean of Air

As a boy from the highest hillsides above our town I watched the winds depart our valley empty and return laden with spoil, and I came to know the sky's upper reaches as a domain of tempests and whirlwinds from which poured torrents and hail and other phenomena that suggested Nature was in combat with herself. Pliny urged us to consider the marvel of the heavens, that immense space where the vital fluid to which we give the name of air flows in all of its diffusion and mobility, and so I followed the ascension of clouds that rose like capitals on invisible columns of air, and imagined even then an aerial machine that might take advantage of the prevailing currents of the higher atmosphere the way sailing ships ply the trade winds.

Life in the countryside and solitude left me well fitted to the study of natural phenomena. I was congenitally retiring, and neither conversation with my peers nor my increasing age further emboldened me. I felt as if I were dark to all the world or, like the amphibian, disposed to live in two antithetical realms, the first within my fancy and the second forever pulling me toward society. But from my earliest days, my capacity to speculate and invent resolved me to the heavens.

My brother and I are Jacques-Étienne and Joseph-Michel Montgolfier, the fifteenth and twelfth of sixteen children born to Pierre and Anne Montgolfier. Étienne was always entranced by what he considered the magical space of my imagination, and I always assumed I would submit each of my ideas to his more mature discernment, despite his being five years the younger. He was esteemed for his capacity and reliability whereas I seemed to be forever indulged for my fecklessness, and so we envied each other's positions. But we also understood that in any of the tasks and explorations we contracted to undertake together we would never refuse our time, begrudge our thought, or deny our commitment.

I had been intrigued even as a boy to read as much as I could about every discovery concerning the constituent gases of the atmosphere. I was sent to school first at Annonay and, when that failed, to the Jesuit college at Tournon. The latter institution drove me to such active rebellion that at the age of twelve I stole away on a barge down the Rhône before being retrieved. My teachers were fond of citing me in order to impress upon the group the limitations of human knowledge. One theorized that I had absorbed less theology than any other charge with whom he'd had the misfortune to work. But in my secret folders I had already systematized for myself the nature of various forces and the structures of matter, and my self-education proceeded by the experimental verification of various propositions, though my development was impeded by my having had to evolve my own methods of calculation, as the Jesuit Fathers had rejected the utility of mathematics.

I made my first balloon in Avignon when I was meant to be

studying law. One cold winter morning I sought to warm a shirt over the hearth and noted that the fabric billowed and lifted with the heat. The image stayed with me, like the sun's warmth brooding over the waters, and on a rainy November evening a few weeks later I found myself examining a print I'd tacked to the wall depicting our country's futile siege of Gibraltar. The fire in the grate below it carried its sparks upward through the flue above. Why couldn't that force be confined and harnessed? No access could be gained to the fortress by either sea or land, but my shirt's behavior reoccurred to me and I wondered if reinforcements might not arrive by air.

The next morning I constructed a first machine of silk stretched over the slenderest of wooden frames, a polyhedron. It would be made lighter than the air it displaced by the expansive power of heat, and was half my height with an internal capacity of forty cubic feet. I burned paper for its heat source, and soon after, the assembly floated from its cradle and hovered beside me before rising farther to bump along the ceiling to the window. I immediately wrote to Étienne that if he laid in a supply of silk and cordage, I could show him one of the world's most astonishing sights.

Thérèse Filhol was my earliest memory of the model of a sensibility that consorted and sympathized with all things. One of my first images of her was of a tanned, glossy-haired seven-year-old wearing behind her ear an intricate flower made of paper, crouching naked in a pond to examine a leech she'd laid along the top of her hand. Five years later I spent an afternoon alone with her and her schoolbooks, the pair of us curled in a set of her mother's armchairs. At one point she remarked that the Greeks believed Olympus to have been so high that it never rained on its summit, where the air was always still.

Since she was four years my junior, I almost never spoke to her. She seemed to cherish her own contradictions, as if she did not wish to throw any part of herself away. When three years following that afternoon we finally kissed, and I asked if she'd been aware of my interest, she swept her hair back, her eyes half closed and her mouth half open at the thought, and said but of course, everyone had.

We were first cousins, and married when I was thirty and she was twenty-six, against the wishes of my father, who considered such consanguinity indecent.

She maintains on our bed table her own private cabinet of rarities, including a miniature painting of a sea meadow on the ocean's floor, and with such gestures she reminds me that we carry with us the wonders we seek throughout the world. She pursues within me all those evasions I assay in the realms of the spirit and the heart, and she demonstrates with her daily attention how participating natures can unite across incomparable distances, and how we might build and sustain the bounty of our compact, even in the face of my profligacy, just as, at God's bare word, all of creation started up out of nothing.

Whispering in the dark, she has conceded the various ways in which I remained a mystery even as she has celebrated the shared and preternatural transparency of our enjoined hearts. She fancies in me a diffused benevolence and interest in others that they appreciate no matter how distracted I might seem.

I rely upon her faith. My father has said I am so absentminded that upon retiring I once tucked the cat into bed and put myself out the door. In various travels I departed one lodging house without my horse and another without my wife. The latter case had been only two weeks into our marriage. Arising before dawn for a constitutional, I had so quickly entangled myself in thought that I had walked straight through to our destination, remembering I had left Thérèse asleep in the inn's bed only when our hosts, upon my arrival, asked after her.

My letter arrived in Étienne's hand at a propitious moment. For two years he had been negotiating to make the Montgolfiers the first papermaking concern in France to adopt the new manufacturing machines developed in Holland, and the laborers, frightened for their livelihood, had organized a strike, whereupon he locked them out. He wrote me back that he would be pleased to take up a project that wasn't endlessly vexing, and that might also bring credit to the family name at a time when it was being slandered in the streets.

I hastened home to meet him and we began work on larger models. Thérèse was called to her father's side to help with his faltering ribbon factory, and was for three months a presence only in her letters. Did I miss her during the course of my days? she wanted to know. Étienne and I lived in our little workplace, hardly coming round even for meals. We investigated the lifting potential of every vapor and especially considered steam and hydrogen before settling on the dilation of ordinary air by heat as the simplest and most inexpensive technique. Realizing there was much to be learned by the burning of various materials, we ignited an array of woods, wet, dry, and decomposed, as well as sodden straw, chopped wool, old shoes, and rotten meat. We had our best luck with a fire of straw and meat, perhaps because of the greater lifting power of the combination of mephitic and inflammable gases. All of this I explained to her. Her letters in response were enthusiastic, if not everything I might have hoped for.

Our machines rose well, as anticipated, but the force propelling them soon dissipated as gas was lost through minute holes and imperfections in the silk. My brother was no more discouraged than I, though, since from the tenderest age he also had refused to put any limit on his hopes, and we spent two weeks experimenting with methods of sealing the fabric. We could dream our designs, but it was only when we put our calculations into physical form that we could judge their practicality.

Paper-backed taffeta proved the most successful solution, and on a bright December morning when even the carriage wheels were covered in frost we repeated the Avignon experiment in the seclusion of the new garden just north of the house with the family gathered round. Our little polyhedron rose eighty feet into the air and rode the breezes to the southwest for a full minute. Once it returned to earth, my brother and I repaired immediately to our workroom, where for the next three weeks we fabricated a balloon three times the size. It rose with such vigor that it broke its tether and disappeared over the trees to the north, only to be destroyed where it landed by some alarmed passersby.

The new garden is one of the few spaces near the house large enough to accommodate the entire family. Our dining table seats forty. While unmarried daughters might avail themselves of the religious orders and younger sons might attempt a commercial venture or the priesthood, those of our relations who find no place for themselves in the world—the ne'er-do-well, the artist, the widow, the plainly discouraged—are all granted shelter in our household.

Family tradition claims the Montgolfiers have been producing paper since the twelfth century, our ancestors having apprenticed in the art starting in Damascus during the Second Crusade. One hundred years ago another pair of Montgolfier brothers married the daughters of a rival papermaking family and settled in Annonay, a region with ready access to markets and raw materials and a climate mild enough for sizing paper the year round. They built their mill deep in a ravine through which the Deume pours from the surrounding hills before reaching the town, the river's water clear and soft and fine for rinsing rags and pulp, its pitch powering the mill wheels with commendable vigor except in the summer's driest months.

Pierre, our father, was one of nineteen children, and as the eldest surviving son he succeeded to his inheritance at the age of forty-three. He has since maintained his place at our table as patriarch for thirty-nine years. Under his hand the firm has earned the King's patronage, and the seal of Royal Paper Manufactory.

The factory is in fact a series of additions to an ancient farmhouse, and as toddlers we thrilled at the thundering of the mill wheels and the flume on the massive wooden blades and the groans of the cyclopean joists and axletrees. It was only when we were permitted to forage sufficiently upstream or deep into the woods that we could hear ourselves think, or listen to the wind in the poplars.

Our father rose every morning at four and performed his ablutions out of doors in the millrace whatever the season, and for the rest of his day oversaw every task in operation. Any and all deficiencies would at some point be uncovered in his survey. He retired without fail at seven following supper, and until he did light conversation was forbidden.

He seemed particularly pained by the sight of me. Étienne, as the youngest son, had gone off to study architecture in Paris, but the death of our brother Raymond meant that each of the elder brothers was now in ill health, the Holy Orders, dead, or temperamentally unsuited to business, and so Étienne renounced his dreams so that he could become head of the concern.

We harbor no illusions in our family about one another's qualities, and ask of each other both what we do well and not what we do not. We avoid the unkindness of requiring more of a loved one than it would be reasonable to expect. From my earliest memories of the factory floor, and hearing the nursery songs about women and children sorting rags, I knew that when it came to the affairs of commerce I could not persuade myself to honor what that practice demanded. I continued to search for success with no notion of where to find her.

Étienne was, unlike me, well educated in mathematics and self-discipline, and not hopeless at commerce. Having escaped the Jesuits, I had drawn on my experiments for my first commercial venture, fabricating dyes I'd hoped to sell at fairs and markets. When this failed, my father had provided me, and another of my younger brothers for whom no one could find a useful sinecure, with a lease on two small paper mills in Dauphiny; but to that concern I had also remained inattentive. Even while studying law at Avignon I had mortgaged enough credit to have spent a week in debtors' prison. Yet my home remained open to me, as it did to each family member who caused my parents pain.

Even before our little balloon landed, Étienne had expressed to me his anxiety that we might be cheated of whatever advantages our invention might yield. He wrote to an influential friend in the capital to request that our ascending machine be registered with the Academy of Science, and his baffled friend asked him to provide an improved drawing and more detailed specifics. My brother responded with an adequately comprehensive dossier on our success and added that our novel speculation likely could ferry heavy weights at very little cost, and also that it might immediately be useful for sending messages or supplies into cities under siege. He further stipulated that the particulars about our next, much bigger machine would be withheld until we had tested it.

Our entire family was then drawn into the project, our father suffering the machine to be built only on the condition that we swear a filial oath never to ascend in it. It was arranged that our second-oldest brother, Jean-Pierre, whose health had improved, would assist in daily proceedings at the mill, and our brother Alexandre—an abbé at Lyon, he liked to say that his career in the Church was unmarked by devotion, success, or chagrin—would oversee all correspondence and sales.

We spent six months constructing the machine for the first public demonstration. Having determined that a spherical form would provide the maximum internal volume, we soon discovered that shaping sheets of taffeta of the necessary size, before lining them with paper and enjoining them together with thousands upon thousands of buttons and buttonholes, was something no seamstress had ever attempted. The monster was assembled out of segments that together formed three lateral bands with a dome fitted over the top, all reinforced by a net of stout ropes encompassing the entire exterior. These ropes converged beneath the envelope in a frame securing the iron brazier that would hold the material to be burned. In a test we conducted in late spring, again in the privacy of our garden, two laborers let the cords fly through their hands and two others were pulled aloft until they released their grips and fell back to the earth with panicked cries. We retrieved our machine undamaged from the adjoining property.

The debut took place in our town square on the morning of the 4th of June in the Year of our Lord 1783, with the provincial assembly among the spectators gathered. It was raining. The extravagant mass of the taffeta was piled on a wooden stage beside the bridge over the river, and two detachable ropes ran through a wheel set atop a mast with their ends fastened to an eye sewn into the center of the fabric. At our instruction the laborers positioned the envelope's maw over a hole cut in the stage, beneath which we'd set ablaze in the furnace a great quantity of wool soaked in alcohol, and the balloon's upper reaches were then hoisted prior to its inflation by means of the two ropes.

Within minutes our creature was bridling at its restraining lines and commenced bucking and twisting like a fairground animal while four of our burliest laborers endeavored with all their weight to rein in its fury. Then Étienne and I together ordered its release, and the great sphere bounded upward and spiraled to a fantastic height.

As it rose, the congregation's discordant minds were aligned in a state of astonishment that held sway until the silence that we had created ended in a roar of acclamation. All present described the ascent as majestic and beautiful beyond compare, and many were amazingly affected. A small boy yelped and slapped at his face again and again, and an old woman beside me clutched my arm and wept. If savants could achieve such a miracle, she said, what else might they accomplish?

The currents of the wind carried the machine a half league to the south while we all gave chase, before it finally came to grief on a stone fence where coals from the brazier spilled across the envelope, setting the entire mass afire.

Thérèse had requested I delay the ascent until she could attend it, but I was so taken up with various vexations that I neglected to do so. Her expression upon arrival was so dismaying that Étienne was forced to interrupt me to finish relating the account of our triumph. And even as I stood listening to his exultation and gazing upon her displeasure, I was served with three promissory notes for which I was badly in arrears, and about which I had told her nothing.

That night in our bed I marveled at how close the footfalls of exhilaration and frustration and misery tread upon one another. She said she understood my childhood was one of indulgence, and that I had imagined I could endlessly have everything a home could provide. She understood as well that, unlike many of her friends, she had been spared a life with a husband who differed so materially as to prevent her happiness. She thanked God there were so many mornings when she found she desired more of the same for the morrow, and so many nights when under my hand she savored all the felicity a woman was allowed.

She suggested every marriage was a story of indebtedness, and that she had tried to convince herself, when considering my irresponsibility, she was looking at the wrong side of the picture; that if she just turned things around, or balanced the accounts between the two extremes of my behavior, she would then find ample reason to be joyful. She reminded herself that during our engagement I had jokingly urged her to bear with me, for I knew that someday I would come out all right. She understood there were husbands who needed to be managed as well as obeyed, and that sometimes it was her duty to remain silent even when she believed I was in the wrong, and that married life was not so much about choice as about living with the choices already made.

But she also had to realize that such days as this demonstrated I was one of those men who granted themselves endless absolution in advance, considering themselves occasionally weak but never wicked. I acted as if in my mind the quotidian was veiled with dread. She was expected to express excess when it came to affection, and restraint when it came to our household affairs, while I seemed to believe I was discharging a task well suited to my natural generosity when I squandered whatever security we might achieve. What a sense of obligation she had to bear, because of this most generous of men!

Such was her state of agitation that I twice had to restrain her from leaving the room. We squabbled the long night through. Eventually I entreated her forgiveness, then told her I cared little of what came to cheer me if she drew away. I promised to repay each of our creditors monthly until all were satisfied.

She asked where we would find the money and I reminded her that the very next day Étienne intended to petition Their Lordships of the Estates to formally acknowledge our success and establish our priority and thereby persuade the King to support our project, since we meant to improve our design in order to make it more broadly useful. I urged her to imagine no end to the amount of wealth that might be generated.

She was quiet for some minutes and finally murmured that whatever funds we received would be instantly devoted to reimbursement for our machine's expenses and further development. I pledged I would set some portion aside to address her distress. And after another silence she reminded me that in a family if one suffered then so did all.

"You chide me for taking no delight in things and yet you force me to keep our accounts," she said.

I was sorry to make her weep, I told her.

"And when you return to my bed I'm supposed to be seduced by you once again," she cried.

I understood her disappointment, I conceded. Perhaps this was a matter of age turning bad dispositions into worse habits.

We attended a commotion from our stable yard that featured donkeys and our terriers, who always set up a fearful barking whenever something turned up outside the gate.

"I expect you to govern our household as if you cherished it," she said, and I promised that I would. And through such resolutions we seek access to the mansions of our restored selves, even as we fail to banish those unanswerable doubts that torment the wisest agreements.

Eventually in her exhaustion and sadness she fell asleep, and I took her hand and listened to her breaths. I know now, as I knew then, that I loved my wife even before myself, which was not to say I loved her enough, or that I still didn't fail to fully credit the extent to which I carried my own domestic enemies within.

We were informed that the Academy of Sciences had appointed a committee to investigate our machine, and that the committee included Lavoisier. It was decided at a family council that Étienne should go alone to Paris to secure our fortune, since I was too unworldly to be of any help there, and that I should remain behind to continue our experiments and oversee the construction of new balloons.

Mention of our machine had already appeared in Paris: the *Feuille Hebdomadaire* had printed a description of the flight provided by one of our neighbors, an account neither good-natured nor accurate. Still, it was said that the Controller General of Finance himself had felt his imagination fired by the invention.

So the morning post held a special fervency for us. Étienne had left his wife seven months pregnant, and only two of her previous four girls had survived their infancy. It was agreed that he would produce two sets of correspondence: one concerning general developments that could be read in our father's presence, and another addressed to his wife containing news about the machine, which information she could share after our father had retired for the evening. Among the former was our hope to capitalize on our machine's fame to win further privileges for our mills. As Jean-Pierre put it, why compete if we could fix the game?

Étienne wrote that he found himself contending with the young J. Charles—whose laboratory in experimental physics had enjoyed such a string of successes that the American Franklin was said to have remarked that Nature could not say no to him—for the right to pursue our discovery. Charles had his own balloon, only twelve feet in diameter but filled instead with hydrogen that he generated in a barrel through a reaction of iron filings and oil of vitriol.

Étienne's letters expressed mostly his fears that as a provincial businessman he was out of his depth in such a great capital. He claimed to have little aptitude for the calls to be paid to ministers and courtiers, and little feel for the salons in which he should play the lion and which the lamb. He reported to be afflicted by turns with irritation and depression, and Alexandre wrote to remind his younger brother that patience was a drug impossible to overstock. He added the further reassurance that Adelaïde was maintaining her spirits, though her condition made her sleepy in the mornings. Jean-Pierre appended a postscript urging Étienne to obtain some American orders for paper from the famous Franklin.

A month later Étienne wrote to report that Charles had released a tethered balloon that had ascended one hundred feet into the air, and that two days later it had been set free on the Champ de Mars before an estimated fifty thousand spectators, where it had risen until it disappeared into the clouds. And that Franklin, having heard someone suggest the invention was of no practical value, was said to have responded, "Of what use is a newborn babe?" Étienne added that gossip had been put about that he had been turned away from his rival's demonstration for want of a ticket.

. . .

Left to my own devices, I spent my weeks drawing up plans for a balloon one hundred and fifty feet in diameter and one hundred in height. This might cost over sixteen thousand livres. But why settle for less? I conveyed my excitement to Étienne and urged him to suggest, if the commission balked, that we might take our invention to England, where there were plenty of wealthy patrons.

He responded that the commission had undertaken to pay our expenses, though only for a machine of the size he had proposed: fully a third smaller than my leviathan. The Controller General had indicated the King's interest and authorized those at court who could arrange a demonstration before the royal family at Versailles to do so. The exhibition was scheduled to be mounted on the great patio before the château on 19 September, with a private trial to be staged for the Academy a week earlier.

Even for a machine that size we were anxious about the durability of the taffeta and paper. I proposed silk coated with varnish, but Étienne rejected that option due to the expense. I wrote back that only he would make economy a point of honor after having been accorded carte blanche.

It was decided that this time we would not be content to match the spectacle of the Charles balloon with a grander machine of our own; instead, we would bear living beings into the air. But which animals should go aloft? When Étienne first proposed a sheep, I responded that it might go unnoticed. What about a dog, whose barking could be heard from high above? Or perhaps a cow?

I inquired if I should come at once to the capital to aid in the preparations, and Étienne answered that his patrons had provided him with all of the assistance he required, and that I was more useful at home. The entire family went silent when Adelaïde read that passage at our dining table.

Construction took place at the Réveillon wallpaper factory, and

Étienne wrote upon the balloon's completion that I had approached its design like a visionary, he like an architect, and Réveillon like a decorator. The result he depicted as a truly splendid object, seventy feet tall and forty-five in diameter with an intricately patterned exterior of cerulean and gold, a machine he pronounced fit to float above a king. In order to align the edges and conjoin the seams, his workers had spread the fabric out in the factory's courtyard entire, since no interior could accommodate the task. When rain or wind threatened, everything had to be refolded with excruciating care and hurried back under shelter.

On the 11th Étienne conducted a trial with Réveillon that went perfectly. On the 12th it rained, and the commissioners failed to arrive at the agreed time. Once they finally assembled themselves with a great amount of fuss, the rain had increased. Étienne made the decision to proceed. In what became a downpour, the paper peeled from its backing and our unhappy machine dragged its gaiety dismally into some nearby trees. Two months of work disappeared in a morning. In his letter he wrote that the spectators were sympathetic.

I reminded him in my response that every success sowed the seeds of potential failure, and that any change in a system might introduce new and ruinous problems. Understanding came from failure and success followed from understanding. We needed only to own up to our roles in the disaster, and thus achieve our absolution. All hope of improvement was rooted in our shortcomings. I refrained from mentioning my earlier suggestion of the varnish.

Within only a week Étienne and his workers constructed a new and smaller machine, fifty feet tall, that would ascend with a wicker cage holding a sheep, a duck, and a rooster. His letter, after the great day finally arrived, described the arrangements at Versailles, where an enormous crowd surrounded a great octagonal stage, below which an apron painted to resemble a velvet curtain concealed an iron stove as tall as a man. Étienne had been privileged to explain the preparations to the royal family before the noxious smell produced by the material being burned forced them to retire from the immediate proximity.

He wrote how electric the atmosphere among the spectators had become when the great fabric had begun to stir and rise. And how the balloon had taken to the air, drawing along beneath it the first aeronauts. The flight covered two miles, and the King himself invited Étienne to observe its landing through his own spyglass. Astronomers used a quadrant to estimate its altitude had reached one thousand five hundred feet, not nearly as high as we had gone before, but the animals had all been recovered in fine condition, although the sheep had pissed in its cage.

Étienne was now negotiating countless dinner invitations, including one from the Queen, who had requested a detailed account of our invention. And the King, upon first hearing of the possibility of sending a man aloft, had suggested a condemned criminal, to which the Marquis d'Arlandes responded that no such honor should be afforded a wretch bound for the gallows, and instead proposed himself. Étienne ended his letter with the galvanizing news that the King had agreed to this notion.

I sent him our congratulations and described our jubilation, adding the further happy news that Adelaïde had delivered to them another daughter, whom she had not yet named.

Once it was common knowledge that men would take to the sky, a mania engulfed our nation with all manner of objects featuring balloon motifs. Étienne sent home to the family four bottles of Crème de l'Aérostatique liqueur, the labels of which featured fanciful images of both our machine and our faces. Every conversation seemed to involve flying machines and the means of managing them. All one heard in Paris, Étienne reported, was talk of inflammable gas and journeys through the clouds. Miniature *montgolfiers* of scraped animal membranes were sold on street corners.

The first upon the scene at our downed balloon in Versailles turned out to be Jean-François Pilâtre de Rozier, who had already made a name for himself at the age of twenty-six by having provided for young ladies of fashion demonstrations of chemical and electrical effects, accompanied by various gallantries and levities. He had a passion for offering his services to scientific causes, and in a rubberized coverall had descended into one of the foulest sections of the Parisian sewers in order to successfully test for thirty-four minutes a breathing apparatus attached to an enclosed barrel of air, an invention that soon was acclaimed for the lives it would save, since those workmen tasked with cleaning the tunnels were so often overcome by the mephitic gases.

The morning following our flight de Rozier publicly announced his willingness to accompany the Marquis d'Arlandes aloft, and since he enjoyed the patronage of the Comte and the Comtesse de Provence, the King's brother and sister-in-law, Étienne wrote that he found the young man to be exceedingly well qualified.

The ascent of the Marquis d'Arlandes and de Rozier was arranged for the morning of 20 November at the Château de la Muette, a royal hunting lodge. Étienne wrote at the end of every day to describe the progress of our preparations.

In our bed in the middle of the night, after I thought Thérèse was asleep, and having heard Adelaïde read one such letter in its entirety to the assembled family earlier in the evening, she whispered to me, her palm cool and soft along my cheek, "How has he not sent for you? Why have you not gone to him?"

This machine would be our grandest yet, with Réveillon having assigned eight workmen to the decorative touches alone. The main envelope would be indigo and royal blue, with red and gold fleurs-de-lis and eagles rampant, and with signs of the zodiac encircling the great dome. The aeronauts would ride in a wicker gallery surrounding the aperture for the burner, the gallery curtained by a lightweight cloth painted to resemble drapery. The entire contrivance, including passengers, was calculated to weigh sixteen hundred pounds. The burner once aloft would be tended with straw by means of lightweight pitchforks. On our own experimental machines, constructed separately, we had calculated the distance of separation required to keep the brazier's heat from setting fire to the fabric above.

It was decided that experimental tethered flights might be a prudent prelude to a manned, untethered voyage, and so Étienne placed a notice in the *Journal de Paris* that on 17 October tests would be conducted exclusively for scientists. Of course this created even more excitement, and a week prior to these events he reported with both pleasure and dismay that it was clear that many thousands planned on attending, and that a multitude had already arrived upon the site.

Our father's apprehension that Étienne himself would participate in the ascent became so intense and ungovernable that both Alexandre and Jean-Pierre soon threatened to leave home. Jean-Pierre finally wrote that our father required Étienne to allay his distress by warranting that he would not ascend in his machine, and the old man countersigned the letter himself. "If he were to be lost, I do not know how I would carry forward," he announced to our family at dinner the following evening, apropos of nothing.

On the appointed day the tethered flight took place under threatening skies. The American Franklin, who resided nearby in the Hôtel de Valentinois, was among the vast assemblage. De Rozier ascended alone, first, to eighty feet, with a one-hundred-pound sack at the opposite end of the gallery to balance the weight. As I read Étienne's account, in my mind's eye I beheld him soaring on rapture's white wings. As he drew back toward the earth, he apparently remarked for all to hear that it had seemed as if the whole country was alarmed and transfixed.

The following day a heavy wind prevented de Rozier from rising any higher. The day after he floated at some two hundred and fifty feet for eight minutes, and on the next flight he climbed to over three hundred feet, thereby becoming visible to the entire city. On the third day he was accompanied by the impatient Marquis d'Arlandes, who upon his descent predicted aerostatic ships that would one day carry guns and strike down our enemies from above.

In my exile from the invigoration and euphoria of those great events, which all of France save myself seemed to have witnessed, the dreams that took shape in the solitude of my workshop filled vast sheets with unparalleled extravagance: A rectangular balloon two hundred feet high and capable of lifting a horse and wagon. A cylindrical machine six hundred feet long that would float by burning two hundred pounds of wood per minute. Vessels without equal in size in the history of the world.

With an air of distraction noticeable even in his letters, Étienne praised my ambition and suggested I first attempt small-scale models. Though he joked that my notion of small, he feared, was rather larger than that of other men. When I wrote that my new machine would ascend far higher than any ever had, he answered that my fantasies might be well and good if we both were twenty and unshackled by responsibilities, but that Thérèse had confided to him details of my financial situation, and he wished to remind me that we could no longer be certain of an endless supply of funds. Our father had privately made it clear he would do no more to enable my profligacy, and that even in England the rich didn't toss their wealth out the window any more readily. Étienne recommended I instead concentrate on improving the impermeability and lessening the weight of the envelope.

Subsequent to the Marquis d'Arlandes's remark, my brother wrote, he had been calculating the military applications of our invention, including the possibility of ferrying bombs over walls to be dropped onto fortified positions. He had long been upset by the complaint that aviation ministered only to the vanity of scientists, as if the royal family's thoughts on our endeavor extended no farther than the entertainments they staged and enjoyed. Because of us, after all, the skies were now as open to exploitation as the seas. What most excited him, though, were the opportunities for commerce, the lifeblood of the ordered world, especially for the transportation of bulk goods at low cost.

I wrote back to confess that what drove me now was the potential for not a monopoly but a community of learning. He apparently found this notion so pitiably naïve that he chose not to respond to it at all in his next letter.

But trade itself is nothing more than a galaxy of the imagination, wheeling through a marketplace of services and commodities. Confidence and anxiety, each utterly ephemeral, are infinitely more powerful than any solid materials. Consider credit, with its ghostly power to buoy its servants and carry them forward, even as they register how diaphanous it remains—only a vapor—when they attempt to grasp hold of it.

I relate this conviction to Thérèse in the middle of the night, and having been pulled from sleep she concurs so as to be left alone. "You still have to pay what is owed," she murmurs, her back to my front.

On such nights, having once again renounced the arms of my

wife, I'm unsettled by a sleepless and prowling sadness, and struck that the conceits of this world may be as dreams in the next, just as the phantoms of darkness are dispersed by the clarities of the day.

Thérèse seems even more herself in slumber, and yet more worthy still of my devotion, so I peer down at her expression in repose and remind myself of the intimacy which remains despite all of the obstacles I have strewn in its path, much as the memory of a troubled dream relates to the awakened mind a confused and broken tale of what might truly have passed.

We continue to fall short, like the objects we create. We can only pray, on our rounds, *"Let me not injure the felicity of others."* And wait for sadness to grow tired of her office, and to provide us some respite. And for labor to vibrate more forcibly on the chords of our heart than the most harmonious music.

I wake Thérèse again and she sits up in the cold of our bedroom, drowsy as a child but concerned enough about her husband to counsel herself to patience. Her forbearance itself is an indication of the intimacy whose resilience I fear. "If you want to go to Paris, then go," she tells me, believing this to be the cause of my distress. A better man would awaken her more fully to what's coming, but this one only sees to her comfort with a blanket and sits beside her until she eases back into sleep. So that even the clarity with which I can discern the ongoing pattern of my withdrawal refuses to occasion in its master a shift.

I often have fancied that man in his relation to the sky resembled marine organisms confined to the ocean's floor, and that in order to discover the true conditions of the atmosphere it would be necessary to observe them from considerable heights. We live in the depths of an ocean of air.

Étienne writes that the Marquis d'Arlandes urges all speed in readying our craft for its first untethered flight, since our competitor Charles is now also at work on an improved hydrogen balloon for the same purpose, and the Marquis confides that persons of the greatest eminence have made clear that being the first to launch a man in free flight would attach the final seal of glory to our invention. Jean-Pierre has written to remind his brother that he should accept no distinction that did not apply equally to me, and when Étienne wrote to reassure me on the subject, I told him that if the King had only one ribbon it was Étienne who should have it, and Étienne who would no doubt put it to better use. As for me, the more I am informed of the pleasures of society, the more I am drawn to my solitude. Jean-Pierre then showed me a letter Étienne sent to him privately, in which he noted that apparently the success of my experiments had elevated my imagination to a height so grandiose that I could not easily lower myself to attend such base considerations as providing creditors with payment. He accused me also of playing Achilles in my tent.

I have exhausted the funds remaining at my disposal, including those I pledged to Thérèse, in order to complete my own improved machine. Under cover of darkness, with the household asleep, I have made all of the final preparations for ascent, with only the terriers as my spectators. My balloon is much smaller yet its envelope is reinforced with varnish, and my brazier and fuel supply are double the size of Étienne's.

It is very late before I'm ready. The terriers circle below the ever-expanding fabric above them, wary but quiet. When the balloon is filled to capacity and the restraining ropes vibrate with tension, I slip the knots and feel myself leap upward into the darkness. One terrier barks and I hear two others pursue me for a short stretch, just as children chase a butterfly, before falling away below.

At three hundred feet, the tether arrests me with a thump that knocks me to my knees. Once my little basket stops swaying on its ropes, a stillness reigns over the air.

I now can hear only increasingly hoarse and far-off barking. Then that, too, fades and even the wind is hushed to a calm by the canopy of constellations above.

I gaze upon stars new and unheard-of. I can make out the glow of furnaces from the blacksmith's in town. Otherwise a black plunging gulf surrounds me on all sides. I sip some water and drop the empty bottle out of the basket and listen to it whistle as it descends. I remain as still as I am able, laboring under the grandeur of the moment, until just before daybreak, when the cultivated fields begin to materialize below, bordered by embrowning hedges.

In the gray light of morning, smoke emerges at last from various chimneys. Highways and rivers appear just as if laid down on a map. Rising hills to the east afford pasturage to dotted flocks of sheep. My father I'm sure is already awake and about, and no doubt puzzled by the ropes and tools in the courtyard.

The barometer stands at twenty-eight and the thermometer at thirty-one. I untie the tether, which helixes away below, and vault upward. The act makes me the first man in the world to engage in unbound flight.

I can gauge from the horizon the accelerating speed of my ascent, the balloon spinning gently on its axis. I close my eyes and turn my face to the sun and imagine that somewhere down below Thérèse has done the same.

The barometer now stands at eighteen, having fallen an inch since my release. The temperature has dropped to twelve and seems to be decreasing uniformly with the height. Passing through thinner and more striated cloud, I don the sheepskin from the bottom of the basket and wait.

A van of mallards passes over the far-off river. According to the barometer and my timepiece I have achieved an altitude of over eight thousand feet in just under nine minutes.

At some point I loose a small shout of relief and joy before covering my mouth in surprise. The mallards, now almost invisible, continue on in their direction.

Finally, with a cord attached to a valve, I release some of my store of heated gas and halt my ascent.

The balloon pendulums alarmingly, then stabilizes. The wind picks up and I move horizontally through yet more mist. From the fabric's shape it's clear that the rarefication of the air has diminished the envelope's volume even further. I imagine Étienne's expression were I to tell him of all this.

Thérèse will wake to my absence and find all the evidence of my departure among the chagrined and confused terriers. She'll wonder if what I've done is possible, and if I'd really risk a voyage that could bring us to complete ruin. But we ride our lives' trajectories as swallows sometimes race from fair weather to foul, and at least at my most self-aware I have striven to remember that all too often the only world I choose to regard is myself.

The cold is sharp and dry, though not unbearable. When I survey the astonishing course of my experiences, I call to account the finger of God and the scepter of His mercies for having delivered unto me these gifts of imagination and love, hubris and achievement. Posterity will applaud each of my brothers before they take their place in that perpetuity unto which all of us must finally relinquish our reach.

But were I to be saved, and were Thérèse to forgive me, we would still be gone before we could witness, in the years to come, aeronauts departing on the trade winds for America or the tropics, to return laden with passengers and goods. The fruit of my machine is beautiful to imagine but not available for us to sample. This is a tree planted for our children.

I remind myself that Thérèse is the patron who made me ready, in the happiness of being known, and through our common faith and cause, to assail such heights. Through what she has enabled I have been delivered all that I dare call happiness on earth.

The balloon, still shrinking, has begun its descent. My hands beneath the sheepskin are numb. My reasoning feels light-headed. There's a pain in my ear.

I examine each sensation in tranquility, standing in the center of my basket and lost in the spectacle afforded by the immensity of the horizon at this height.

So many below me remain in the dark where I left them. So many allied themselves to me only to see that they were groping for a wraith. So many farms and houses are still in shadow that the sun seems to have risen for me and me alone, gilding the basket and fabric above with its light.

Positive Train Control

As a kid I always thought I'd take any train anywhere I found one, anywhere it was going. I wanted to learn something. I wanted to surprise somebody. I wanted to surprise myself. I wanted to end up some place where someone was happy to see me.

Nine or ten years old I used to go down to the station to meet my father when he worked for the railroad. Even then I couldn't find my brother. The station was half a mile away past some serious intersections, but when my mother complained I told her I was good at looking both ways. She told me I wasn't allowed to go and I didn't argue and went anyway. My father liked to say you got out of life what you put into it, so at night in bed I'd go over what I'd put into it and usually came up with the same thing: nothing.

He also liked to say that I led the league in complaints and wasted time, and one day I said to him, "What league?" and he laughed. He called me "the Kid Without Enthusiasms," but my brother told him, "Hey, he likes trains. That's something."

So my second year of high school when somebody told me the

Burlington Northern Santa Fe was hiring for the summer, I asked my father about it and he said he'd heard the same thing, but that they weren't looking for beachcombers. I asked what that even meant and he never answered, so I filled out the one-page application and then didn't think about it. A week later they called me in for a physical. A week after that I got a call from somebody who said he was the crew dispatcher and that they needed me to cover the 5:30 commuter train to Aurora. I said, "Does that mean I'm hired?" and the guy said, "Didn't I just ask you to work?" I hung up and told my father and he laughed and said he guessed summer hiring was a little more casual. I didn't have a uniform and I'd never been on a train to Aurora and had no idea what I'd be doing, and when I called back they said wear dark pants and a white shirt and we'll give you a tie when you get here. And when I showed up at the crew dispatcher's office he handed me the tie and a punch and a conductor's revenue book, which listed what the fares were between all stations at all times, and then he showed me where to look for what I needed to know. I said, "Is that it?" and he found me a trainman's hat and badge, and while I stood there he put the hat on my head and pointed out the track for the 5:30 to Aurora.

And I did all right. The first stop on my timetable said Belmont so when I felt the train slowing down I called out, "Belmont! Belmont next stop!" and got some looks. Then when the doors opened the station sign said Downers Grove. An old lady pushed by me on her way out and said, "This isn't Belmont and you're not the conductor."

Now it's a little more of a big deal, conductor training, but the OJT—on-the-job training—is about the same. Most guys once they get some seniority in don't make the change from passenger to freight. Usually it goes the other way. But I learned under Mr. Robichaud, so when he switched so did I. He gave up twenty-one years' seniority as a conductor to start all over again in the engine service, and when people gave him grief about it he said, "I just thought, if you really like trains, hey, what's the top position? The guy who drives them."

Burlington Northern is a Class 1, one of those mega-railroads with a rail network of thirty-two thousand route miles that generates 300 million in revenue every year by running about 1,600 trains per day, most of them those hundred-car freights that hold you up for thirty minutes at level crossings. And if they're the deep end when it comes to trains, then the deepest parts of the deep end are the hazardous-materials trains, the ones where if something goes wrong you lose a whole town, like up in Canada.

My mother the last time this came up said the guy I worked with sounded okay, and my father said crude oil trains were too much stress and responsibility, and I said he was and they were. She asked if my trains were that dangerous, and my father told her she didn't want to know, and she said that she did, and then when I wasn't more helpful on the subject she asked about Mr. Robichaud again, and I told her he'd been with the Burlington Northern since the days when a train rolled into town with the trainmen standing at the half-open vestibule doors, that he kept a rented room near the switching yard, and that when he first had me in for coffee on a layover I asked what I was smelling and he said hoop cheese and roach powder. I told my father he always wiped the grab irons with a rag when he came on shift because he said some of the boys got careless when they took a leak off the gangway. I told my mother everybody liked him because he had a good eye for trouble, and that he said that's what came of twelve- and fourteen-hour days spent watching the track ahead for some other guy's mistakes. She asked if he'd ever been married, and I said he had, once, way back when, and that he said his ex still lived in town and after thirty years still crossed the street when she saw him coming. My father asked if he ever had trouble with a schlump like me as his number two, and I said he liked me. My father said maybe he liked everyone, and I told him no, and that in fact he said we were lucky because a huge number of assholes found their way to rail work and so sooner or later every crew ended up with one.

In freight you spend a lot of time going over what you need to deal with, so you'd better hope you get along with your engineer, since it's just the two of you in a cab the size of a bathroom. You got to work together because even on level ground the biggest challenge is controlling the in-train forces or slack: each joint between the cars has several inches of play, and if you times that by 120 cars, it can add up to twenty-five feet or more, so if you start too fast you can pull your train in half, and if you let the rear run in on you, the kind of jolt you get when fifteen thousand tons pile up behind you can spill a lot of coffee. It means you're always thinking ten miles ahead to planned stops or straightaways, or other traffic, and everything else you have to juggle.

You can be on call 24/7 with two hours' notice. Forget being home on holidays or making an appointment for something a week out. A lot of guys are single. Divorce rates are high. The pay's pretty good, but you have to put in 250 hours a month to get it.

You'd think there'd be plenty of work on the oil trains for those who wanted it, since over the last ten years that traffic has increased 5,000 percent. Burlington Northern alone last year was hauling 600,000 barrels of crude a day across its network, most unit trains having a minimum of a hundred cars holding 34,000 gallons apiece. That oil traversed almost every county between the production fields in central Canada and the Great Plains and the destination facilities, ten on the East Coast, eleven on the Gulf, and twelve on the Pacific. Train after train after train going through a station near you. And for a long time the production of crude kept going up and up.

None of this would matter to anybody besides guys who hang

around hobby shops in their engineers' caps if it weren't for what happens when an oil train derails. The one that exploded in Quebec three years ago incinerated forty-seven people in their beds. The oil we haul is way more volatile than your average crude: its higher gas content generates more vapor pressure, and it has a lower flash point.

But we'd still be just earning our pay if it wasn't for the state of most of our railway infrastructure, which on a good day can look like the shittiest Third World footings and tracks on a bad day.

Eight years ago as part of the deregulation fiesta the statesmen who ran DC passed what they with their sense of humor called the Rail Safety Improvement Act, which announced among other things that the federal government was ceding authority for over 100,000 rail bridges across the country to corporate or municipal owners, who could determine their own load limits, their own engineering standards, and their own inspection and maintenance and repair schedules, with no oversight from anybody else. It meant whoever was inspecting no longer needed an engineering degree, and that any safety issues that were discovered didn't have to be reported to federal agencies.

See if you can guess what happened next. Or if you don't like guessing, row a boat underneath the nearest railroad bridge and take a look up. You'll see broken pilings. Exposed rebar. Split crossties. Missing bolts and spikes. Fractures in the structural steel. You'll even see metal straps wrapped around braces and beams, like someone's idea of a truss. And if a train goes over while you're under there, watch out for falling concrete.

When anything compromises what's holding the rails in alignment, all that forward force and weight takes over and a train leaves the tracks. This isn't a theory. For a while this was happening at the rate of ten to twelve derailments a year. And then a lot more oil trains started running, and they turned out to be some of the heaviest trains out there: the longest could scale in at twenty thousand tons. Some lines carried twenty to thirty million tons of freight a year. You could see what that did to the ballast in the roadbeds, or the wood ties, or the rails themselves: it was causing track failures even in new sections laid down less than a year before.

With oil derailments mostly there were spills and fires instead of explosions. But there were more and more of both. And when the Pipeline and Hazardous Materials Safety Administration set the minimum evacuation area at one square mile, that meant twenty-five million Americans now live in the blast zones.

The DOT's own hazardous-materials division sent out flyers reminding us that given crude oil's volatility, there's an increased risk of a significant incident because of the volume being transported and the distances it's going. So at least they did that.

All sorts of things could've made this work safer, and deregulation gutted every one of them. Going slower's always safer, but the speed limit for extremely hazardous materials got bumped up to forty miles an hour. In emergency stops, electronic braking systems can keep the cars from piling into one another, but the companies said they were too expensive. Shorter trains have a much lower chance of derailing, so our union asked for a 30-car limit, but most of the trains now haul 100 to 120. Pressure-relief valves on the tank cars reduce the risk of explosions but are only recommended, not required, by the National Transportation Safety Board. And with the track problems, better inspection would help, but here's how big a job that is: even Amtrak, the runt of the litter, operates over twenty-two thousand miles of track.

And of course we could go around the major cities. But travel time converts to running costs, so we go right through downtowns. We go by schools. By stadiums. By neighborhoods that people like me grew up in, so nobody worries too much about it. Deregulation even meant that first responders never got told about what was coming through: all the company had to do was designate the shipment as security sensitive, and it got wiped off the local responders' ledgers. Because of what happened up in Canada, the DOT issued an emergency order stipulating that all carriers operating trains ferrying more than a million gallons of crude had to inform each state through which the trains would travel, but that EO wasn't even codified in a lot of places. And given that most towns don't have enough fire equipment to do the job, after an accident the responders mostly have been evacuating the area and waiting for the fires to burn themselves out.

One thing my mother and father do agree on is that at my age I shouldn't be living at home. She asks isn't it lonely keeping to my room, and I tell her of course it is. She says don't I get tired of just either working or being up there, and I say of course I do. She did what she could to raise me but she didn't have much to work with. When I was a kid, she'd set me down next to some other kid and I'd head off in the opposite direction. I'd tell her I didn't want to go to this or that birthday party and she'd tell me she didn't want me to end up like my father. "What's wrong with his father?" my father would ask, and she'd go, "His father has no friends."

My brother she didn't worry about, because he was always out of the house. She thought that made him the smartest thing on two feet. "*He* doesn't get stuck around here talking to himself," she liked to say.

"Your mother's only happy if it's a camp meeting," my father said when she complained, and sometimes she'd ask him if he at least talked to people *before* he got home, meaning at the bars. I was almost grown before I realized my father didn't get out of work at seven. "I don't go to gin mills to make friends," he'd tell her.

Mr. Robichaud told me that I'm the same way and that's why he's given up on introducing me around. At our last union meeting the local's vice chairman talked about each of us doing our bit to reach out to other unions to get them onboard for this new Safe Freight legislation, and Mr. Robichaud jerked a thumb at me and said, "Yeah, that'll happen when this one brings a college girl to Karaoke Night." Even the guys who didn't know me thought that was funny.

Part of what the union is so pissed off about is this new collision-avoidance system called Positive Train Control, a mix of GPS and computer technology designed to eliminate human error, which naturally made all the railroads think that with a system like that in place they could shave the crews down to a single engineer. They'd take it down to zero if they could and do all the piloting by satellite. They've already been slashing labor costs for decades with what they call anti-featherbedding legislation. Add that to the right to abandon branch lines and you start to see why Class 1's are such cash cows and that Warren Buffett knew what he was doing when he bought Burlington Northern. When some drunk in a bar heard what I did he asked me why any train needed more than one guy on it. "What's involved, anyway?" he asked everyone around the bar. "You start, you stop. It's not like you have to steer. Shit, crank it up, hit the brakes every so often, and let the scenery roll by."

The Canadian train that killed all those people was over a mile long and had a one-man crew, and the guy on a routine stopover shut down everything but the lead engine to keep the air brakes powered, set some handbrakes, and went off to his hotel for his sack time. A ruptured fuel line on the locomotive started a fire, so the local fire-fighters and a track maintenance employee shut the engine down. Once the fire was out, everybody went home. But with the power off the air brakes eventually lost their pressure, and that big a train—each tank car's 120 tons—carries so much weight that even on a very small grade it'll start to roll. After the emergency responders had taken their quick look around and left, all ten thousand tons started heading downhill. By the time those cars hit the sharp bend in the middle of town they were going seventy miles an hour. The lead engines with their lower centers of gravity stayed on the rails, but centrifugal force took over with the tank cars and they followed the path of least resistance, and when one derailed it torqued the car behind off in the opposite direction and they accordioned together. The investigators said the blast was like nine hundred tons of TNT. It flattened forty buildings in the downtown area like tents in a hurricane. Burning oil sprayed three hundred feet into the air and acted like napalm on any of the houses that weren't knocked down. In photos of the site every building was taken down to the foundations. Family members had to identify most of the dead through DNA or dental records.

Even though I was paying rent my father asked once or twice a week what part of "You need to move out" I didn't understand. He said I was twenty-nine years old and that he had plans for my room, and when I asked what kind of plans he said I didn't need to know what kind of plans. My mother said that lately when I came down to dinner she had to decide whether to just set out the food and leave or sit in on the argument.

After he went to bed one night I asked her what kind of plans he could have for my room, and she said she had no idea. She liked to sit up late and smoke like she was punishing herself. I asked how they'd gotten together in the first place and she said the first time they met he kissed her and she let him finish what he was doing before she slapped him. He'd been working for the railroad even back then, out at a way station that was nothing but an old boxcar up on some blocks, and her mother said she should've taken that as a sign. The boxcar he took her out to see had no running water but he told her at least there was a bathroom, pointing at a bucket in the corner. She said in those days he always wore a hat that said *"Southern Serves the South."* She said that because of the schedules he somehow missed every one of her birthdays for the next four years.

I asked why they hadn't had any more kids and she said, "I don't know how we had you." I asked who'd been the bigger pain when we were little, me or Kevin, and she just shook her head. I asked if my father had always been worried about money and she asked if it was Dolly Parton who'd said, "You'd be surprised how much it costs to look this cheap."

I told her I had a line on a couple of places and she said all I had to do was give one of them a call. We sat there while she smoked some more, and finally I said it wasn't much of a family, was it? I was surprised at how bad it made me feel. She watched me get ahold of myself and then she said, "Are you gonna blame us for that?" Then she added, "When we offered to pay your way to Chicago to look for your brother, what did you tell us?"

I was through explaining about that so we just sat there. She looked at me like she'd caught me going through her wallet.

"When I was in the hospital for my cysts, you know that Mrs. Simms was the only one who came by?" she said. And I reminded her that I'd been out on three different runs for twelve days in a row before I could deadhead it home, and she said, "I'm talking about *after* you got home." And then, after we sat there a little while longer, she told me to turn off the lights when I went to bed.

I was still upset enough the next day to go look at some of the rooms that were advertised, and then ran into Mr. Robichaud even though we both had the day off. He was in a booth at the back of the Blue Flag, a crew hangout, and the guy he was sitting with got up and left a few minutes after I sat down.

He asked if I was all right and I said sure, and after I watched him drink for a while he said he'd take me on in shuffleboard since the table was open. We started playing and two girls waiting for the ladies' room teased him about his clothes. Some of the young guys called him Workout because his pants bagged at the knees and sagged in the seat. He told the girls he'd lost forty pounds and they asked when, and he said just recently, and when they asked why he said he just hadn't wanted to be that size anymore. Later, back in the booth, he told me that when he'd been a big eater he used to keep two waiters at a time short of breath. The girls had never come out of the ladies' room and he asked what I thought they were doing in there, and I said they were probably talking about me, and he laughed.

At times like that he drank enough that you thought he had to be drunk, but the only way you could tell was that one story led right into another.

I asked if he'd liked school, and he said, "School?" and I said, "Yeah, school," and he rubbed his eyes without taking his glasses off and said he was just a dumb kid come out of the sticks to go work for the railroad, and that he'd started as a call boy in Milwaukee, riding his bike up and down the river and banging on doors to call crews to cover the schedules, and they'd all sit there with their blinds drawn, stupid with sleep, bare feet on the floor, fumbling to sign his call book. I said, "What's that got to do with school?" and he never answered. Then he told me he'd helped the trainmaster's clerk keep the runboard straight so there'd always be crews on tap. And he'd gone on to conductor from there.

He looked like he was waiting for me to say something back, so I shrugged.

He said his first engineer was one of those guys who thought the conductor worked for *him* and would go over his head to talk to the dispatchers, and that when he complained about it the guy'd tell him to shut up and go check his passengers' tickets. But then his next engineer was Carl Laudenslager, who was only four years older, and they'd had themselves a wonderful time and sort of grown up together, even to the point of embezzling each other's girls, and this was the guy who'd given him the idea of becoming an engineer himself. He said nothing ever fazed Carl and that they'd worked that Amtrak derailment in Maryland that the investigators thought was caused by a sun kink when the heat buckled the track. Anyway, the event recorders recovered from the cab totally backed up their version of what had happened. The wreck sent a hundred people to the hospital, though nobody got killed. He said their engine had seemed to be tracking good and doing about sixty when all of a sudden she just headed out into a cornfield. She'd gone over and thrown Laudenslager clear, and once the rest of the crew climbed out the windows it had only taken them an hour to get everyone out of the four Superliners that had also rolled over. When the big crane finally showed up and they re-railed the engine, it turned out the front end was smashed, her headlight gone, and she had mud all up and down one side. She was a real mess, and they pulled into the next town just as all the second-line investigators were arriving. When the station-master pointed out their broken headlight, Laudenslager called back that it was okay because they weren't looking for anybody anyway.

I asked where Laudenslager was now, and why I'd never heard about him before, and he said Carl had made the change to freight too, and that a few years later he'd had his second derailment, with a load of coal, and that the only survivor, their Tail End Charlie, told everybody their engine had flown so far off the curve it was like it just took to the trees.

I got back late that night and figured I'd tell my mother in the morning that I liked one of the rooms I'd seen, but I woke up to my father making noise at the foot of the bed with his toolbox, and when I came back from the bathroom he was starting to take my bed apart.

"What's he doing?" I asked my mother, and she said, "It looks like he's taking your bed apart."

"He couldn't even wait for me to find a place?" I asked her, then asked him the same thing when she didn't answer.

"Guy asked me if I had a bed I could sell and then offered me fifty dollars for it," he said. "I'm not walking away from fifty dollars."

I went downstairs and made some coffee while he banged away in my room. She stayed up there with him. She had a shopping list out on the counter and I drew lines through all the things on the list. I called Mr. Robichaud but he didn't pick up. I told myself I wasn't going to get mad and then I said to myself if you're so worried about getting mad, why are you crying, and I grabbed my coat and left.

I was sitting in Burger King feeling sorry for myself and my phone buzzed and it was Mr. Robichaud asking if I ever checked my messages and letting me know we had a run from North Dakota to Philly and that we had to get there by Tuesday morning. This was a major deal, a long haul, with 103 cars of Bakken crude along with 2 buffer cars loaded with sand. He said at least the tanker cars would be the new CPCs instead of the old DOT-111's. Supposedly the CPCs had thicker tanks and head shields. "Anything that helps," he said when I didn't answer.

I went home and started packing. My room looked even dirtier without the bed. My father stopped by the door and didn't say anything for a few minutes.

"Where's Ma?" I finally asked.

"'Where's Ma?'" he repeated. "Why? You want to complain about me again?"

"Now you're going to start?" I asked.

"I'm not starting anything," he said. "You know how sick your mother is and you keep acting the way you do."

"Yep, that's me," I said. There wasn't a single pair of underpants that didn't have holes in it. "You know I don't even have a decent pair of underwear?" I told him.

"So go buy some," he said. "What're you, five years old?"

"Where is she?" I asked, but he didn't answer.

"How come you didn't take apart Kevin's bed even *after* he left?" I said.

We didn't know where my brother was or if he was even alive. Last we heard he was somewhere in Illinois, but he'd been gone for three years. My mother had gotten a card from Rockford. He first hurt his back in the state regionals in high school and went on pain pills, then got off them, and then back on them, and when he really got bad he started robbing our house blind. Checks were always missing from the back of the checkbook and any cash they left anywhere disappeared. The low point was probably when my father came home one night and flopped down on the couch and clicked on the remote and there was no TV.

"He doesn't have any underwear," my father said to himself while I zipped up my bag. He kept shaking his head.

I asked if my mother was having more trouble breathing. "She won't even *go* to the doctor," I said. "Never mind every so often doing what he tells her."

"She hasn't had a good night's sleep since your brother left," he said.

"You know what she gave me for my birthday when I was sixteen?" I asked. "A framed picture of me and him."

"Maybe she was trying to tell you something," he said.

"She was. That picture was from his All-Star banquet," I said.

"Poor you," he said.

"I'm not complaining," I told him. "I'm just saying."

"She's over at Mrs. Simms's," he finally said when he saw I was ready to leave. "The old lady's lung thing is back and she's hacking like a seal. Your mother's sitting with her. You should go see them before you take off."

"Otherwise you'd be disappointed in me?" I said.

"You're a sour son of a bitch, you know that?" he told me. He seemed surprised to have to say it.

When we got to dispatch we had to wait for a ride out to the depot and then somebody sent the wrong paperwork and then we had to be driven offsite to fetch our engines, so by the time I was ready to test the air brakes we were already an hour behind and could hear over the radio how much the trainmaster was itching to get us out of the fucking yard. I radioed the dispatcher that we were still brake-testing the cars and the trainmaster cut in and asked how many we'd done and I told him sixty-something and he said that sounded fine and we didn't need to worry about the rest because the whole string had tested okay on the last run.

I told him that was against regulations and got off. While I was dealing with that Mr. Robichaud had walked halfway down the train and was talking with somebody who'd gotten out of a company pickup. The train was so long I could barely tell who it was.

"Is that the guy you were sitting with at the Blue Flag?" I asked when he got back. He said yeah and when I asked what the guy was doing all the way out here he said he was with Employee Performance Accountability.

"I didn't know that was a position," I told him.

He said it was, and that he'd been on the guy's shit list for a while. I asked why and he said for any number of reasons that were none of my business.

The trainmaster radioed again to ask why it was taking so long. I told him we'd gotten a late start and that it took a while to take each brake pipe down to zero. He said he needed the yard space and that we didn't have to cross every tiny fucking *t* and to get this thing moving.

A few minutes later he was on my ass again and when I gave him some lip he said he wasn't going to argue about it over the radio. Mr. Robichaud didn't say a word about anything. "You all right with this?" I asked him, pointing at the receiver in my hand, but he just shrugged.

Two minutes later we got a call from the assistant terminal superintendent, who needed to know if we were ever going to get out of the depot or if he had to call in a replacement crew. He asked if the engineer was ready to move or not.

"I'm ready," Mr. Robichaud told him.

"And what about the conductor?" the ATS wanted to know. Any

sign of trouble and they'd switch out conductors at the drop of a hat. Hell, they were getting ready to phase us out anyway.

I looked at Mr. Robichaud as if to say, *"You don't want to do this run with somebody else, do you?"* But he just took hold of a grab iron and put a boot up on the step without looking at me. I'd always pissed and moaned about the company's corner cutting and he'd always said that even if they *were* going to make us run under shitty conditions, we should do our best to make sure they were at least as safe as *we* could make them. And that if we stepped away, what if the next guy on tap couldn't even handle the problems *we* could?

"The conductor's ready too," I told the ATS.

"Then see if you can't make up some of this time," the guy said.

My brother had always been one of those guys who nobody thought was as bad off as he really was, partly because he was so good at pulling shit off at the last second. The first time I found him completely out of it I called 911 and by the time the paramedics got there he already was on the sofa with his feet up watching CNN and he looked so surprised to see them they only checked him out for a minute before making faces at me. He asked if they wanted any coffee. I told them how I'd found him and that I thought he'd taken some pills, and my mother shouted from the kitchen that he hadn't taken anything and she'd been with him all day. So later on a cop came to lecture me about fake emergency calls and said if it happened again I'd have to take a class or pay a fine.

Another time coming home from somewhere he told me to pull over at a cemetery, and when I asked why he said, "It's Ma's birthday, you fucking idiot," then came back to the car with this bouquet he'd pulled off a grave. "Can we say it's from both of us?" I asked, and he said, "It was my idea."

"You forgot?" she said to me, after she put his flowers in a water glass.

There were so many times we didn't know how he'd ever got home. Once we found the car up on the sidewalk with so little room between two trees that it took us an hour to get it back on the street. "He didn't hit either tree," my mother said later that night, standing at the front window.

Before he took off for good I asked him what his secret was, and he said he must've had some kind of autopilot. And when he saw my reaction he said, "I don't know what to tell you. All I know is, I get fucked up and make it home without a scratch, and you're Mr. Teetotaler and you inflict damage just walking through a room."

For a while I stood beside Mr. Robichaud's seat at the main instrument panel. Though it was one of the newer cabs there was enough noise that we had to talk to each other on our headsets. I kept accidentally kicking his duct-taped duffel bag on the floor until he finally slid it under his seat. I asked what was wrong and he said he'd stepped off a moving engine back at the yard and thrown his back out.

I said I'd heard Burlington Northern was cutting down on oil shipments and he said nobody'd do that, at least not until somebody built a two-thousand-mile pipeline from North Dakota to Philly or through the Rockies. The oil companies wanted their money now, not in ten years when some pipeline got finished. I said I still didn't feel good about the air-brake thing and he told me that if I hadn't felt good about it I should've registered a formal complaint, and that nobody wanted derailments, least of all the company, but after I didn't say anything back he got glum again and said there was always a lot of talk about safety being the top priority but let's get serious: if safety was the top priority, would everybody be having all these accidents? And that wasn't counting all the shit that *didn't* get reported.

I said if I had to bet I would bet that they were way behind in rail inspections, and he said how could they not be? And that he'd heard they'd already started a program using drones for that, and that the FAA'd already given them the green light.

"You telling me some drone can see everything a track walker can pick up?" he said. "Somebody who's been looking at rails and ties and roadbeds for thirty years?" And that made us quiet for another hundred miles.

He didn't say anything else until we passed a passenger train on a siding. This close to the holidays the train was packed and the windows all steamed up. He said he felt bad for the guys who'd put in all those years and still didn't know what it was like to work the head end. He asked me to double-check the slowdown orders again. We had any number of them coming in about which new track sections were so bad we needed to cut our speed back even more.

After another fifty miles I asked if I'd ever talked to him about my brother, and he said he'd never had kids and that he'd never fallen off a high pole, either.

So we were quiet for another fifty. Even at such a low speed we could feel the bridges and roadbeds flexing and swaying and slumping when our weight went over the rotted ties. I gave him a look and he gave me a little smile and said that sometimes even the best engineer couldn't make it ride like a Pullman.

My brother called home just once in those three years after he left, on my mother's birthday, though at that point I don't know if he even remembered. I was alone in the house, and after I said hello he said, "How's the railroad man?" And I had to sit down when I heard his voice.

"How're you?" I said, and he said back, "How're *you*?" He sounded out of it. I asked where he was and he said he'd gotten this good job and was living with this great girl. I said that was great and he said yeah, it really was. He asked how everybody was doing and I told him they were all about the same, and when he asked if the old man was still busting everybody's stones, I said more than ever. He said, "How's Ma's what-do-you-call-it? Phlebitis?" and I told him the doctors said it was something even worse, and I found where I'd written it down and read it to him: deep-vein thrombosis. He asked what that was and I told him her legs were always swollen and she could hardly get around at all and there was a pretty good chance of a clot going up to her lungs.

He didn't say anything for a while. "You fall asleep?" I asked him.

"I'm here," he said. But it sounded like he *had* fallen asleep.

"Everybody's been worried about you," I said.

"Yeah," he said, like I'd been talking about the weather. "So listen, is she around?"

I told him they were out. It took him a while to concentrate on what I was saying but finally he said he'd give me a number and to have her call. He'd try to be there for the next few hours anyway. It was a 331 area code and I remember wondering if he was just down the road in Aurora.

When my mother got home she didn't look in on me and I didn't check on her. I'd already called that number a couple times and nobody had picked up. I was listening to the radio and waited until my show was over and then opened the door to her room. She said, "What?" and looked at me like something bad had happened and I hadn't told her. When I told her he'd called, she got up and moved me out of the way to get to the phone number in the kitchen. She stood there calling him back for so long I finally went back upstairs, and she started yelling why hadn't I told her right when she got home? My father came in and she told him the whole story and they both took turns with me. The neighbors had to call to get them to quiet down.

After they calmed down they left me alone for a while and then in the middle of the night they came into my room together and said I should go look for him, but by then I wasn't talking anymore. The next morning they called the police but the police were even less help than I was.

"Maybe he'll call again," I heard Mrs. Simms tell my mother in the kitchen a few days later. "He did it on purpose," my mother said, meaning me.

The second night out we hit a storm so intense all we could see ahead was the whiteness of the rain in our headlight. Northbound trains came out of nowhere and rocked us even more than usual. The next morning it turned to snow and Mr. Robichaud joked that I should put away my phone and I said I was just checking the time and he said his pal Laudenslager's big motto was that a lot of guys died because either they weren't paying attention or somebody else wasn't, and then he told me again about the guy in the switching yard whose boot slipped through the stirrup of a moving tank car and he got dragged half a mile while the ties beat him to death.

I said he didn't need to lecture *me*. "Hey, *you* pay attention," I told him. "All I'm supposed to be worried about for the time being is the log and the waybill."

And the air brakes, he said. And *all* mechanical inspection of the rolling stock. "You might think that's funny but I don't," he said when I didn't answer. "Every air brake that's working is good news in any situation," he told me, and I said, "You don't have to tell *me*."

That stopped our joking and after a while he asked a few questions that I answered with a nod or a shrug. I thought about my mother and brother, and he broke out his lunch and ate it without offering to share any of it. I waited a little while longer and then around one broke out my own. I took off my headphones and did my work.

When we hit Illinois I put them back on and for something to say asked what he remembered of his first run as an engineer, and he shrugged and said he was cold all the time because the cab's heating unit had been on the fritz.

He slowed us down and then slowed us down even more, and when I wondered where we were he said a little west of Galena. I asked if that was where they had the big festival and he said yeah, in the fall, and that he'd been talking to a woman who was an alderman there and she told him they'd been trying to get a passenger train through there for years, but Amtrak said no because the track isn't in good enough shape for their trains.

We worked that over in our heads for a while.

We were rocking and swaying even more and he slowed us down another notch and said about the roadbed, "Isn't that just perfect," which was what my mother always used to say.

We'd all been sitting there cheering for him when my brother hurt his back in the state regionals. He'd barely made his weight and was favored to win it all, and I still remember his face after he tried to get back out there on the mat and realized he couldn't. That whole night I cried more than he did, and once he stopped my mother came in and sat with me. My father stood out in the hall and reminded her that I wasn't the one who got hurt. But my brother told him to leave me alone, and I always remembered how good it felt to have surprised him. And when we woke up next to each other, he asked me to stay home with him and I did, walking back from the bus stop after our parents were out of the house.

One thing I hadn't told him the time he called was what the doctors said about that clot thing and the way they thought even with the drugs she was taking it was likely that a clot could move, and they couldn't up the anticoagulants because of something with her kidneys. I was going to tell him that when I called back, but he never picked up.

When I was nine or ten at one of my confessions the priest got so tired of hearing the same things over and over again from me that instead of Our Fathers and Hail Marys he wanted me to just make a list of all of the things I loved about my family and that they did for me.

At first I wasn't going to, but then one night I got up and turned on the light and started writing. I don't remember what, exactly, but if I made another list now I'd include that when I had to get up and out by four or five in the morning my mother left coffee in the pot for me so all I had to do was warm it up. That she insisted I always get home for cake on my brother's birthdays, and he get there for mine, because when somebody had a birthday or you were sick, she said, you should always be home. That she told us how when she was a kid too her mother fell out of bed one night and died right on the floor, and how much that always panicked us. And that she wished she could remember her mother doing something besides work. That when she toasted both me and my brother on his sixteenth birthday, even my father looked happy, and how years later he angled the conductor's cap on my head one morning and said, "There. Now you look even more like a railroad man." And that Kevin took me into the woods and made me promise we'd never let each other die on the floor. That he told me before leaving the first time that we couldn't *both* be fuckups when it came to our parents. And that before the second time he said, "I don't care what you *mean* to do. It's what you *do* I don't like."

I held my phone up to the side window and started filming. *I should show them what I do,* I thought, and the rail joints rattled us past scrapyards and warehouses and woods, and somebody's ratty backyard with an old truck with tires rotted to the rims. I got some video of a broken-down house on top of a long hill. Of two girls trying to make snow angels in the frost and of a station wagon at a level crossing with all four doors open and a kid beside it pointing out our shadow to his brother when it jumped the fence rows.

Those kids were still in my head when we tilted and jolted and started slewing and skidding, the high grinding screech telling us a rail had given out. And Mr. Robichaud grabbed for the throttle and brake levers through the shearing of metal on metal that filled our headphones, and in the rearview I could see the tank cars tumbling into the tree line behind us, one of them telescoping and lifting the buffer cars like a drawbridge before a flash of light blinded us and flung us forward, taking our breath and lifting us into the dark.

Telemachus

To commemorate Easter Sunday, the captain has spread word of a ship-wide contest for the best news of 1942, the winner to receive a double tot of rum each evening for a week. The contestants have their work cut out for them. Singapore has fallen. The *Prince of Wales* and the *Repulse* have been sunk. The Dutch East Indies have fallen. Burma is in a state of collapse. Darwin has been so severely bombed that the naval base there had to be abandoned. The only combatants in the entire Indian Ocean standing between the Japanese Navy and a link-up in the Gulf of Aden with the Germans, who are currently having their way in Russia and North Africa, seem to be a single Dutch gunboat that we came across a week ago with a spirited crew and a crippled rudder, and ourselves.

We are the *Telemachus*, as our first lieutenant reminds us each morning on the voice pipe: a T-class submarine—not so grand as a U but not quite so dismal as an S. Most of us have served on S's and are grateful for the difference, though we do register the inferiority of our own boat to every other nation's. The Royal Navy leads the world in battleships and cruisers, we like to say, and trails even the Belgians in submarine design.

In the chaos following Singapore's surrender we've been provided no useful intelligence or patrol orders. A run through the Sunda Straits between Java and Sumatra ended in a hail of enemy fire on the approaches to Batavia. At our last dry dock, the Ceylonese further undermined our morale by invariably gazing out their harborside windows at first light to see if the Japanese had landed. We have no idea whether any subsequent ports will be available to us now that we've shipped back out to sea. Nor if we will have access to more torpedoes once we've expended our store. "Heads up there, boys," our captain joked to those of us within earshot of his map table last night. "Is there anything more exhilarating than carrying on alone out on the edge of a doomed world?"

"Sounds like Fisher's childhood, sir," Mills responded, and everyone looked at me and laughed.

They view me as a sorry figure even by the standards of their meager histories. As a boy I was a horrid disappointment, pigeon-chested, gap-toothed, and as grandiose as I was untalented. The only activity for which I was of any use at all was running, so I ran continually, though naturally not in competitions or road races but just all about the countryside, in both fair weather and foul. It brought me not a trace of schoolboy glory, though it did at times alleviate my fury at being so awful at everything else.

The characterization my parents favored for me was "out of hand," as in "Something must be done when the boy gets out of hand." My stepfather inclined toward the strap; my mother, the reproachful look. Her brother had been killed in the first war and her first husband had come to a bad end as well, and my stepfather never tired of pointing out to us that a disapproving countenance was her solution to most of life's challenges. He said about me that by the time I was out of short pants and he was forced to introduce me at pubs or on the street, his friends sympathized.

My father had been presumed lost at sea on a bulk cargo ship that went missing between Indonesia and New South Wales. When I asked if he had loved me, my mother always replied that it hurt too much to recall such happiness in any detail. When I required particulars of her nonetheless, she said only that he had been quick to laugh and that no man had possessed a greater capacity to forgive. When I asked my aunts they said they'd barely known the man; and when I asked if he'd been pleased with me, they said they were sure that had been the case, though they also remembered him not much liking children.

My stepfather viewed my running as a method of avoiding achievement or honest labor and marveled at my capacity for sloth. He pressed upon me *Engineering Principles for Boys* and *Elementary Statistics* and all sorts of other impressive-looking volumes I refrained from opening. He asked if I was really so incurious about the world of men and I reassured him that in fact I was very curious about that world, to which he responded that in such case I must bear in mind that this world was also the sphere of industry; and I clarified that I meant the *adventurous* world of men, the arena of tropic seas and volcanic cataclysms and cannibal feasts and polar exploits. He said that if I wanted to grow up a fool I might as well join the Navy, which was precisely what I had already resolved to do.

When he arrived aboard Mills told everyone that he'd been one of those posh boys who'd gone to boarding school, where at great expense he'd been provided rotten food and insufficient air and exercise, so therefore submarine duty oddly suited him. His father had been great with speculation until it had all gone smash and he hanged himself. Mills remembered his mother sitting in the drawing room during the following months with all the many bills she didn't dare to open, since there was no money to pay them, and he'd thought it would be a good thing if she had one less mouth to feed. He'd been a chauffeur, a silk-stocking salesman, a shipyard hand, and the second mate of a sailing ship before signing on with His Majesty's Navy.

As gunner's mates we bunk in the torpedo stowage compartment, between the tubes. He calls me "the Monk" because in this tiny space I never bother with pictures or photographs. I carry what I want to see in my head. Everything else feels like clutter. "Our mate here doesn't know how to take things easy," he says by way of explanation to our fellow torpedo men. He seems to believe that he panders to my whimsies with resigned good humor.

Mills had been assigned to us at Harwich as a replacement for a mate we'd lost to carbon monoxide poisoning when a torpedo's engine had started prematurely in the tube. He'd asked me confidentially what sort of boat he was joining, and I recounted for him our most recent patrol, which I described as three weeks of misery we'd endured without sighting a single enemy ship. We'd run aground and been unsuccessfully bombed by our own air force. We'd also damaged our bow in a collision with the dock upon our return. He said that on *his* most recent patrol they'd surfaced between two startled German destroyers, each so close abeam that their bow wakes had spattered onto the submarine's deck. On the bridge he and the captain had simply gaped up at the Germans above them, since for the moment they were beneath the elevation of the German guns and too close to ram without the destroyers also hitting each other. He said they'd pitched back down the conning tower ladder with the Germans still shrieking curses at them. He said they'd mostly worked the Arctic reaches out of Murmansk, sinking so much German tonnage that the Russians had presented them with a reindeer.

He said he was pining for a nurse he'd met in the Red Cross

who last he'd heard had been sent to London and now no doubt was pouring lemonade over the wounded in the East End. Her father on first meeting him had cordially asked, "And who or what are *you*?" and upon his reply her mother had remarked only that people had been doing dreadful things at sea for as long as she could remember. He said that when he managed to arrange some privacy with the nurse and attempted a liberty with her she begged him instead to "do something useful," though he *had* been encouraged by her remark about her father that no man had ever behaved so badly with the ladies and gotten away with it.

Occasionally when he was particularly displeased with the lack of vivacity in my responses he'd say he didn't suppose that I had any experiences of my own to relate, and I'd assure him I had very few, though before I'd left home I had in fact conceived of an intense and inappropriate fondness for a cousin on my mother's side. Margery's own mother displayed in her house a photograph of herself and my lost father alone under an arbor, peering at each other and smiling, though when I'd asked about it the woman had appeared faintly stricken and was no more informative than my mother. When I was fourteen and my cousin twelve I lured her into a neighbor's garden and in my overheated state had crowded my face in close to hers, much to her alarm. Bees were drowsing above a flower she was examining. She then fixed her eyes on my mouth and when I moved still closer she backed farther away. She was chary around me during our visits afterward but had also taken my hand under the tables in dining rooms and once, having run into me unexpectedly in a hallway, had put a finger to my lips. In my fantasies I still imagined an unlikely world in which I would be allowed to marry her and she would happily agree to this. In the packet of correspondence I received when arriving in the Pacific my mother noted that my cousin had let on that I was writing *her,* at least, and in her response to my letters Margery asked apropos of nothing if I recalled a day years earlier during which I had acted very odd in the garden beside my home. When off duty I lay on my berth between tubes 5 and 6 and wondered what others would make of someone who could imagine tenderness for only one other being, and an improper tenderness at that.

Our hallway encounter had occurred the month following my eighteenth birthday, soon after which I served my first sea duty on the HMS *Resolution,* an elderly battleship that had been hurriedly refitted, and still dreaming of my cousin I stumbled around its great decks on those few tasks I was able to execute, grateful for the small mercy of remaining unnoticed. We sailed around the Orkneys in seas so tumultuous that during one gale our captain threw up on my feet. The other excitement about which I was able to write my cousin transpired one calm morning when we all turned out on the quarter-deck to witness the spectacle of the second pilot ever to be launched from a seaplane catapult. The first had broken his neck from the colossal acceleration. This one had been provided with a chock at the back of his head for support.

I detailed for her my impressions of my first submarine, *Seahorse,* and how I'd almost fallen overboard when hurrying across the nar-row plank onto its saddle tanks while the chief petty officer watched from the bridge, expressing his displeasure at my insufficient pace. How intimidating I'd found its interior, the lower half packed with trimming tanks, fuel tanks, oil tanks, electric batteries, and so on, and its upper all valves and switches and wiring and cables and pressure gauges and junction boxes, and how I'd had to learn from painful experience which valve was likely to crack me on the head over each station, and the revelation that above the cramped wooden bunks were cupboards and curtains for sleeping. I explained for her how the conning tower became a wind tunnel when we surfaced and the diesels were sucking in air and how the diesels themselves were a

pandemonium of noise in such confined space. I described a rare
look through the periscope, as I glimpsed far more clearly than I had
expected a flurry of tumbling green sea that blurred the eyepiece like
heavy rain on a windscreen and then swept past.

There was much I chose to spare her. On our first sea trial the
piston rings wore away and exhaust flooded the engine room, and
everyone had to work gas-masked at their stations, sweating and
panting and ready to faint. On our second, one of our own destroyers tried to ram us and then, after we'd identified ourselves, reported
that it had just pursued without success two German U-boats. On
our practice emergency dives everyone threw themselves down the
conning tower ladder, trampling one another's fingers, and not even
shouted orders could be heard above the awful klaxon. On training
maneuvers we lost the torpedo-loading competition, the navigation
competition, the crash-dive competition, and the Lewis gun competition. On our second practice torpedo attack everything went according to plan, and when I reported accordingly to our torpedo officer
he said, "Are you hoping for a prize?"

With nowhere to go we are headed vaguely toward the Andaman
Sea off the west coast of Indochina, diving by day and gasping in
relief in the cooler surface air at night. Every few days the captain
announces our itinerary. He long ago resolved whenever possible to
keep the crew informed, since in his belief we have a right to know
what we are doing and why, and because security is hardly an issue
aboard a submarine.

It is impossible to verify whether the wireless silence has to do
more with our forces' standing orders not to give away our positions to the enemy's direction finders or with the total unraveling
of our efforts in this region. The captain finally patched through to

HQ Eastern Fleet and was told to stand by and then nothing more. A week later a Dutch merchant ship we raised on the horizon shared its understanding that the Eastern Fleet had abandoned even Ceylon and fallen all the way back to Kenya. That, the captain informed us, for the time being left the decision to us whether to quit the field or to strike a blow with what we had. His preference was the latter.

The crew is divided about this verdict. On the one hand, as our torpedo officer advised us, at such a dark time perhaps even an isolated victory could buoy morale. It took only one U-boat to sink the *Royal Oak* in Scapa Flow. On the other, if we attack alone and unsupported a fleet of any size at all, our chances of escape would be infinitesimal. But run into the right ship, he said, and we could find ourselves in all the papers. Run into the wrong one, Mills replied, and we'd find ourselves with seaweed growing out of our ears.

The captain has elected to ignore the few enemy merchant vessels we spy in order to hoard our likely irreplaceable torpedoes for capital ships. When we surface and the circumstances seem safe he has the wireless operators continue to request information. Upon crossing the 10th parallel he announced over the voice pipe that as far as he knew the entirety of the Royal Navy's fighting strength has now fled the Indian Ocean for the Bay of Bengal.

Despite the limitation of shifts to four hours, with everyone so cramped and hot and miserable it's an ongoing effort of will to recall what we are supposed to be doing or monitoring for every waking second of such a long patrol. In the head a lapse of focus can have calamitous results, as any mucking up of the sequence of valve operations to empty the lavatory pan will cause its contents to be pressure-sprayed back up into the inattentive crewmen's faces.

Because of the chaos in Ceylon we were revictualled with one type of tinned food only: a peculiar soaplike mutton that's been breakfast, lunch, and dinner for the past three weeks. Those who complain are reminded that everything else tastes of diesel oil. We have weevils in our biscuits, as if we're serving under Nelson at Trafalgar.

A bearing seized in one of the engines and the engineers spent three days disconnecting and slinging the piston; the resulting vibration was so severe that our lookouts on the conning tower couldn't see through their binoculars. Now that this has been addressed we await a ship or ships large enough to engage, and those who complain about the uncanny solitude are reminded of what the alternative would be.

Off duty in our berths Mills suggests that it's a miracle we've made it even this far. He came aboard sufficiently early in our Norway patrols to wish he hadn't, and he often compares the two theaters for their relative miseries: in Scandinavia we couldn't cook on the surface because it was too rough, whereas here it's impossible when submerged due to the heat. He claims we then were even more fatuous. When the French surrendered we were all upset since it meant the end of shore leave for the rest of the summer, and we spent those months living quietly, fed by wireless rumors, and one day intercepted a plain-language signal pleading for rope and small boats from anyone in the vicinity of Dunkirk. As we were hundreds of miles north, all we did by way of response was to wonder at the reason for the break in radio discipline while we sailed about like imbeciles, puzzled by such empty seas.

After Dunkirk the expectation was that the Germans would invade from either Normandy or Norway, and the RAF had to concentrate on France, so it was left to our submarine fleet to provide adequate advance warning of any flotilla approaching from the north.

The Royal Navy had a total of twelve submarines to dedicate to this mission, including ours. Together we were responsible for thirteen hundred kilometers of Norwegian coastline, although the good news was that military intelligence had already decided we should concentrate on those few ports from which a sizable offensive force could be mounted. Our orders upon sighting such a formation were to report and then to attack. The former would require us to surface within view of the enemy, which would render the latter irrelevant, unless their gunners were blind, and the real question was whether we'd even finish the broadcast. Each submarine had been provided with a padlocked chest of English pounds and Swedish kronor so that any of us bypassed by the invasion could in the event it was successful refuel in Göteborg or another neutral port and then cross the Atlantic and carry on the fight from the New World.

To evade Luftwaffe patrols, particularly given the onset of white nights, by June we were submerged nineteen hours daily and gambling that we could recharge our batteries and refresh our oxygen supply between enemy air sweeps. Those who lost that bet were destroyed on the surface. At the end of nineteen hours our atmosphere was so thin that matches wouldn't light and even at rest we heaved like mountain climbers. American and German submarines were equipped with telescopic breathing tubes that could breach the water like periscopes, but when we proposed the same for our own we were told there was no tactical requirement for such a fitting. Our Treasury refused to spend a million pounds to save a hundred million, our captain said bitterly, and its ranks were filled with mincing clerks cutting corners.

As our periods submerged lengthened, our medical officer lectured us in small groups about the danger signs of carbon-dioxide poisoning. Night after night, just as breathing became all but impossible, we were saved by a little low cloud providing just enough cover to surface. With the hatches opened the boat revived from the control room aft to the engine room, though that didn't do much for the torpedo room, so Mills and I and our mates were allowed to come to the bridge two at a time for fifteen minutes of fresh air.

But we weren't safe even below. In fair weather the Norway Deep is clear as glass and we could be seen down to ninety feet, as we learned on our first day off the coast when six dive bombers took turns with us before heading home.

Around the solstice some nights never did get fully dark, and in the horrible half-light one after another of our boats was destroyed when they were finally forced to surface: *Spearfish, Salmon, Sturgeon, Trusty, Truant, Thames.* By July the losses totaled 75 percent of the ships that were engaged. During one of our agonizing waits on the surface two Me-109's dropped out of the clouds and we could hear the pom-pom of their cannon fire over our watchman's screaming as he plummeted down the ladder, and while we submerged a gunner's mate snapped in his distress and beat himself senseless by pounding his forehead on his torpedo tube. He had doubled his jersey up over the steel first, to muffle the sound.

When the invasion failed to materialize we remained on station nevertheless, weathering the autumn and winter storms. During the worst of them we alternated at the watch, poking our faces and flooded binoculars into the gale, riding up wall after wall of steep and chaotic waves, maintaining a round-the-clock vigilance in case the preposterous happened and an enemy funnel materialized, the captain struggling to keep the sextant dry long enough to snatch a star sight and gain a clue as to our whereabouts. In the heaviest weather the breaking waves poured in over the conning tower and filled the control room below, sparking the switchboards and washing through the entire ship. The hatch had to stand open because the diesels stalled when they could no longer draw air, so a stoker with a great suction hose had to squeeze atop the conning tower beside the watchman, absorbing the battering as he pumped the water back out.

. . .

One moonless night soon after surfacing I was on watch with the captain and two others when all around us in the darkness ship after ship appeared out of the mist, the hulls of transports rising above us like cliffs. We had run head-on into a full convoy, ascending inside the ring of their escorts, whose attentions were all trained out to sea. There was no time to dive and attack from periscope depth, or to estimate the correct angles.

"What's the old saw?" the captain whispered, extending his hand toward the first transport. "If the enemy is slow, give him nine degrees of lead, or the width of a human hand at arm's length." Using his fist as a gun sight he set the firing interval through the voice pipe, and then shouted, "Fire!" At the launch of each torpedo we could feel the ship lurch slightly backward, and before leaving the bridge we watched a column of water erupt from one of our targets, followed by the concussion. He shouted, "Dive!" and plunged down the ladder, and underwater we heard two more huge, far-off bangs at the correct running-range intervals, and the entire crew cheered. Then we went deep for hours, hanging silently, those of us off duty forbidden to move since even the clink of a dropped key could expose us, while we listened to the sub hunters' depth charges getting closer, then farther away, then closer, until finally the German Navy seemed to run out of explosives.

On my last leave at home after the Norway patrols my cousin insisted on bringing me round to her favorite pub, where a whole series of men with whom she seemed utterly at ease insisted on buying me drinks. "I didn't know you cared for pubs," I told her, and Margery said, "Why should you?" She added that I should meet her friends, and that her background had not prepared her for the amount some girls could drink. I asked if she had a favorite friend and she cited a girl named Jeanette, whose up-to-date mother allowed them to smoke in the house. I continually had to repeat myself over the din of the place and when she finally asked with some exasperation why I couldn't speak up, I told her that almost everyone in the crew had what the doctors called fatigue laryngitis from having reduced our voices to whispers for months on end in the attempt to outwit the enemy's hydrophones. She apologized, and when I told her it was nothing she took my hand.

One of her friends from a table nearby asked me, after a harangue with his mates, to settle the matter of whether the English had in fact invented the submarine. Not hardly, I answered, and he said but hadn't the English always led in naval innovations? Who'd invented the broadside? Who'd converted the world from sail to steam? From coal to oil? And what about turret guns? "What about them," I asked. And Margery chided him that I wasn't allowed to talk shop, and that we needed some privacy to discuss family, thank you.

Once we were left alone she asked how my family *was* getting on, and I told her my mother had reported that she was enduring both my absence and the nightly bombing raids with a puzzling calm. When I asked after her family, she reminded me that they all remained greatly concerned about her older brother, Jimmy, who was with the RAF and had already lost many friends. She said that when he returned home on leave her mother and sister now wore hypno-tized looks and their conversations never strayed from speculations about the weather. And that Jimmy had in confidence told her some horrible stories. I suggested that perhaps he shouldn't have, and she responded that she'd known since childhood that the world beyond her home was stunning and heartless, and that all she'd ever heard from her mother about the protection afforded by an adherence to the rules was wrong. While she was speaking she seemed to scan the room before focusing on the nearer details of my face.

On the walk back to her house in the darkness of the blackout she said she'd always been fond of me, and I said she couldn't imagine how fond I was of her, and then she pulled me into an alley and kissed me, and my chest felt like it did when I was running as a boy, and as her kiss continued her mouth flooded mine with pleasure. When I got hold of my senses I gripped her head and kissed her back. Finally she pulled away and said we had to get home. While we walked she remarked that *there* was some rule breaking for you: first cousins kissing.

We stopped on her front step. She was lit for a moment when someone waiting up for her peeked through a blackout curtain. She said I should take care of myself. I grasped her hands, still dumbstruck and happy. She asked if she could tell me something, and then waited for my assent. She said that during some of the family gatherings we spent seated beside each other at dining tables it had been for her as if the stillness we made together were like a third person who was neither of us and both, and that when she'd felt the most sad and alone it had helped to imagine herself creeping into that third person who was half hers and half mine.

Did I have a sense of what she meant? she asked after a moment. I told her I thought I did, though some part of it had confused me, and I worried that even in the darkness she could hear that. Well, she said, maybe it would come to me, and then she said good night and kissed my cheek, and the next morning I was off to the Pacific.

We sailed through Gibraltar for Singapore with a merchant convoy bound for Alexandria and left the convoy to stop over in Beirut, which provided our first sight of a camel outside of a zoo, and where we painted our gray ship dark green for its Far Eastern tour, and from there proceeded to Haifa and Port Said and the Red Sea and through to Aden and the Pacific theater. Before we left Harwich the captain had addressed the crew, announcing that we could all settle back and prepare ourselves for a long journey filled with indescribable discomforts. We'd taken him to be joking.

Our initial view of Singapore was a towering column of black smoke on the horizon. When we docked at the naval base the captain went ashore in his whites to inquire as to where to lodge his men. He found everyone in headquarters burning records, and was told that our allotted accommodation had been destroyed by bombs that afternoon.

While he searched for an alternative we remained aboard. The bombing resumed and because the harbor was too shallow to dive the hatches had to be kept shut or else the great splashes from the impacts would swamp us. A few of the torpedo men beside me who I thought were dozing turned out to have fainted from the heat. The rest of us just waited. We were all losing so much sweat the decks were slick underfoot. After an hour of the concussions one of the stokers went wild and tore down all of the wardroom pinup girls before his mates restrained him.

Around sundown the captain returned with the news that he had finally located the rear admiral for Malaya inspecting the chit book in the rubble of the officers' club, and he'd offered us his house in the hills. A commandeered truck transferred those of us off duty, and the rest of us had to remain in the boiling confines of the boat.

The next morning black clouds hung over the entire waterfront from the burning oil and rubber dumps as we refitted and loaded any supplies we could find amidst the chaos. The last provisions aboard were crates of Horlicks malted milk and Australian cough drops. When we cast off, an old woman with a spade was digging herself a private air-raid trench in the garden of the Raffles Hotel. The sky to the east was filled with high-altitude bombers and once clear of the harbor we submerged, and as we rounded the channel buoy the captain, standing at the periscope, reported that a convoy of our own troop transports was arriving. He could make out the standards of the Argyll and Sutherland Highlanders. The whole ship went silent at the thought of what they were disembarking into.

We chugged three thousand miles west. We started leaking oil. One night I walked into the wardroom, where the chief and the captain were sitting and talking quietly so as not to disturb the sleepers. They invited me to join them and chatted about where they might be this time the following year, and the perversities of women, and the most brilliant pubs they had known. I fell asleep with my head on the wardroom table and for days they joked about how much they apparently had bored me. The gunlayer on his watch at last spotted a swallow and the next day a stoker sighted an old boot, and in the end we made Colombo Harbor in Ceylon. For the final two weeks no one had spoken except to give or to acknowledge orders.

The captain suggested we use our week in port to become human beings again. Mills responded that he was going to commence his rehabilitation with an invigorating fuck. Our chief was carried ashore with dengue fever and instructions to rest up and then to report with a clean bill of health and no nonsense. Despite the direness of our situation those of us on liberty took real showers and shaved our beards on the harbor tender and then disappeared to the four corners of the city. I found myself at the Colombo Club, which given the circumstances had been opened to enlisted men. I passed the time strolling about lawns and staring at women. I listened to their husbands' leisurely comments about sporting events. The captain positioned himself in a deck chair every morning and, after a few drinks, took to playing something he called bicycle polo, which always left him limping. A lone Hurricane flew over trailing smoke, circled back, and belly-landed on the club's green, after which the pilot climbed out and proceeded directly to the bar. Upon drawing any attention I quickly disappeared. Nights I dreamt incessantly and awoke so soaked with sweat I could smell my room from the hall.

I returned to my running, ascending the steep steps to the top of the cable tram, where I'd arrive bathed in sweat and then come right back down while bystanding natives looked on, amazed. They seemed to be wondering if Englishmen were prone to this sort of thing.

I went out drinking by myself. One night I happened upon Mills and our stoker petty officer, who soon slipped on some stairs, rolled down to the bottom, and then vomited. Mills said, "You know what they say: 'If that's the Navy, all *must* be well with England.'" After I woke in the gutter of a bazaar without my billfold, Mills insisted I no longer go out drinking alone.

We bought rounds for crew members of the *Snapper,* celebrating the sinking of a Jap submarine. The Japs had attacked a Dutch merchant ship and then machine-gunned the survivors in the water, so after the *Snapper* sank the sub its crew beat to death with spanners the two Japs they'd fished out of the water. They said that off the west Australian coast they'd been laboring into harbor in heavy seas when an American submarine had surfaced and ripped by them like they were standing still. They said that in Australia, girls welcomed sailors at the gangways with crates of fresh apples and bottles of milk.

We met Mills's cousin, who'd been left behind in hospital when his ship had fled the port. He'd served as a mess cook aboard a destroyer in Manila and said he loved the Philippines because there he had multiple girlfriends and Scotch cost all of seventy-five American cents per bottle. For scarcely more he'd maintained a love shack in the bush, a one-room hut up on stilts. The toilet and shower emptied below without benefit of pipes and the only running water was from heaven. All the palm trunks nearby were encircled with steel mesh to keep rats from stealing the coconuts. In the bar he stripped off his shirt to show us his tattoos, including a smiling baby's face over one side of his chest that was labeled *"Sweet"* and another on the opposite side that was labeled *"Sour,"* and another that featured *"Twin Screws, Keep Clear"* on the small of his back.

He loved hearing how the *Snapper*'s crew had rescued those Japs only to beat them to death. Back in Manila he'd befriended a sampan man who'd rowed British officers around the harbor to visit the town or shoot snipe, and for years the man told anyone who would listen that soon the Japanese would invade, and he'd been more accurate than any prognosticator in London. And when the Japanese did arrive they crucified him on his boat for having ferried the enemy. Mills's cousin had spied the body as his destroyer fought to escape the port.

Three more went down with dengue fever before we departed Ceylon: our mess cook, which allowed Mills's cousin to come aboard as his replacement; the junior engine-room rating; and a torpedo man. Mills and I showed the latter his station, and while he peered with dismay at the hideous and antiquated confusion of corroded pipes and valves and levers, Mills advised him that another way of looking at the situation was that hardly any other crew had been granted our abundance of experience and survived.

A merchantman that staggered into the harbor turned out to be carrying a mail packet that included letters for both Mills and myself. Mills's Red Cross nurse had also sent a photograph, and he teared up when he showed me. After noting my response he protested that just because he was no celibate it didn't mean he'd forgotten her.

I received three letters posted over a span of eleven months, from my stepfather and the prelate's daughter and my cousin. My stepfather had attached to his note some newspaper clippings about the bomb damage to our street. He wrote that my mother had discovered the neighbors' cat dead in the rubble of the back garden gate, that she was keenly hurt by my refusal to write, but that she dispatched her regards nonetheless, along with the news of an old classmate of mine, also in the Navy, whose wife had just given birth. He added that when it came to me he often wondered if I would ever reach the top of Fool's Hill.

The prelate's daughter had also sent a photograph of herself, and confided that she'd shared with her father what we now meant to each other and that he'd then asked her to leave his house. She wanted to know what she should now do. She was referring to a night I'd been on leave from the *Resolution* and had encountered her outside a tearoom in Harwich. It transpired that she was teary from another sailor having failed to meet her as promised, so I offered to walk her around the navy yard in consolation. She put an arm around my waist and cheered herself with my stories of my own haplessness. We necked next to others in the darkness under the Halfpenny Pier and she opened her skirt to me. She whispered how fondly we felt toward one another, and it sounded so piteous that I stopped, and she seemed to think we'd gone far enough in any event. She'd saved her chewing gum in her palm and signaled we were finished by returning it to her mouth. Before we separated on Kings Head Street she wrote down my name and posting and her address, handing me the latter.

Margery wrote that she hoped I was well, and that at her family's insistence she now languished in a remote place where nothing momentous was likely to happen. She wrote that previously her nights in London had been mostly long periods of enforced inactivity in her building's shelter, waiting for the all-clear, and that after one bombing she had emerged to find a woman's body covered in soot and dust and stooped to uncover its face. She wrote that in the middle of the memorial service for one of her mother's best friends she'd retired to a dressing room and wept at her own cowardice. She said her family often inquired if she had any word of how I was getting on, and that her little niece had asked her if I sank all of the bad people, could I then swim back home? She said she recognized that our relationship had at times been an unconventional one but that she hoped I wouldn't hold this against her, and that with whomever I chose to share my life I would be happy. She also enclosed a photograph of herself, in a sundress, almost lost in the dappled light and shadow of a willow tree. I began any number of responses to her letter, all of which I rejected as insufficient.

Once rumors started circulating about our impending patrol I spent mornings looking for myself in the mirror, as if hoping someone else might reappear. In the days before our departure a senior medical officer from the hospital gave us each the once-over. "Here's an interesting phenomenon," he remarked. He asked to see our fingernails. I held out my hand and he indicated the concentric ridges. "Each ridge is a patrol," he said. "The gaps between correspond to the length of your leaves ashore." I stared at him. "Purely psychological," he told me.

On our last night in Ceylon all of the offshore watch returned in various states of intoxication, and the captain sentenced them, somewhat wryly, to ninety days at sea in the loathsome heat and overcrowded confines. "Very good, sir," one of the drunken mates said in response, and the captain answered that he could now make that one hundred and twenty days.

After two weeks in the Bay of Bengal everyone is feeling lethargic and suffering from headaches. Some of the crew haven't shaved during the entire patrol and resemble figures from another century. Running on the surface at night we pass sleepy whales bobbing like waterlogged hulks. Our medical officer taps out on his tiny typewriter a new edition of his *Health in the Tropics* newsletter, which he has entitled *"Good Morning."* This week's tip: "If you have been sweating a lot, wash it off, or at least wipe it off with a hand towel, since the salt which your sweat has pushed out of your pores will irritate the skin." The only ships we've encountered have been trawlers and junks, and the captain has decided that in such cases we'll lie doggo and watch them move past. We find our new torpedo man all over the ship, his eyes moving around our feet looking for fag ends. When we're off duty Mills can instantly sleep and I lie awake. When I no longer can stand my own company sometimes I go to the wardroom. There I find the captain or the chief alone at the table with his binoculars slung round his neck and his head on his arms.

Mostly we're immersed in a haze of inertia. We dove to evade a flying boat sighted by our starboard lookout. A heavy bomber flew directly overhead on a northerly course but did not appear to have noticed us. The 0400 watch reported that three small vessels he couldn't identify altered course toward our location, then turned in a complete circle for no apparent reason before continuing on their transit.

We are perpetually in one another's way, tormented by septic heat sores, stinking bodies, and endless small breakdowns in the ship itself. The only clean-off available is a dab of torpedo alcohol applied to the rankest spots. Wet clothes can't dry. Condensation is everywhere. Shoes are furred with mold and our woolens smell worse than the head. The batteries have begun to fume and refuse to charge. The periscope gland leaks. In the night we passed one of our own bombed-out merchant ships, listing miserably. The tinned mutton when opened is now often slimed over, and even the roaches

won't touch it. Mills claims he can't imagine this going on much longer, but his cousin says that if this has to be done it's better that we
should do it, since we know what we're about and newcomers would
likely cost their friends their lives.

I'm jolted from my bunk by a tremendous explosion, then a second
and a third, and when I reach the wardroom everyone is celebrating
and it turns out that our target was an ammunition ship. The captain is permitting the crew to go up to the bridge three at a time to
enjoy the spectacle, and upon my turn explosions are still sending
flame and debris high into the sky. All of us who've been bellyaching
for days and begrudging anyone a civil word are suddenly thick as
thieves and the best of friends, since with one solitary success all the
clouds are dispelled. But soon after that come the sub hunters and
we hang still for twelve hours at one hundred and eighty feet while
they thresh around above us like terriers at a rabbit hole. Off-duty
crew lie in their bunks trying to read thrillers or magazines. Those
at work sit at their stations trying to make as little noise as possible.
The chief pores over a technical journal. The captain draws the green
curtains round his berth. With the first depth charge a few lights are
put out and a cockroach falls stunned to my chest. The second cracks
the glass gauge before me and the welding on a starboard casing.
The third knocks me onto the floor and the remaining lights go out
and water spritzes from a joint. Pocket torches flash in the darkness
before the emergency lamps come on. More detonations reverberate
farther away and closer, farther away and closer.

The hunters persist until the humidity coalesces into an actual
mist and the thinning air plagues everyone with crushing headaches
and nausea, and then finally our hydrophone operators report that
our pursuers are moving away.

.   .   .

When we're running on the surface again I find Mills contemplating his photo of the Red Cross nurse, his chin on his filthy mattress.
I ask her name but he responds only that one of the last things she
requested was for him to take time to consider what she might want,
and what she might like, but that instead he gave her the sailor's
lament that he'd soon be shipping out and perhaps they'd never see
each other again, so she'd allowed him the kiss and some of the other
liberties he'd been desiring. Before his train departed she told him
through the carriage window that he was the sort of man who was
always at the last second catching his ride in triumph or missing
it and not caring. "I think she meant I was selfish," he finally adds,
and then turns to me to discover I still have nothing to contribute.
"What do you think of selfishness, eh, Fisher?" he asks, and some of
the torpedo men laugh. "So here we are," he concludes. "Sweating
and grease-covered and alone and miserable and sorry for ourselves."

And a memory I banished from my time with Margery surfaces:
we stood on her front step, after our kisses, and she waited for me
to respond to what she had confided about the stillness we made
together. While waiting she explained that she was trying to ascertain where she could place her trust, and also where more supervi-
sion would be needed. And when she received no response to that,
either, she said if I wanted to swan around the world pretending I
didn't understand things, that was my affair, but I should know that
it did cause other people pain.

Another long stretch of empty ocean, which the captain announces
as an opportunity for resuming the paper war, and everywhere
those of us off duty get busy with pencils writing patrol reports and

toting up stores expended or remaining. Our boat continues to break down. Each day something or other gets jiggered up and someone puts it right. The chief initiates a tournament of Sea Battle, a game he plays on graph paper in which each contestant arranges his hidden fleet, consisting of a battleship, two cruisers, three destroyers, and four submarines and occupying respectively four, three, two, and one square each, while his opponent attempts to destroy them by guess-work, each correct guess on the grid counting as a hit. I'm drawn to the competitions but decline to participate. "That's how he acts on leave as well," Mills tells everyone. "The Monk only likes to watch."

Off Little Andaman Island we pass a jungle of chattering mon-keys that cascades right down to the shore. For safety we stay close in to the coast in the darkness, and the oily-looking water is so filled with sea snakes and jellyfish that when we surface at nightfall hor-rid things get stuck in our conning-tower gratings and crunch and slide underfoot. The captain takes a bearing on the black hills in the starlight and no one on watch can hear anything except the water lapping against our hull and the fans quietly expelling the battery gases. Every so often a rock becomes visible. A vacant little jetty. In the morning we dive in rain that resembles sheets flapping in the wind.

The mattresses grew so foul the captain had them rolled and hauled up through the conning tower and thrown overboard. The coarse pads left on our bunks rub open blisters and sores and our medical officer recommends cornmeal and baking soda to dry up the mess. Our new torpedo man had the fingernails and top joints of his first three fingers crushed in a bulkhead door in a crash dive. I helped the medical officer with the bandaging and afterward was surprised by his annoyance. "You could have answered a few of the boy's questions," he complained. "He's new on the ship and looking for a friend."

Mills has begun agitating quietly with other members of the crew to petition the captain to head home, wherever home now remains, before it's too late. He explains that his philosophy is to be neither reckless nor overly gun-shy, and to evaluate the situation in light of whether we have any chance at all to make a successful attack and survive to report it. He claims that while the miracle of encountering a lone ammunition ship is all well and good, it's only a matter of time before we confront an entire convoy. When he asks for my help to rally support for his position and I agree, he says we can start with the torpedo officer, because his shifts and mine align for the next few days. Each night when I return from duty Mills asks if I've talked to the TO yet and I tell him I haven't had the chance.

The next night the watch reports a debris field and the captain goes up to have a look. When he descends to the wardroom, the wireless operator says, "It seems we've finally given them a dose of what they've given us, eh, sir?" and the captain answers that it's British wreckage that we're sailing through.

At breakfast there are complaints about the mutton and to provide perspective Mills's cousin tells of having eaten in a mess so rancid they'd had to inspect each mouthful on the fork to ensure there was nothing crawling on it.

Twelve bleary hours later I'm seven minutes late for the dawn watch. The captain is on the conning tower as well, and the enraged mate I'm relieving shoulders past me and heads below. The fresh air smells of seaweed and shellfish. In the heat the sea is so calm it looks like metal. Mist moves across our bow in the morning sun. I apologize and the captain remarks that as a midshipman he was flogged for "wasting two minutes of a thousand men's time" by piping a battle cruiser's crew tardy to its first shift. I tell him that when I'm sleepless for long periods I sometimes don't properly attend to details, and after a silence he answers that he had a great-uncle who always admitted to the same shortcoming and who as Lord Raglan's aide-de-camp during the Crimean War was more or less responsible for the Charge of the Light Brigade.

He stays on the bridge with me, evidently enjoying the air. "Did you know that in Greek Telemachus means 'far from battle'?" he asks. I tell him I never studied Greek.

In the face of the blank sky and still water I return to the problem of how to respond to my cousin's letter. I imagine describing for her all of those dawns I've collected on watch: gold over the Norway Deep, scarlet off Singapore, silvery pink in the China Sea. I imagine recounting the morning the sun was behind us and a fine spray from the bow was arching across the deck so that we carried along with us our own rainbow. In my last attempt I wrote that there wasn't much I could say about my position, but that things were presently quiet and I was in excellent health and that she shouldn't worry, and then I stopped, because every other man in the crew had the same fatuous and unfinished letter in his locker. I imagine telling her how vividly I could see her face as we left Harwich, the dockyard walls slipping past us like sliding doors, opening up vistas of the harbor, our stern coming round as docile as an old horse. I imagine telling her how some part of me anticipated the Pacific might allow me to discover my father's fate. The sadness of our final glimpse of our escort vessel as it signaled its goodbye and dropped back to its station on our port beam.

Later that day a commotion pulls me from my bunk. The watch spotted something far-off in the haze and the captain has taken us to periscope depth. When I get to the wardroom he's climbing into his berth and telling the chief he'll resume observation in ten minutes since it's going to be a long approach. In the meantime the chief is to redirect our course to a firing bearing, instruct the torpedo room to stand by, and order the ship's safe opened and the confidential materials packed into a canvas bag and weighed down with wrenches.

The torpedo men are excited, as most of them believe Thursdays and Saturdays are our lucky days. Mills is not hiding his dismay. He suggests to the TO that the captain use the wireless to inquire if the Admiralty thinks the action worth the risk, but the TO reminds him that any message at all would reveal our position. When Mills informs him that much of the crew shares his unease, the TO looks around at each of us until finally Mills tells me that if I'm not on duty I'm just in the way. As I turn to go he asks when I stuck the photograph over my bunk but doesn't ask who it is.

Back in the wardroom the captain is out of his berth and at the periscope. When the sweat dripping over his eyebrows steams the lens, he wipes it clear with tissue paper the chief hands him. He finally murmurs that the convoy appears to be five miles out and he estimates it will pass about a quarter mile in front of us. He reports that we've chanced across an escort carrier, and the convoy's rear is lost to the distance, but in its vanguard alone he can make out two destroyers and three submarine hunters.

"In this calm and in this channel, once they see our torpedoes' wakes there will be nowhere for us to hide," the chief tells him, as though reciting the solution to an arithmetic problem, and the captain keeps his face to the eyepiece.

"Perhaps the wise course is to live to fight another day, sir?" our navigator asks. No one answers him. In the silence it's as if my stomach and legs are urging me on to something.

The chief questions whether we should put on a little speed to close the gap still further, and the captain replies that in this calm any telltale swirl or turbulence would give us away, even at this distance, and that instead we'll just settle in and get our trim perfect and let them come to us.

We can hear our own breathing. The captain orders the forward torpedo tubes flooded and their doors opened. Our hydrophone operator indicates multiple HE's bearing Green 175 and closing rapidly. "Are we really going to do this?" our navigator asks now, barely audible. The captain senses the oddity of my presence and glances over before returning his attention to the eyepiece. "Our shipboard wraith," he jokes quietly, and the chief smiles, and I feel a child's pride at the separateness I've always cultivated.

Then the captain clears his throat and regrips the periscope handles and calls out a final bearing, and gives the command to fire numbers 1 through 6, and the entire ship jolts with each release. Mills confirms in a strangled voice that all tubes have fired electrically, and soon after that our hydrophone operator reports all torpedoes running hot and straight.

And the image of what I wish I could have put into the letter to my cousin at once appears to me, from the only other time I was allowed at the periscope, along with the rest of the crew, when on a rough day near a reef in a breaking sea we found the spectacle of porpoises on our track above us, leaping through the avalanches of foam and froth six or seven at a time, maneuvering within our field of vision and then surging clean out of the water and reentering smoothly with trailing plumes of white bubbles, all of them flowing together, each a celebration of what the others could be, until finally it seemed as if hundreds had passed us and in their kinship and coordination had then vanished into the impenetrable green beyond our reach.

Forcing Joy on Young People

Torey was a fund-raiser at his alma mater—one of the mid-majors, the kind of school where the campus went batshit every ten years when they won their conference and qualified for March Madness—and after some administrative reshuffling a few weeks after he got there, he found himself in what was now called the Development Office/Alumni Relations. He wouldn't have thought it was his type of job, since he didn't even answer the door when repairmen or the Girl Scouts came around. Someone came to the front or back, he was super busy. And if Tara wasn't home, the kids would just ignore it, so whoever was knocking was out of luck.

They were here for Tara and the job she'd scored as a part-time lecturer teaching Contemporary American Literature. Torey hadn't been crazy about coming back but hadn't been against it, either. He was the youngest guy in his office and stood out in other ways too, as his boss liked to put it. She always looked like she was headed for the cocktail party after the regatta, but Torey mostly worked the phones and updated spreadsheets, which he could do in Volcom and Darkstar shirts that hung on him like tents. He liked to imagine they thought of him as the sickest of the skateboarders, and one time he took his deck to work and during some lunchtime screwing around stuck an Ollie North, and after that he wanted everyone to call him Bam but nobody did.

His job title was "coordinator" but so far he hadn't coordinated anything. For the most part they worked around him, but he would have said they liked him anyway. He was upbeat. He was cheery. He had good skin, and looked like the kind of guy who took his kids kayaking, which he did.

His wife told people they'd been having a little trouble settling in. She was worried that her course evaluations the first few times around hadn't been so hot. After she'd added a Joy Williams collection that hadn't gone over so well, she started privately calling the course Forcing Joy on Young People.

When they moved back from New Jersey, where she'd been teaching as a grad student, the two realtors who'd rented them the house had argued about whether they were in the Midwest or the western end of the East. "How about just the sticks?" Torey suggested, which is what he'd thought when he arrived as a freshman, and both the realtors and Tara had looked at him and then gone on with whatever they were saying.

The thing was, he was seriously depressed, which would've been news to everybody else, given how much he got done when anybody asked him to do anything. "You're not *depressed*," Tara told him the one time he brought it up with her. "My *mother* was depressed. My *brother* was depressed." "What *am* I, then?" Torey wanted to know. "You're an anxious procrastinator," she said. "Tell the kids the tacos are ready." Like her diagnosis was more insightful.

She did say every so often that he had the lowest horizon of anyone she knew and didn't even think about Thursday, let alone the upcoming year.

"I think about the future all the time," he argued at one point when he decided to stick up for himself. She'd been running him down pretty good with some people they'd invited over for dinner, and they'd all had some big laughs.

"Oh, yeah?" she said. "What do you think about it?"

"I don't know," he said, realizing everybody was waiting to hear. "That it's coming?" Which had gotten another big laugh.

"But you don't think that if we're going to have flank steak for dinner, you need to pull it out of the freezer in the morning," she said.

"*I'm* happy if my husband cooks at all," somebody else said, and Torey said, "Ka-*boom*. Exactly."

The week after Reunion turned out to be mostly about watching wipeout videos at his cubicle. In the dead time before everything ramped up again he was supposed to be going over the Staff Handbook, which was 527 pages long. There was other stuff to do as well, probably, but none of it was urgent.

The new capital campaign didn't kick off until the fall. He'd agreed to welcome everyone to the 40th Annual Alumni Golf Tournament on July 2nd, and had been told that that was a big enough deal that they ran a lottery to fill the hundred and forty slots. In a little spasm of team spirit and with his wife in mind he'd told the boss that he had her back on that one and she wouldn't need to cut short her Cape Cod vacation, since she wasn't a golfer anyway. But even with that, as workloads went he couldn't exactly complain, and he wasn't knocking himself out about what he was going to say. He wasn't a golfer either, though, and when he imagined standing up there in front of all the plaid pants and pink polo shirts, it made him sad, if he really wanted to be honest. He reminded himself that he'd been flexible enough to come back in the first place. So for a stretch every day he went in late and came home early and hung out at home, playing with the kids and annoying his wife, who was trying to come up with some alternative readings for the fall, especially more women of color. "How about if I proposed a *course* called Women of Color?" she asked him. She was always trying to wrangle new ways of getting more work, and it was a sore spot that so far his new job hadn't seemed to help. "*I'd* take it," he told her, but she only made a face. "I feel like I'm bothering you, being at home like this," he told her, and she said, "Because instead of concentrating on my reading I'm trying to figure *you* out." And when he asked, a little flattered, what there was to figure out, she said, "Do you think we're *that* different? Don't you think *I'd* like to just sit around and play with the kids all day?"

Rodney, who was already eight, wanted to be a BMX racer and spent his time trying to drop his bike down the six-foot-tall woodpile beside the garage, and only wanted to see his dad after he hurt himself, so Torey mostly played with Nyjah, who at four precociously insisted on an undersized wooden bat and a real softball instead of a Nerf or a Wiffle and even got good wood on it periodically, and when he did, since they faced the house, it sounded like a rifle shot on the shingles.

Whenever the door opened in response, Torey made an exaggerated *we've-been-busted* face and Nyjah dropped the bat and asked his mother what that noise had been.

Tara would tell them they were going to break a window, and they'd wait a few minutes before starting up again. They tried facing away from the house but then lost too many balls in the undergrowth down the hill.

She and her mother had had a huge fight over what to name

the second kid—"Let me know if you want *my* input on any of this," Torey told her at one point—and finally Tara got so fed up with her that she told Torey he should pick, and then he came up with a name that neither of them liked. He couldn't be serious, Tara said, but for once he stuck to his guns, and she finally figured she'd call the kid by her favorite even if it was his middle name. Once, on campus, when he shouted for Nyjah to get down from a walkway railing, a passing undergraduate heard and said, "Like the skateboarder?" But that had been about it in terms of people who approved of the name. At least Nyjah seemed to like it. Tara called him Peanut.

He'd planned on finishing his golfers' welcome, but Tara reminded him that first she had her TRX workout and then he'd promised she could hit the library, so he had the kids for the afternoon. After he moped about that for a while, after she was gone, he found the boys huddled around Rodney's phone and asked if they wanted to play that game he'd invented with the plywood ramp and the milk crates called *Evel Knievel: Triumph and Tragedy.* They didn't. He took himself outside like he'd been turned down at the high-school dance. Okay, so he wasn't strictly needed anywhere. He dropped off the little deck and tramped down the hill. Farther down it was overgrown enough that soccer balls shanked into there were lost until the fall, and below that the slope dropped off into a creek. He did this every so often: went off into the woods and thought, *No one's going to come looking for me.*

A white van turtled around their cul-de-sac before parking, and for a few minutes no one got out. There were nature noises behind him, but when he turned to look he didn't see anything. He crouched and sifted loamy dirt through his fingers like brownie mix.

He heard the van's door open, and when he peeked over the top of the slope a guy about his age was getting out and heading up the driveway. He disappeared from sight and the doorbell rang before Torey lost interest and sat down in the dirt. One of the times he'd made his boss laugh during his job interview was when she asked if he'd like to meet *her* boss, and he answered that strangers made him nervous.

"What are some other words for this kind of thing?" he'd asked his mother the first time he spent a whole day in bed, and his mother said, "Well, one would be 'laziness.'" He'd been fifteen. She'd sat near his feet and rubbed her eyes like she couldn't get any more tired, and then reminded him that he had things to do, and he answered that maybe that was part of the problem, and after a minute she told him that the *problem* was that he wouldn't get himself out of bed.

He'd survived that and high school and then college. At her funeral he saw his father again after however many years, and mentioned how bad some of his episodes had gotten, and his father gave him a look and then asked if he was going to make even *this* about him. And when he didn't answer, his father added that Torey's mother had always said that when it came to making himself miserable, her son was a genius at building something out of nothing.

The night everyone had such a good time at his expense he'd complained about it to Tara in bed, and she told him that he had more trouble being happy than anyone she knew. "But I'm *not* depressed?" he asked, and she said, "Oh, my God." "What?" he said, and she said, "Being happy is a decision." "So I just don't want to make that decision?" he wanted to know. "I have to get up early," she told him.

He tried to bring it up again the next morning and was surprised

at how upset she'd gotten. "What would happen if *we* were a priority?" she asked him. "What would it be like if you thought about *us*
first?" Then she loaded the kids in the car for camp, and they hadn't
talked about it since.

It sounded like somebody was crying off in the house, so he stopped
to listen. A mosquito hummed around his head. He stood up again
and looked. He could see the living room but nobody inside. Tara
would've suggested that he go check what was going on. He thought
about her all the time, he said to himself again, and how often did he
pop into *her* head?

Rodney shouted out for him like someone had stuck him with a
pin. It scared him and he hustled up the hill and onto the deck and
slid the glass door open. He heard running in the yard and then the
van starting up. In the kitchen, blueberries and their Tupperware
pint were scattered across the floor. Rodney called him again and
came around the corner in front of him. "Somebody was here," he
said. "Something happened to Nyjah."

Nyjah was on the sofa in the family room and yelled at his father
not to open the window, though Torey hadn't been about to. He knelt
in front of him and Nyjah said the man had asked if his parents
were home and then had hugged him very tight. Torey asked what
that meant, and Nyjah said he'd hugged him very tight. Had he done
anything else?, Torey wanted to know, and Nyjah said he'd hugged
him very tight.

The front door was still open. When Torey checked it out, the
van was gone. He asked Rodney what had happened and Rodney
said he'd been up in his room on his headphones and when he'd
come down this guy was holding Nyjah and then got scared and
took off.

"What do you mean, holding him?" Torey asked, and Rodney said, "Holding him."

Torey got back in front of Nyjah and said, "Are you okay? Did he do anything other than hold you?" But Nyjah didn't seem to understand the question. Torey went back to the front door and looked around again and then shut it. "Did you get a good look at the guy?" he asked Rodney.

"Shouldn't we be calling the police?" Rodney asked him back.

"Why would we be calling the police?" Tara asked from the back door. She dumped her backpack full of books on the floor and then noticed Nyjah. "What's wrong with him?"

It took a while to explain, and even after the explanation his wife kept looking at him like something didn't add up.

"Where were *you*?" she asked.

"Where was *I*?" he asked in return. "I told you where I was."

She asked again what he'd been doing down there, and he said just hanging out. Walking. Whatever. When she said, "Did you hear the guy come to the door?" no specific lies came into his head. She looked at him like this time he'd surprised even her.

"And you haven't called the police," she said.

"I got here right before you did," he told her.

"Peanut, you're sure you're okay?" she asked Nyjah again, kneeling in front of him. He nodded pretty convincingly. She got up and pushed past Torey and he got down on the rug in front of Nyjah, taking her place. Nyjah jumped up and ran over to her.

In the kitchen she had the phone to her ear. She hefted Nyjah onto her hip and held him there.

Rodney was wandering around inside the garage. When Torey stepped inside he moved down the driveway, where his father caught up to him and roped him in with one arm and lifted him up. The kid seemed to appreciate it but still looked away.

Back in the house Tara had hung up the phone and taken Nyjah upstairs. There was water running in the tub.

He dumped Rodney onto the couch and walked to the bottom of the stairs and asked if she wanted help. She said no. Rodney pulled his legs up and turned on ESPN.

With nothing to do Torey walked through the downstairs and looked in every room before coming back to the kitchen and pulling some paper and a pen out of the drawer so they could maybe write down what they remembered. Rodney started surfing with the remote and then went back to where he started.

"You all right?" Torey asked.

"I'm okay," Rodney said. They could hear splashing and low talk upstairs.

When the cop got there, they were watching ESPN. The cop was a dad they knew from youth soccer. After they told him what they could, Nyjah did too, bundled in his towel next to Tara, his hair still wet. The cop asked if they'd noticed any weird people hanging around before this, if there'd ever been any sign of anyone else in the house, if they'd seen anything like a weapon, if it looked to Torey like the guy had been on drugs, and if he had any other information about the van besides that it was white. The cop wanted to know why they thought the guy might have picked this house. Tara asked if anything like this had happened in town before, and he told her there'd recently been one other possible home invasion, but not like this. Rodney asked if he thought the guy would come back, and the cop said he really didn't think so. Nyjah held his wet hair away from his head with his fingers and looked at it.

Finally the cop put away his little notebook in its carrying case and said to call if they thought of anything else, and that he'd be in touch. He said to Nyjah on his way out, "That was pretty scary, huh?" and Nyjah nodded.

.   .   .

For the rest of the day the kids and Tara were a little trio and every so often he joined the group. At one point he noticed her backpack still on the floor by the door and asked if she wanted her books in the study, and she said no.

The first time she'd broken up with him, she spent the night before talking him into a six-hour bus trip from Athens to Meteora on their junior year abroad, and the next morning, once he'd overdone his hangdog thing about having to move his pack in the overhead rack so hers would fit, she stored hers in the front of the bus and stomped back to her seat and told him she'd had it, and that they were history. He'd asked what she was talking about, then asked her a few questions about it, before finally giving up, and they sat shoulder to shoulder in silence for the next six hours.

They'd gotten back together on her birthday and then broke up again over how he'd reacted to her sister's being sick, and then finally got back together for good after, at his mother's suggestion, he'd taken stock and written Tara a long letter about just how comprehensive an emotional fuckup he'd been. He begged her to meet him in a coffee shop, where he laid out how he was going to change, and at first she didn't believe him, but eventually she'd come around. He told her as partial explanation of his behavior that before he met her he just hadn't felt like he ever brought very much to the party, and she answered that maybe that would change if he ever actually went to a party, and he said absolutely, and he'd gone to three in that week alone with and without her.

He went to bed early that night and no one noticed. Eventually Tara passed through the room carrying a load of folded laundry and towels. "If your speech or whatever isn't finished, you might want to work on that," she said from the bathroom.

"Thanks," he said. She put away some T-shirts in his dresser and left the room.

When she finally got into bed later that night, she asked if he thought Nyjah was okay. She asked if he ever thought about how *they* felt when he did stuff like he did today. He started to defend himself and she told him to stop. She asked if they were going to have to keep having these conversations. He wanted to tell her that his father—now *there* was a guy who could disappear. He told her that he was going to do everything he could not to let her down. "Oh, honey," she said, and it was equal parts *I won't give up on you* and *I already have.*

He woke in the middle of the night remembering his talk was going to be at the clubhouse near the first tee, and that the assistant head of Alumni Relations would address the group afterward. But Torey would be up at the podium first, just standing there in front of all those happy impatient faces. He'd start with the lottery system, since that was supposedly controversial but couldn't be *too* controversial since everyone there had benefited from it. He'd explain how each name had been pulled out of a hat by the golf pro. He'd talk about the assigned pairings, and how the partners' combined handicaps had to be within a certain range, and add that he wanted to take this moment to officially wish the best of luck to all. And while he was making wishes, he also wanted to let everyone know that he wasn't planning on going quietly, in terms of having to settle for being the guy that everyone thought he was.

He would let that sink in for a minute before he went on. Then he'd let everybody know that he just wanted to go home. That he *didn't* ignore what was ahead of him but in fact worried about it constantly. That it wasn't like he didn't *know* about the way he was and how it made things harder for everyone. He'd open up to all those mid-to-high handicappers. Maybe when they saw him like that they'd call a doctor. Maybe they'd call his wife. But even as he wallowed in the poor-me turn that the story had taken, he could feel the old Torey coming back, the one who *knew* he was a good guy. The one who didn't think it mattered what he always did or what was coming next. The one who'd watched his kids in the backyard trying to rehoist a collapsed tent in a heavy rain. "What're you *doing*?" he'd called out to them, stupidly. And Rodney had told him, "You *know* what we're doing." And Nyjah had told him, "Don't *look* at us."

Intimacy

By the time Gladys May Sparks dropped her soaked leather portmanteaus on the veranda of her new home in Barrow Point, Queensland, the rain had started to come down very heavy. Her new husband, Tommy, busied himself with a welcoming pot of tea and she remained where he'd left her, a puddle spreading around her feet. It seemed unlikely that a single item inside the portmanteaus was still dry. Her first impression was of a place where everything was covered with vines, including the two cane chairs and the breakfast table and the hammock, and out front she noted a mandarin orange tree and a prickly pear hedge. The rain was now so heavy the mud was strewn with bougainvillea petals, and when she stepped inside the house all the crawling things had come out: a fat bird spider was creeping up the curtains and ants had gotten into the jam. Tommy helped her with her wet clothes. Something was wrong with the fireplace damper and as much smoke was pouring into the room as was going up the chimney, and that gave her license to cry. He put his cheek to hers and his hand on her shoulder. While he rubbed some warmth into it she looked out the little kitchen window at one of the plots he had cleared. In the downpour a magpie was bathing in one of the stumps.

The entire journey had been demoralizing. On the railway north from Brisbane the heat was a clammy misery, and once the rain commenced the road beside the tracks became a channel of mire. They passed any number of drivers of bogged drays sitting like sailors atop foundering ships. In some ravines the road disappeared entirely and the jungle swept right down to the train windows. Every so often boys on horseback would appear in the clearings for mail sacks thrown from the locomotive, waving gaily at her as it raced by. In more open areas they passed enormous, queer-shaped tombstones that the conductor explained were anthills, and on her only trip to the toilet she discovered a monstrous yellow frog in the washbasin.

She'd had to take a Cobb & Co. coach from the railway terminus and for two hours was the only female passenger. Then once the other passengers had disembarked she was entirely alone. Soon she'd been in such immense distress at needing to relieve herself that after peering out the window at length into only wildness and turmoil, she seized on the sizable crack at the bottom of the coach door and arranged herself as closely to it as she could, and then upon arrival she begged the driver's pardon for having spilled a bottle of wine, and after hearing her out he sniffed the carriage floor and said that if she liked he had a cork that would fit that bottle. She didn't tell her husband this when he rode up in his trap.

They had met when she worked at an inn that served as a changeover stop for that same coach company, and Tommy returned three or four times after she'd caught his eye, and once they made their affections known they hadn't been at all dilatory in settling the matter of their love.

At that point he'd been working as a railway fettler but had had enough money saved for a selection up north where he intended to breed cattle. Before that he had started a fruitless venture involving a plantation cultivating a palm tree that he claimed would have made splendid billiard cues. But Gladys had been the last daughter living at home and her responsibility for a full year had been to her ailing parents, until her father passed on in his sleep and then within the week her mother had risen from bed one night, washed and dressed herself in clean linen so as to not give trouble, and then laid back down again with her hands folded on her breast, and by morning Gladys and her siblings were orphans.

She and Tommy married soon after and spent their first week together in Brisbane, while he was embroiled in a dispute with his drovers. When he returned to her each evening burdened with care and strife, she understood it to be her periodic task to remind him of the silver lining of their intimacy. One morning he wrote her a love note that he left at the breakfast seat explaining there were many things he ought to say to her that were better put to paper than spoken directly. But as often as she reread his words, even before he left for Barrow Point, for all her contentment she felt she had held her soul away from him, and wondered if he'd done the same. Still, she said nothing about it, perhaps because, as Tommy sometimes teased her, she disliked skirmishes even with her cow. She did think, though, of that adage about sailors in the storm: they vow to amend their lives and yet don't, because if drowned they can't and if saved they won't.

Iris Beryl Finnimore had come over on an assisted-passage ticket on the *Darling Downs* via the Suez Canal and disembarked in Brisbane after a voyage of one hundred days. She had been twenty-three and unaccompanied by any of her family, and she had come because of the publicity in Ireland about the Queensland government's assistance to migrants for this new colony. The circulars had described a demand in particular for farm laborers, vine dressers, mechanics, and domestic servants. Her younger brother had wanted to come with her but had not been allowed to do so by their parents because of his age.

Despite what she'd been told, upon arrival she found Brisbane to be filled with perfectly good and proper streets, excepting for their open drainage gutters, and one of the first things she'd done was to purchase Professor Halford's snakebite cure, operating on the notion that her life would not be safe for a day without it. This consisted of a hypodermic syringe and an evil-looking elixir, each nested in a leather tray. Ultimately during one of her subsequent relocations it went astray and was never again seen or missed. The next thing she bought, for threepence, was a large pineapple that she ate alone near the docks in the shade of a eucalyptus, thereby realizing a childhood ambition to finally get enough of that delicacy.

She inquired at a local agency about domestic service but then resolved that almost any other situation provided superior inducements, reminding herself that no one lost any dignity by performing physical labor, and that indeed it was just the reverse: the more a woman could do for herself, the better she would get on. Eventually she took a position with a milliner for twelve shillings a week in Rockhampton, some four hundred miles north, and before leaving Brisbane had been informed that if she didn't die of malaria or wasn't cut to pieces by the blacks on the journey, that would simply leave more for the crocodiles, since most young women's first river crossings that far north were also their last.

She'd arranged herself a room in a good home in which she made herself comfortable, even if she was unable to boast of any style about the place, and had written her brother John Henry that here she was in tropical Australia having traveled as far as the railway proceeded, and when she peered out her window it really looked as though she'd reached the end of the world.

But she neglected to write of the habit she'd formed of every Friday night watching the special train come in with its disembarking passengers and all of its hubbub of husbands meeting wives, and sisters embracing, and children reuniting with parents, and all sorts of other joyous people who, unlike her, were not alone in the world. And how severely it pained her to witness any number of gay departures from the station platform which in every case swallowed the participants into the darkness forever as far as she was concerned. She chose not to trouble her brother with her fear that she would have no friends and few acquaintances. Though she did sign off her letter with *"Amid these uncoveted solitudes I wander by the silent moon."*

Nellie Murray's grandfather migrated to North Queensland after extensive tin deposits were discovered in the Wild River area, and worked thereafter as a tin miner at Flaggy Creek. He arrived in midsummer and reported to the family a scorching wind so intolerable as to obstruct respiration. He also noted a vast number of reptiles and large insects, all of which raised an incessant clamor. Before moving north he had married May Catherine Carrick, Nellie's grandmother, in the rites of the Methodist Church at the Centenary Hall in Sydney, and had had three children: Nellie's father, James; a second son, Joseph, who died of bronchial pneumonia at the age of four months; and a third, Thomas David, who was lost to a brain fever. Grandmother May then died of pulmonary tuberculosis and was buried with their two infant children. Prior to her passing she asked her closest friend to look after her surviving boy, and then added that the best means of doing so might be to marry the boy's father, and that was what her closest friend had done.

Nellie's father worked for a few years at the Mount Abundance Station ferrying wool from the shearing sheds to the railway and saved enough to buy some land to raise his own sheep farther north, where Nellie grew up helping her parents on their properties. For her early education she attended the provisional schoolhouse only three miles from her home, and when small she helped prepare the lunches for her father and brothers, and when a bit older was allowed to carry those lunches on horseback to where the men were working. During the shearing months there were always long lines of teams on the western roads as well as a scarcity of shearers, with some sheds shorthanded. When she was especially good her father let her accompany him the nine miles into town to visit the general store known as the Little Wonder that sometimes stocked dry goods from England and France. The wooden sign atop the store read *"The Biggest Wonder Is How We Do It."*

By the time she was eighteen her three older brothers had gone west together and her mother had died of wind on the stomach, which had affected her heart, and her father's response was to drink himself blind drunk five nights a week, but she absorbed those losses and moved on. Unlike many girls her age she was content to have things around her a little rough. When younger she'd seen a transient carrying his swag rolled in a blanket and remembered admiring his independence of everyone and everything. She never minded isolation, whereas her brothers were like squadron horses on scouting work that were always fretting to return to their kin.

She met her husband, Ernie, when she was nineteen and he was forty-one. He had worked on a surveyor's gang, stripped bark, and dug for gold. As a younger man he often made three-day rides between stations with his only provisions a pocket full of oats, a water bag, and a little sugar. He'd been hired to help around the shearing pens and they bantered for weeks before she agreed to marry him over the washtub in which she was soaping her arms, and once she rinsed off they proceeded directly to the magistrate to have the ceremony performed. She'd roused her father from his hangover to show him the ring. And soon she discovered that in marriage her husband was a quiet man given to sulks and nursing his grievances in a dignified aloofness.

Out of spite toward her brothers her father had provided in his will for her to have life tenancy, stipulating that the property could be sold only upon her death, and the week following his burial she buried her husband as well, after his horse pitched him over its head, and she then enjoyed a run of excellent seasons when the price of wool rose after the drought of 1889. She and her husband had remained childless, and he had informed everyone around the station that they'd been like the fishers of Galilee who toiled all night and caught nothing. After his death his favored sheepdog ran away, never to return. Nellie commonly told herself that it was no use looking on the black side of things, as it never made matters any better. But after three years of running the place alone, when her spirits sank she pondered her want of success hitherto in life, and the improbability of holding on to this station as her own. And she registered that it had become increasingly wearisome to toil in such a place where people lived so far apart and so often thought only of themselves. She herself had administered to three different young women who'd been without nurse, doctor, or a female neighbor at the time of their deliveries, and the postman passed her station twice a month on his three-hundred-mile circuit. At night on her veranda the melancholy thought would occur to her that to her south were thirty thousand acres of exposed country on which there grew no tree or shrub higher than a candle, and in the darkness out beyond her lamplight, all was still, except for the thumping of her dog's tail at her slightest stirring, and the occasional and solitary bell that indicated where one of her horses was grazing.

Gladys and Iris had already, as Nellie had long since, heard the stories about what the blacks called kooinar, the great wind that flattened trees and turned the country into an inland sea. These storms were sensationally chronicled in the colonial newspapers and formed by monstrous whirlpools of air over three hundred miles across that came scything down out of the Coral Sea and into the rainforests of northeastern Australia with such ferocity that the governmental and amateur meteorologists investigating afterward reported their findings in expressions of awe and horror usually reserved for the most extravagant fictions. Between January and March the storms assaulted the coastline between Cooktown and Rockhampton with such a fierce regularity that three years after its founding every building in Cooktown was blown down and that first set of survivors crawled out from under the wreckage and headed south, never to return.

Two years before Iris's arrival in Rockhampton, downpours had already been unceasing for a week when the first cyclone of the season hit Chillagoe, just north of Nellie's section, and dropped thirty-five inches of rain in twenty-four hours. Her property, being on higher ground, had missed the worst of the flooding, but three of her neighbors' homes were carried away and the Mission Station near them entirely destroyed and all who'd sheltered within it had perished. And the *Brisbane Courier* reported that off the coast at Cairns, two mothers swept out to sea had tied their toddlers to each other's back and urged them to cling to their hair, and that the mothers were retrieved from a reef some miles offshore but the children had died of exposure in the night. And some months after that, a black who'd hitched a ride with Nellie's cart driver pointed out to them the shattered remains of a rowboat sixty feet up in the branches of a bottle tree and said he'd survived the great flood that put them there.

The first sunny days had cheered Gladys more than she might have hoped, and she had had to concede that theirs was an extremely picturesque station, with its largest grazing portion running parallel with the beach along the sea. Most days were sunny, though the gales that blew in rioted southward as though intending to cross the entire continent to the Pole beyond.

Tommy had done much to improve the place in anticipation of their life together, adding extensions to the original hut for bedrooms and a veranda, and it wasn't as isolated as she'd feared: letters and newspapers were delivered twice a week by packhorse mailmen who also brought any telegrams that might have arrived, and their neighbor was only a mile or so off, though he was a peevish, conceited old man who took no pains toward civility and whose wife, an invalid, Tommy depicted as having been too good for this world, adding as if to prove this that the previous year she'd succumbed to a spider bite.

Tommy carved *"Tommy & Gladys Sparks"* onto a sign he hung over the hammock. While he never swam, on hot Sundays she flopped from the rocks offshore like a water hen, and one such morning on the strand found a curious hollow stone that might serve as an ink bottle. She spent the end of her weekends on garment repair, tacking on patches from her piece drawer and setting tucks before the sewing she would take up to bed. Most nights her husband would lie patiently beside her. And when in the course of his daily rounds he suffered setbacks, and rejoined her questions with grunts, or let his glance pass over her, he was willing after a day or two of her answering silence to proclaim himself sorry from his hocks to his hat top, and she was able to remind herself that counsels of perfection were easier to teach than to practice, and that many a cloudy morning turned into a fine afternoon, and so we take that which God provides while striving for the better. And there were clear nights when, holding hands atop their roof, they registered the stilled stupendousness of an ocean plain before them star-brightened around the lengthening gleam of the moon.

As a wife she sought to be neither vindictive nor morose about trifles. Yet on rainy days her fire's smoke would still blind a bullock, and puddles still ran inside from the veranda, and whenever their horses came to the little creek to water and she undertook to pat them hello, they evidently imagined they were being harnessed and galloped away. And she still sometimes thought that she didn't wish to know anyone very intimately, for fear that person would spy her many imperfections and esteem her even less. Her mother had said of her that she was like a cat with one trick, and her sole accomplishment had been reading. Her husband when his gaze took her in saw a pleasant-looking woman of middle height, her hair tucked up in her tortoiseshell combs, but inside she felt herself to be a nest of complaints and privations and erratic desires, an alchemist's crucible with its multicolored fumes and mephitic odors and occasional gleam caught only briefly through the bubble and seethe.

Iris's solitude had evaporated once word had adequately gotten around Rockhampton about the pretty new arrival. Any number of swains had wooed her, some lean, some obese, some pious, some disconsolate. One had spectacles, and one no hair at all. At first this bustle had pleased Miss Laycock, who ran the shop, but then she'd had to intervene and would-be suitors required other excuses to stray into

Iris's path. When Iris finally remarked with some embarrassment about her situation, her employer explained that the colony was full of gentlemen who had squandered their capital and fallen off the social ladder, and that the bush was swarming with broken-down swells, many of whom had been sent to Australia because they'd been considered liabilities in England.

Most commented upon Iris's accent and proceeded as though the entire arc of their courtship would need to occur in a single afternoon. Some seemed to offer all the affection the most craving heart could desire. Still, she had no patience for men who carried on like this not because they were poor but because they didn't know any better or care to, and when she turned them away the majority were cordial and sincere in their good wishes. Even so she felt, as they gaped at her, like an impatient schoolmistress forced to track the slow mastery of a simple rule.

Yet she accepted so many invitations that her employer felt the need to sit her down for a scolding, which later that night back in her room Iris found she resented. She was tired of knowing that someone was sure to be shocked by whatever a woman might do. Remain at home and you're a mystery, go out and you're a gadabout, sit quietly at a dinner and you're a dullard, be vivacious and you're a flirt. She joined the local Suffrage League and particularly liked the second talk she'd attended, the main argument of which had been that a society couldn't raise free men from enslaved women, and that at no period in the world's history had women given so much thought to the social conditions that affected them. She raised the matter with Miss Laycock the next morning when opening the shop, and was reminded that if she really sought to get ahead as a woman, she might fret less about rights and more about influence and how to achieve it.

She met Ned outside of town on a hill that was used as both an

observatory and a picnic spot. For a change that day she had parted
her hair on the side. It was so terribly hot—in Rockhampton nine
drunkards had died in just four days—that even in the shade he had
sought relief in a wet towel wound around his head. She found that
white ants soon rendered her water bottle unfit for use, and Ned
offered her his. When she'd first noticed him she thought he looked
quite the farmer's boy, but he came from Woolloongabba, where he'd
been a cart driver. Like so many of his age he was lank-limbed and
sunburnt. She spilled what he'd given her and he wondered if she
needed help as well with pouring, and she thanked him and assured
him that when she did want some help she would ask.

He inquired as to her history and then related his own. He had
gone west and worked as a stockman mustering and branding calves,
though within a week he had wanted desperately to return home,
but had hated the idea of doing so as poor as when he'd set out, and
in debt besides, and laughed at in the bargain. Then he'd gotten the
position as cart driver and it had all mostly come out all right.

They met every day for the next week and when taking his leave
of her on the second Sunday he asked in a teasing way why she was
still single—was she so difficult to please?—and urged her to look
for someone with good sense as a husband, and further cautioned
that she would never be content with a man inferior to herself when
it came to understanding. She asked if he assumed she was easily
led into error, and he said no as though they hadn't just been teasing each other. Before she'd left Ulster her mother had reminded
her that it wasn't great deeds that were necessary for a happy bond,
but only kindly action and the loving look, but that night, back in
her room, Iris wanted to write her mother to say she wished to add
to that accounting the wholly engaged kiss, the free immersion in
which suggested a bond that brightened the darkest shadows. And
that such mutual caresses could be the physical expression of the

deepest spiritual truth, since that was where, however rarely, difference and separation were vanquished.

As solitary as Nellie was, she wasn't working her section alone, but had two stockmen, Georgie and his brother, Arthur, also known as "Squeak." For a few years they'd humped as gangers for the railway out of Quilpie, and while Georgie was right as rain, Squeak was the kind of worker who every three months would demand his pay and a few days' leave, after which he would return without his money, horse, saddle, or, once, even his clothes. Before hiring on with Nellie they had minded a flock so remote that it took them a month to get there from Townsville by foot and dray. After settling in on her station, they revealed they preferred this sort of work with sheep to shepherding, since the latter had inclined them toward a neglected appearance and strange and cranky ways, and said that if shepherds, given their great isolation, didn't need to be mad, it was nevertheless a great qualification. Georgie as a fencer was a prince with a mortising axe, his posts always upright and the same height out of the ground and as straight as you wanted them, and his corners and gateposts marvels of stability. He considered his brother a good hand as well, by which he meant Squeak never complained and didn't care what he ate. They lived toward the north end of the property in their own hut with two wooden chairs, two camp beds, and one box for their swag. They were particularly proud of their beds since each featured canvas sheets.

Squeak did complain, however, that he didn't have his brother's knack with the blacks, who were often passing through along the creeks and could be relied upon for the occasional odd chore. He thought the tame blacks had picked up all of the worst characteristics of the white race and had lost some of their own, and that of course there was nothing to be done with the wild ones. At some sheep stations farther west he'd seen aboriginal women confined behind fencing for the use of the white station hands, and had known one stockkeeper who kept his woman chained to a log but then discovered she'd run away with his only shirt, which he'd given her out of fondness. It seemed to Nellie listening to them talk that even the humane had abdicated to the general ruthlessness, that it had become in effect a question of which race would survive, with each man's vote cast in favor of his own. Still, she strove to treat everyone fairly, with the result that even when migrating tribesmen, provoked by maltreatment, inflicted outrages on others, they preserved their kindness for her.

After those profitable seasons following the drought she'd been able to add to her father's holdings, and five years after taking the lease on an additional 160 acres she made successful application to freehold it. The night she hung the deed of grant over her threshold Georgie and Squeak had knocked on her door to help her celebrate, with the assistance of two jugs of an unidentifiable liquor provided by a local dram-shop owner whose wares were said to be so poisonous that he had a special burial place for all those customers insufficiently hardy to survive his hospitality.

That January, from Nellie's section all the way north and east to Gladys and Tommy's, the flies were very troublesome for everyone's eyes, even on windy days, and a number flew into any opened mouth and could be expelled only by a violent fit of coughing. This was followed by a period of rain so unrelenting that all outdoor chores became dreadful work, and in the worst of it Gladys pointed out to Tommy that their cartwheels were so thickly coated with mud they resembled Christmas wreaths. At last the weather cleared and the night was radiant with stars and the full moon emerged so gloriously that Gladys read the newspaper by its light. Then the atmosphere became unusually still.

Iris noticed the stillness as her train was arriving in Brisbane. She'd been sent there to fetch Miss Laycock's brother Nicholas and to not take no for an answer. He had lost a good job in a cotton-yard warehouse and since then apparently transferred his energies to running up debts and granting favors to dubious friends. He had agreed to come stay with his sister in Rockhampton, but with him all resolutions were quickly formed and just as immediately abandoned. Miss Laycock told Iris she would have gone herself but her mother and father were both ill and she didn't want to be out of reach should anything happen to them, and she had the little ones on top of that. She further noted that with trade being rather dull at the present and few prospects of a rapid revival, she could spare Iris for the few days this errand would require. She counted on Iris to not be turned aside by her brother's charms or recalcitrance, and warned that she hadn't grown up with the boy without having become aware that he was a very awkward animal to lead or drive, though she recognized he might say the same of her.

The coach from the train dropped Iris outside the inn where her employer had arranged for her to stay, and she noticed the pennants on its façade had gone oddly limp. The coach horses shied and shook. Safe in her room, she made her toilet, put out the lamp, and laid atop her bed in the heat and the silence, remarking to herself aloud after a few moments that there was nothing like lying and listening alone in the dark to promote anxiety.

———

Nellie was by her section's largest creek, soaking her feet, with a head aching from a cause she couldn't identify, her dog patiently waiting for her to be up and about again. With the moon now gone it seemed intensely dark, and she also noted the lack of insect noise. She set her hat on the earth beside her, dented the crown, and poured in some water for the dog. He appeared attuned to something worrisome, which she imagined to be her. She'd been short with him lately, and feared she turned to him an expression of at best only haggard cheer in the face of a world she felt had grown ever more dismal.

Off to the north she could hear Georgie struggling with his wagon and its exceptionally heavy load. He would blaspheme until refreshed and then fill his pockets with stones to throw at his team and go at it again. Some aspect of his voice reminded her of her father, who had so disliked company that he had regularly claimed that people gathered socially principally to make themselves disagreeable, and she wondered how much of her current predicament had been born out of what she was usually pleased to call her frankness with others.

After Gladys retired the night remained uncommonly hot and oppressive, with the eastern horizon lit with distant lightning that disclosed a leaden-black sky. Following a restless hour she rose and returned to her veranda, where she registered equally severe and continuous electrical discharges, now clearly nearer. She watched the flickers and flashes under clouds that spanned the entire panorama.

In his nightshirt Tommy trooped down to the beach and moored their little ketch more securely before returning to the veranda to admire the distant display. Their dog, intrigued by this break in routine, skylarked in the water. Behind him their boat rode quietly on a dead calm sea.

———

Weather reports were limited to nine a.m. bulletins every two days by wireless telegraphy, and that night the Queensland meteorologist, basing his forecast on the most recent and sketchy report from New Caledonia that suggested through the extremity of its numbers that their barometer was broken, advised that while conditions were becoming suspicious south of those islands, no danger necessarily threatened the Queensland coast yet, though mariners nevertheless needed to keep a bright lookout.

At around that same time, the Eight Mile Police Station in Cooktown reported that all communication to the north on the Cape York Peninsula, four hundred miles long and two hundred and fifty miles across, had ceased.

When Gladys finally heard the roaring and recognized the immensity of the disturbance charging over the last miles of ocean toward them, she whistled for the dog and ducked into the kitchen to hoist atop their highest cupboard their cask of corned beef and sack of salt. Tommy only gaped at what was coming and the wind when it hit him was so unprecedented in its force that it blew him over the side of the veranda and out into the yard. Their dog never made it out of the water. Tommy tried to regain his feet and was battered again to his knees and seemed to be trying to catch objects that were flying off the house. Gladys was thrown across the kitchen when its eastern wall collapsed, and took refuge in the bedroom and, considering the bed her most valuable possession, lay atop it in order to hold it down, and from there watched her roof and ceiling tear away along with the other walls until there was nothing left of that side of the house except herself and her bed, and she was eventually blown out of that.

Miss Laycock having found herself unaccountably unable to sleep had put some water on and was contemplating a lump of butter in a stoneware urn covered with a damp cloth when she noted what sounded like a waterfall off to the northeast as the onshore cyclonic winds piled up the sea and, corresponding disastrously with a high tide and a shallowing bottom, swept all before them, and it was only when the clamor grew truly alarming that she rose to her feet and the storm surge blew through her front door and windows in a wave and filled the room to her armpits before she could clamber to the second floor. She got there to find her youngest, a toddler, spread-eagled on his mattress, and before she could reach him the floor split and yawed away, and her half of the house disintegrated.

Nellie took a moment to sniff her fingers, which smelled of yellow soap and beeswax, and heard above her an immense array of waterfowl passing over, and then had a bit more time to be amused by Georgie's abuse of his team before the noise of what was approaching made her stand upright. She was bowled over and the willow oak beside her was ripped out of the ground and tumbled away. Georgie was knocked flat by his team when they panicked at the uprooted tree pitching toward them end over end, and while he clung to the rear wagon wheel a sheet of roofing iron that was part of his load decapitated a bottle-brush tree already bent like a bow before the wind.

And behind the wind came more rain in a 350-mile arc than had ever been recorded on the continent, overwhelming the vast catchment area of the Brisbane and Stanley Rivers. A grazier and amateur meteorologist named H. P. Somerset of Caboonbah, high above the Stanley, woke to a blare akin to an accelerating locomotive and registered that his wind gauge had reached 142 miles per hour before being torn to pieces and then a 70-foot wall of water thundered down the gorge and struck the cliff below him with such impact that it shifted his house from its foundations. Once he recovered his wits and orientation he saddled his horse and tore breakneck through the storm, nearly blown from his mount any number of times, to the nearest telegraph station, to try to warn the postmaster at Brisbane, downstream, of what was coming.

Iris had risen early and remarked on the fury of the downpour to her hostess when being seated to breakfast. She'd found it thrilling at first, as she did all manifestations of excessive turbulence in nature. The woman at a neighboring table was telling her companion that her sister had lost her baby to a fever occasioned by teething, but that her other tot was well. An older woman near the window commented on the storm with the same phrase Iris's mother favored: "What a fine day for young ducks!" And having ordered her bacon and porridge, Iris fretted about her Ned that when it came to her true self he might find her a steep hill whose view did not repay the ascent.

Gladys ended up in a gulley covered in timber, tree boughs, and a few oranges while the rain lashed down in torrents. She cried out for Tommy, who was nearby on his hands and knees but blinded by the wind. Her feet had been cut by broken glass, and as more debris piled around her she crawled under an upturned wheelbarrow and pulled in her limbs like a tortoise and held on. In search of her, Tommy scrabbled up the ridge into rain that stung like hail and looked out to sea and in the darkness made out a great roiling wall of white water tumbling toward the shore and rising upon itself as it came. It swept inland over the beach and trees six feet or more in circumference were ripped out by the roots or snapped off at the ground, and when the surge roared up the slope below him he turned his back to it and ran for the nearest pine. He was twenty feet into the canopy before the water nearly pulled him from his perch, swinging him around the trunk and splintering its bark, but he kept climbing as fast as he could and the cataract finally stopped at his shoes. And from there he searched every treetop still standing above the flood for some sign of his wife.

Within minutes the rain around Nellie and Georgie was such that every ravine was a river and every hollow a lake, and they scrambled for higher ground with the rising water at their heels. They heard the deluge behind them explode down the creek and sweep away Georgie's team and wagon, and they both reached gum trees and climbed for their lives. While they watched, the flood kept rising, the earth so hard-baked it couldn't absorb such a vast volume of water, the extensive rain of the previous weeks having only made matters worse. They shouted to each other over the wind to hang on, and Georgie asked hoarsely if she'd seen Squeak, and eventually the current grew so high that Nellie found herself floating in the flood while she clung to her tree's top branches. But the extra height of Georgie's tree turned out to be worse fortune as hordes of insects and arachnids of every description seeking refuge swarmed over his face and eyes and into his nostrils, and as the surge rose even higher the bark thronged further with centipedes and scorpions who bit and stung him so repeatedly that Nellie heard his shrieks clearly despite the storm.

Even before what was hurtling down the river gorges converged on Brisbane, the town's meteorologist noted in his journal that more rain had fallen in the last twelve hours than in half of the previous year. Miss Laycock's brother Nicholas had been roused early in his rooming house by the tumult of wind and rain, and stood at the window wondering if the weather would spoil the sports program planned for later that day. The wind progressed to a bellow and he watched as fences were laid flat, strong men blown down, and sheets of iron torn from roofs opposite him, carrying high into the air or skimming along the streets. An older house's roof was ripped off in one piece. Refugees from it blundered into the cataclysm and were bowled off their feet and across the roadway while around them severed telegraph lines lashed like stockwhips. The river, further banked by an incoming tide, had already risen three feet in the past two hours when Nicholas heard the boom of the mounting cascade colliding with the Jindalee Bridge, and putting his cheek to the window to peer up the block, he saw wharves, warehouses, sawmills, and factories torn loose and borne away before the obliterating spray reached him and he was blasted from his room.

When the flood carried off the upper story of the home where Ned rented a room in Rockhampton, he saved himself by grabbing at some advertising pennants and pulling himself on top of a store and from there, hours later, he was able to hallo an old friend from his cart-driving days who already was plying the floodwaters in a rowboat hung with a lamp, and the two young men afterward did yeoman's work in going wherever cries for help were audible. They especially reveled in the number of young women clad in the scantiest of clothing who had to be lifted dripping wet into the boat to be ferried to safety. One, having been settled aboard, complained that her seat was wet. Another imperious gentleman on a third-story balcony claimed he had no wish to be taken off but did require them to hold their position before him in the current for the remainder of the evening, should he need them later. On every other roof was a bedraggled cat, or duck, or even cow. All in all they saved thirty-one souls, though one little girl who'd been clinging to a rainspout dropped off into the waters and disappeared before they could reach her, and whenever they delivered their evacuees onto safe ground they were accosted by others who'd escaped yet remained uncertain whether loved ones still out across the flooded expanse had survived.

Gladys had no memory of the sea overcoming her but recalled having been spun and propelled from the gulley in her upturned wheelbarrow two and a half miles on the tide's crest before crashing through the upper branches of a paperbark tree and taking advantage of her barrow's momentary arrest to clamber out of it and up higher. Once she obtained a secure hold the only danger after the water stopped rising came from cattle that swam to the tree and tried flailingly to scramble into her roost.

Iris was still at her breakfast table when the entire room shifted and tilted as the floor below collapsed, and she lunged and caught the banister to the third floor while the woman beside her pitched into the older woman by the window, table and all, and they skidded into the surging water. From the landing she was able to assist two diners who had managed to hang on to the balustrade, and from the third floor, whose lee side had somehow withstood the impact, she stood openmouthed in the face of the vista to the south: a house on a promontory swept from its foundations and rotating intact as it was carried away with three children on the porch visible until it destroyed itself against a railway bridge. A man swirled down the street below on his horse, its tail to the current, and when he attempted to swing it round it turned broadside to the flood and they were overwhelmed. Roofing iron still attached to its framing spun in the cataract like great chopping blades, and any number of buildings downstream gave way under the force of water and battering debris.

At around four-thirty a.m. the wind over Tommy's tree calmed and the barometer at the Cooktown post office fell to twenty-seven inches: the lowest air pressure the instrument could register, opposite the gradation marked *"Catastrophe."* The air became still. In the predawn light the few remaining trees out across the water were blasted and desolate. The bodies of horses, cattle, fish, dugongs, and sea snakes swirled below them. Branches beside him held exhausted seagulls with the feathers torn from their bodies. Two and a half miles away in another tree Gladys confronted her own vista of wholesale desolation. Here and there in the distance toward the western hills she could make out cattle marooned on tiny islands of mud. She wept in her shock and at the pain in her feet while the eye of the largest cyclone any white man in northeastern Australia had ever seen took twenty-two minutes to pass over. And then with a roar the winds reengaged from the opposite quadrant.

The gale's change of direction pushed Nellie around to the other side of her treetop, and she fended off various animals living and dead that slurried by until the storm abated and the waters receded. After an hour she was able to stand on exposed branches, and after another half the tree was visible. Below her a dead bull hung from a forked branch by its horns. By mid-morning the countryside was still flooded if only to a foot or so in depth, and the aspect all the way to the horizon was naked and soundless. Then she heard someone calling and splashing closer but was so tired she just waited, and eventually Squeak appeared, shirtless and streaked with black mud, so she climbed down and led him to Georgie's tree. Once Squeak brought him down, they laid him out flat, holding his head out of the shallow water, and when he was able to speak he thanked them and then, still blinded and swollen with venom, recounted his ordeal before he died.

Ned and his friend extracted from a little rooftop archipelago an additional seven children who'd been orphaned by the first surge, the youngest still carrying a soaked pillowcase with the sole remnants of their household treasures. He next tracked the fortunes of a horse that had maintained its footing for the entire night on a submerged rafter before venturing a swim to higher ground, where it had scrabbled ashore among a crowd of cheering spectators who quickly fed and dried it. And as the flood receded further, many did no more than stand around and watch the show, or call advice to those still struggling, while one group that had salvaged two casks of rum washed from a warehouse tied its boat to a telegraph pole and got openly pie-eyed.

Tommy, too, was surprised at the rapidity with which the inundation subsided. In the early light he counted one hundred and forty head of cattle that passed his tree swimming strongly, and by the time he had climbed down most had emerged safely on high ground. Full of dread he set out in the direction he imagined his wife had been carried, sloshing past the bodies of livestock and great fish, and after an entire day's despairing search he found her at the base of her tree and they embraced while traumatized birds walked fearlessly about their feet.

Brisbane being the epicenter of the massive alluvion's cascade to the sea, its torment was alleviated only much later. Dawn found Iris still on her third-floor lookout with the lower part of the city, including the Botanic Gardens and the red-light district, a vast sheet of water with just treetops and the occasional peaked roof showing. Rescue boats plied to and fro with difficulty against the current. All night over the torrent's roar she'd heard the crash of houses against the downstream railway bridge, and wreckage piled up so thickly against the cross braces that the blocked waters had to cascade up and over them, the girders screeching and groaning under the pressure until finally the bridge itself canted over and toppled into the surge, taking its two foundation piers with it. By midday she could see the bay, now a chaos of mastheads and flotsam. Around what had been the docks, looters worked openly from boats and improvised rafts, the available police still overburdened in their attempts to rescue the marooned.

At noon, when Ned and his friend finally turned their boat over to others and stretched out on high ground near Mount Archer, all was ruin and consternation as far as they could see. His friend fell instantly to sleep and Ned lay back on his elbows and was harangued by a minister who seemed undone by what had happened. Before a young woman with a head wound led him away, he told Ned the Lord had turned the daylight to darkness and had smashed the land like a cup, and that looking down He must be weeping. After he left Ned still couldn't sleep, and wondered not for the first time whether the storm had reached as far as Brisbane and his Iris. He walked with some difficulty through the chaos over to Mount Chalmers and there found a six-legged office desk and its accompanying chair upright in runoff pouring down a mountain of waterlogged wreckage. The paper in its top drawer was mostly dry and a beautiful pen still lodged in its holder, and under a tilted telegraph pole that still writhed with sheltering snakes he sat and composed a letter headed *"FOR IRIS,"* which he began by revealing that his mother once warned him all good men were prone to deterioration once beyond the reach of feminine influence, and that the decline would be evident in a carelessness of dress, a greater license of tongue, and a willingness to turn away from compassion. And he wrote that he felt that lack of benevolence within himself when away from her, and for that reason wished to pledge his love and propose marriage, and in support of his suit he wished her to know he now thought of her so tenderly that even his selfishness abated when he called her to mind, and that this was as great a gift as his having been spared.

. . .

Squeak refused to leave Georgie's body and Nellie sat with them both. By noon the hot sun was releasing spirals of vapor from the scoured terrain. Hilltops were strewn with fish and dead seagulls. Squeak said he'd been sheltering in their hut on his camp bed when two blacks had appeared out of the darkness and told him he had to quit the section because a great water would rise there. He said he owed them his life and then asked Nellie what he would do without his brother, and who would take care of him.

They improvised a pallet and lugged Georgie back through the muck and debris and when they finally reached the site of the house it was as if a cyclopean hand had swept the landscape bare. They were still sitting where their despair had stranded them when a teamsters' traveling camp of four wagons covered by tarpaulins rolled by on what was left of the road, and were then hailed and stirred from their lethargy. The horses were old and broken down, with fly bites all over them, and the harnesses slack. A damp, sorry-looking dingo took a heightened interest in Georgie until its owner and the teamsters helped Squeak and Nellie bury him, and that night they all shared a fire and the dingo's owner offered Nellie his bedding, which was an exceptionally dirty blanket. His companion said about his wife that until recently they had been in the habit of having connection thirteen or fourteen times a night, and that as they had gotten on in years this had now diminished to seven or eight times, whereupon the dingo's owner misinterpreted Nellie's responding silence and chastised the man for his lack of manners. All day long the flies had been bad and at dark the mosquitoes started in, but the blanket was of some help. Nellie imagined her stock scattered far and wide, the survivors struggling on from one hardship to another. And she admitted to herself that she was a natural loner, ready to learn from or break bread with anyone save her peers. And she noted, regarding Squeak's agony in the firelight, that however much some wished to rise toward heaven, the world's excessive fury would hold them down. And she registered that insight as plainly as she understood how little comfort she had offered him.

For the first few weeks afterward Gladys and Tommy lived like those settlers who'd huddled in bark houses and ate wombats and wallabies. He hired a Chinaman cast out by the storm to help with the cleanup and rebuilding and she worried she wouldn't like him, but her husband asked her to give the little beggar a week or two and it would all dry straight. Because one of her cuts hadn't healed properly, she adopted the blacks' resting position of standing on one foot with the other on the inside of her thigh, and from that posture at night she watched the blazing fires her husband built to consume the stumps and bodies and waste wood. And standing beside her he remarked that things weren't what they'd hoped for, but at least they now had a roof overhead, thank God, and a crust to share with a friend. And when she didn't respond he further suggested that under such clear skies they should be lying in a field watching the stars, instead of having to take in such a spectacle of desolation without even enough tobacco to pack one's pipe. He said he still remembered his initial glimpse of the valley's undisturbed downs, and went on to say as if speaking to himself that on this rough journey he wished for a companion to provide cheerfulness and safety, since he knew the lonely man always pushed on too hard and thus was prone to mistakes.

She looked at his felt hat and the calico patches she'd sewn to his trousers, and though she hoped there was every prospect of their new exertions being crowned with success, she was also aware as she considered him that she herself was curious about the quality of her attention and wasn't certain, after having built the life she'd thought she'd been living, that she possessed the energy to go through the motions yet again. She recalled the doggerel her sister had sent upon the news of their engagement: *"When you are married Gladys Dear / A broom to you I'll send / In 'Sunshine' use the bushy part / In 'Storms' the other end."* The last few nights with the setting in of darkness she so regularly disappeared that her husband asked if she was camping up in one of the few standing trees with the birds. Principles were the faction to which he believed he belonged, and against which he thought all the guilty were in league. But in the face of his need she had discovered in herself an oblivious resistance, as if she were an elephant who when stabbed with a penknife would simply stride on unaffected. She felt a part of an age beguiled by forgetfulness, when everyone acted as though no single thing necessarily followed from anything else, and even as her husband took her hand and stroked it she understood her oncoming resolution to sequester herself much as she recognized a sea breeze before even glimpsing the sea.

By late afternoon Iris had been rescued from her roost and ferried to the first-floor balcony of the Gresham Hotel. Sightseers in small boats by then roamed from one point of interest to another, tying up at the balcony's railing and calling for drinks from the bar. She spent the night there in a room with four other women, and woke the next morning to the clamor of young boys diving from the roofs into the flooded streets. A steam launch took the mayor and aldermen around to survey the damage. Police patrolling in other launches were now capsizing looters' rowboats and leaving them to get to dry land as best they could.

For the rest of the day she helped tend to the badly hurt. A bull rescued by lasso showed his gratitude by promptly charging all and sundry. A beautiful young woman in a neighboring house leapt again and again into the foul water to recover the trousseau she'd collected for her marriage, but while Iris watched was able to retrieve only a few cups and a tureen. And throughout the day the greatest anxiety was whether enough unspoiled water remained for everyone to drink.

In the night the flood finally receded and by morning everything was dank and wet and covered with mud. Dead livestock and poultry were buried in the debris, and the smell was sickening. Iris remembered her charge and headed vaguely in the direction of the address for Nicholas that Miss Laycock had provided, and in the sodden ruins she negotiated it seemed everything had been devastated except for mosquitoes and larger centipedes. In one stretch the storm waves had thrown up banks of coral torn from the reefs offshore, under which a stew of crustaceans and fish stank in the muggy heat. Havoc was piled against any obstruction that hadn't been sundered, and beside the collapsed courthouse she passed concrete from the bridge piers and a steel safe and two heavy boilers while men turned unidentifiable reeking heaps over with long bars, and others seemed to be salvaging what they could and dumping the rest into great piles to be hauled away later. Everyone's hands were bandaged since the most insignificant scratches were already developing infected sores, and the dead when encountered were often so unrecognizable that some residents who were recorded as buried appeared again later, unharmed.

She resigned herself with the help of some policemen to the fact that Nicholas's rooming house was gone, along with its entire street, and having done so, she rested amidst the general despondency of a cleared area containing some of the surviving dispossessed. Some were wrapped in blankets despite the heat. None wept or complained, and few even spoke. One little girl who seemed to be alone walked in a circle while waving her arms in the air. There were quiet attempts to relieve a young woman kneeling in the mud of the body of her infant daughter, but the woman refused to release her and in response said only that her baby had been dead all day. Later that evening there was word of wagons serving beans and hot broth, and after locating them she stood beside an elderly woman who appeared to be deaf and ate her way stolidly through every dish with which she was presented. The next morning Iris happened upon a makeshift school, where a knot of children of various ages whose parents were still missing spent an hour on *Caesar's Commentaries* and then working some sums. She took an empty seat at one of the commandeered tables and thanks to one small boy's gift of paper and pencil began a letter to her brother John Henry in which she recounted the disaster and said she was writing to assure him that nevertheless she was well and hoped this correspondence would find him enjoying the same great blessing. She lamented the many thousands of sea miles still between them and reminded him that everyone at home owed her a letter except for him. Having nothing else to say she wrote that she had told him all she could think of for now, that she looked forward to his letter in response to learn how he was getting on, and that she was not, in closing, forgetting a kiss for the little ones. And it was only then that she thought of Ned.

So much rain had fallen on northeastern Australia over the course of that single storm that three days afterward, Captain J. A. Tyree, of the ferry schooner *Allinga* east of Townsville, reported that because of the extent of the runoff a full twenty-four miles out to sea the water when he tested it was three-fifths fresh.

As Captain Tyree marveled that evening at this discovery, Iris awoke on her cot and accepted that it was Ned's face that she bore through the night and his safety to which she had devoted a dreaming space before having turned herself over to sleep. And she saw that whatever their remoteness from security, even with only her meager stock of earthly experience, she knew there were few who acknowledged the feast that the world at its most parsimonious provided every day and night. And it was as if her ego resolved itself in what she beheld in him and what swept toward her. As though, from the proximity of their mouths and eyes as she remembered it from their time together, some vital energy had been prepared to pour: an animation that might overwhelm their endless misgivings and enable them to fashion their future.

Acknowledgments

Most of the stories in this collection would have been hugely diminished without crucial contributions from the following sources: *Sir John Franklin's Journals and Correspondence: The First Arctic Land Expedition, 1819–1822,* and *The Second Arctic Land Expedition, 1825–1827,* both edited by Richard C. Davis; Ejnar Mikkelsen's *Two Against the Ice;* Anthony Brandt's *The Man Who Ate His Boots: The Tragic History of the Search for the Northwest Passage;* Sir John Richardson's *Arctic Searching Expedition: A Journal of a Boat-Voyage Through Rupert's Land and the Arctic Sea, in Search of the Discovery Ships Under Command of Sir John Franklin;* Andrew Lambert's *The Gates of Hell;* Scott Cookman's *Ice Blink;* F. González-Crussi's *Suspended Animation: Six Essays on the Preservation of Bodily Parts;* Helen MacDonald's *Human Remains: Dissection and Its Histories;* Ferdinand A. Fouqué's *Santorini and Its Eruptions;* Leon Pomerance's *The Final Collapse of Santorini (Thera);* D. L. Page's *The Santorini Volcano and the Destruction of Minoan Crete;* Walter L. Friedrich's *Fire in the Sea;* R. E. Gould's *Yankee Boyhood;* T. B. Terry's *Our Farming;*

John T. Schlebecker's *Whereby We Thrive;* Jared Van Wagenen Jr.'s *The Golden Age of Homespun; Cobb's Ordeal: The Diary of a Virginia Farmer, 1842–1872,* edited by Daniel W. Crofts; James Lane Allen's *A Kentucky Cardinal; The Abridged Diaries of Charlotte Perkins Gilman,* edited by Denise D. Knight; *No Priest But Love: Excerpts from the Diaries of Anne Lister,* edited by Helena Whitbread; Claudia L. Bushman's *In Old Virginia;* Catharine Maria Sedgwick's *A New England Tale;* Howard S. Russell's *A Long, Deep Furrow;* Frances Trollope's *Domestic Manners of the Americans;* Sidney Perley's *Historic Storms of New England; Glencoe Diary: The Wartime Journal of Elizabeth Curtis Wallace,* edited by Eleanor P. Cross and Charles B. Cross Jr.; *The Diary of Virginia Woolf,* vol. 3, edited by A. O. Bell; *I'll Stand by You: The Letters of Sylvia Townsend Warner and Valentine Ackland,* edited by S. Pinney; and Henry Hill Collins Jr. and Ned R. Boyajian's *Familiar Garden Birds of America.* I'm also hugely indebted to Vincent Lunardi's *An Account of Five Aerial Voyages in Scotland;* Sir Thomas Browne's *Religio Medici* and *Urne-Buriall;* Paul Maravelas's "The Montgolfiers' Moment in History" and "Joseph Montgolfier: True Ballooning Pioneer"; A. Lawrence Rotch's *Sounding the Ocean of Air;* Charles Coulston Gillespie's *The Montgolfier Brothers and the Invention of Aviation;* Tom Crouch's *Lighter Than Air;* Henry Petroski's *To Forgive Design;* Geoffrey C. Ward's *A Disposition to Be Rich;* Chris Roulston's *Narrating Marriage in Eighteenth-Century England and France; The United States Congressional Hearings on the Collapse of Texas Tower No. 4;* Thomas W. Ray's "A History of Texas Towers in Air Defense 1952–1964"; Z. Jin, R. Bea, and B. P. M. Sharples's "Failure Analysis of Texas Tower No. 4"; C. B. Palmer's "On the Texas Tower"; Francis Jewel Dickson's *The DEW Line Years;* Mary Preston Gross's *Mrs. NCO;* Phyllis Thompson Wright's *A Navy Wife's Log;* Virginia Weisel Johnson's *Lady in Arms;* A. Alvarez's *Offshore: A North Sea Journey;* Patrick Dillon's *Lost at Sea: An American*

Tragedy; Betty Sowers Alt and Bonnie Domrose Stone's *Camp-following;* Charlotte Wolf's *Garrison Community: A Study of an Overseas American Military Colony;* Charles C. Moskos Jr.'s *The American Enlisted Man;* Simon Winchester's *Atlantic;* Edward Young's *Undersea Patrol;* Bobette Gugliotta's *Pigboat 39: An American Sub Goes to War;* Wolfgang Frank's *Enemy Submarine: The Story of Günther Prien;* William King's *The Stick and the Stars;* Duncan Redford's *The Submarine;* Stephen Moore's *Battle Surface! Lawson P. "Red" Ramage and the War Patrols of the USS Parche;* A. F. C. Layard's *Commanding Canadians: The Second World War Diaries of A. F. C. Layard; Colonial Voices: Letters, Diaries, Journalism and Other Accounts of Nineteenth Century Australia,* edited by Elizabeth Webby; *Turning the Century: Writing of the 1890s,* edited by Christopher Lee; Zoe Ferguson's "Running Wild in the Scrub: A Slice of Gippsland's History"; the Memoirs of the Queensland Museum, Cultural Heritage Series, Brisbane; Robert Hogg's *Men and Manliness on the Frontier;* Carl Lumholtz's *Among Cannibals: Four Years Travel in Australia and of Camp Life with the Aborigines of Queensland;* Hector Holthouse's *Cyclone; The Australian Dictionary of Biography,* Geoffrey Searle, general editor; Allen J. W. Murray's *Nineteenth Century Settlers in a Sunburned Land;* Wendell Potter's *Deadly Spin;* Jill Quadagno's *One Nation, Uninsured;* Jo Ann Beard's *The Boys of My Youth;* Howard Bahr's *Pelican Road;* Sean Dixon, Larissa Liebmann, Matt Krogh, and Eddie Scher's "Deadly Crossings: Neglected Bridges and Exploding Oil Trains"; Justin Mikulka's "There Will Be Blood"; the *National Post*'s "The Night a Train Destroyed a Town"; Ashley Ahearn and Tony Schick's "Rail Workers Raise Doubts About Safety Culture as Oil Trains Roll On"; *The U.S. Department of Labor / OSHA Secretary's Findings on Curtis Rookaird;* Ralph Vartabedian's "Why Are So Many Oil Trains Crashing?"; Taylor Hall's "Petro Peril: Shale Oil's Dangerous Journey"; *Headlights and Markers,* edited by Frank P. Donovan

Jr. and Robert Selph Henry; and the Burlington Northern Santa Fe Railway's *Employee Safety Rules*.

The collection also hugely benefited from the archival support and expertise provided by Rebecca Ohm, Elaine Yanow, and Katie Nash, and it owes a special debt to the information generously provided by Henry Benson, Ray Bisha, Antonio Blanco, James Benton Clark, Robert Cotton, Theo Davis, Donna Distefano, Ralph Fisher, Andrew Riley Harkleroad, Paul Harling, Robert Howe, Greg LeRoy, Carl Ardary Love, Alan MacMillan, Thomas McHugh, the New Jersey Maritime Museum, Edith Oldham, Andy Orin, Tony Picarazzi, Curtis Rookaird, C. S. Sanderson, Julian Sapp, Nina Seybold, Jack Small, Rebecca Jane Smith, Mike Tanaka, Madison Rex Waller, and Deb Whitcraft.

And finally, I want to single out for special praise the contributions of those invaluable readers and editors who encountered these stories in their earlier and paltrier stages and whose rigor and optimism did so much to make each project less appalling: Jim Rutman, Peter Matson, Michael Ray, Hannah Tinti, Robert Skinner, Cheston Knapp, and of course Gary Fisketjon—who deserves his own category for crucially helpful—as well as Gary Zebrun, Ron Hansen, and especially the ever-patient, meticulous, and incisive Sandra Leong. And as always I want most to celebrate my first and final reader, Karen Shepard, who remains as justified as ever in reminding everyone within range that she continues to renovate me in all the most crucial ways.

Jim Shepard is the author of seven novels and five collections of stories, including *Like You'd Understand, Anyway,* a National Book Award finalist. He teaches at Williams College in Williamstown, Massachusetts.

A NOTE ON THE TYPE

This book was set in Celeste, a typeface created in 1994 by the designer Chris Burke (b. 1967). He describes it as a modern face, tempered by some old-style traits and with a contemporary, slightly modular letterspacing.

Typeset by Scribe,
Philadelphia, Pennsylvania

Printed and bound by Berryville Graphics,
Berryville, Virginia

Designed by Soonyoung Kwon